The Cosmic Eve

authorHOUSE®

AuthorHouse™
1663 Liberty Drive, Suite 200
Bloomington, IN 47403
www.authorhouse.com
Phone: 1-800-839-8640

© 2009 Susan Isabelle. All rights reserved.

No part of this book may be reproduced, stored in a retrieval system, or transmitted by any means without the written permission of the author.

First published by AuthorHouse 1/26/2009

ISBN: 978-1-4389-1348-3 (sc)

Library of Congress Control Number: 2008909942

Printed in the United States of America
Bloomington, Indiana

This book is printed on acid-free paper.

2012
Rebirthing Mankind
Susan Isabelle,
Al'Lat Le Andro Melchizedek

*So, you think this is a work of fiction,
Right?
Maybe you ought to
Think Again…*

And this is dedicated to the one I Love,
The Creator Of ALL
That Is
Beautiful, True, Loving,
Who is that?
My Father & His Goddess
For now,
I know them Both
And
I shall be like unto them at the end of days
For
I am their Child
And
They have shown me
My Inheritance
And Yours

Table of Contents

Chapter I	Getting To Know You	1
Chapter II	The Project	17
Chapter III	Your Breath Is My Breath	25
Chapter IV	Turning Up The Heat	51
Chapter V	Intergalactic Council Meeting	59
Chapter VI	Be Not Deceived	83
Chapter VII	Any Old Time You Can Call Me	105
Chapter VIII	The Great Divide	121
Chapter IX	Goddess Of Wisdom, A Mystic Star	129
Chapter X	*The End Of What?*	*139*
Chapter XI	Ruby and Sapphire	157
Chapter XII	Play That Again, Sam	167
Chapter XIII	Fly, Fly Away	179
Chapter XIV	A Song, A Song, A Singing In The Night	193
Chapter XV	The Cosmic Eve	203
Chapter XVI	Time For Us	229
Chapter XVII	A Visit From Adama	247
Chapter XVIII	A New Life	263
Chapter XIX	A Tangled Web	271
Chapter XX	England	283
Chapter XXI	The Dimensions	293
Chatper XXII	Questions	301
References		311

Foreword

Originally, I had intended Book III to be titled *In The Eye Of The Goddess; Assignment England*. This is an unexpected change of title, but also a revealing of sacred knowledge.

As I began writing, Spirit interceded and desired that I tell you the whole story. That which happened prior to my assignment in England, I found difficult at first to reveal; it was much too personal, intimate, and has been kept very private until now. Even my students, who had no knowledge of the amazing events that were unfolding around them at the time, are going to be surprised!

I wrote as I was directed, put the whole story on paper and before I knew it, a complete new book appeared! *The Cosmic Eve! 2012, Rebirthing Mankind* came into being. I thank Spirit now. *This incredible story has to be told!*

The Rebirthing Of Mankind is coming soon. A great promise to humanity, that has only been hinted at in the scriptures of old, is now about to be revealed. 2012 is coming: time is short. I feel that you need to know this information. I gained permission from Richard, my partner in this work, and we have decided together to share this incredible story of our private lives and the birthing of The Cosmic Eve with you.

Times ahead may become a bit rough,
For the seas of humanity are rising in more ways than global warming.
You will need to have knowledge.
Wisdom is contained within this writing, wisdom that will enhance your awareness
And greatly contribute to your progressive, spiritual action and

ascension.
Read carefully.

Many of my readers have discovered, I share with you in each book I have written, a true- life textbook; a spiritual training ground; mine. As Richard and I experienced the Higher God Realms, our Twin Flames energies, Creation, the pain and the challenges, I wrote. My journals written during that time have become this book. The spiritual teachings and the procedures are factual. Spirit wanted me to inform you, to teach and share spiritual truths we learned through our experiences. God and Spirit want you to know;

The Cosmic Eve is the future hope of humanity;
She was planned long ago, at the very beginning...

Knowledge of her will bring you much peace. I am excited about our future! What is contained within this book will bring you into a place of refuge in any storm. The unfolding of the Divine Plan around us gave us no knowledge in advance; all had to be kept hidden, even from us. Why? Because what we had to do required our actions come from the heart with complete love, total, unconditional love, alone. You'll see.

In All Love, Susan Isabelle

Chapter I

Getting To Know You
September 23, 2001

"How did you know? How did you know? They died! Couldn't you have done something?" My emotions burst out at the sight of Richard entering through the front door of the Shambhala Meditation and Training Center. His long trench coat flowed out behind him.

Despite my verbal assault, he casually glided over toward me. The sight of him enraged a part of me and I stepped back, away from him. Just a couple of weeks earlier he had warned me, I remembered. He had said there was about to be a disaster that would shake up the entire world. He knew about it ahead of time, and I knew he knew. I fumed inside. He ought to have done something!

He stood straight and tall as he stared right in my eyes and answered, "I did, I told them but no one would listen. No one believed me, *not even you.*"

My anger and self-righteousness instantly diffused. He was right. I hadn't believed him. I did now, as well as those he had warned. I sighed and realized that over the past few weeks I had judged him, blamed him. I had just been covering my own anger at feeling such powerless by placing blame. I now felt regret for my being so short sighted. I turned away from him. The memories of planes crashing into the Towers flooded my mind.

"I am so sorry. I am so sorry. Over three thousand people died in the Twin Towers. It was horrible! Couldn't we, I mean, could I have done more?"

Susan Isabelle

"Susan," he said as he touched my shoulder and turned me to face him. His dark brown piercing eyes looked deeply into mine as he spoke. " You did exactly what you were supposed to do."

I looked up at him with wonder. What did he mean? Did he know? Did he know what we had done? If so, how had he heard? He wasn't around when it happened…

He spoke gently, "The Guides wanted me to return. We need to talk. They want me to work with you."

"What?" I couldn't believe what I'd just heard. "What do you mean? What Guides?"

"Let's get out of here to talk, that is, if you can." He spoke as he looked around the Center.

We were standing in the Center's store area. It was filled with noisy chattering customers that roamed about shopping. They were just waiting to hear the latest scuttlebutt. A few had heard our exchange and nudged in closer to hear more. As the Founder of the now thriving store and metaphysical training center, people were curious about me. An argument with a handsome stranger would just make their day!

"Ellen!" I shouted around behind Richard toward the front office, "I'm going out for   lunch, can you cover for me?'

"Sure, Susan." She spoke rather absently as she walked out from the office to see what was happening. She stopped short when she saw Richard. I could see it in her face. There was a moment of fear and then, confusion.

A question flashed across her face. Why? Why was Susan going to lunch with that man? He didn't look like anyone Susan would be going to lunch with. She immediately scanned him, up and down.

She looked with some disfavor at his long trench coat and more so with the long black hair that flowed over his collar.

I could feel his growing discomfort with her assessment and interjected, "Ellen, I want you to met Richard. This is the man I told you about who told us about the Twin Towers a few weeks ago. We're going out to talk. I want to tell him about what has happened here recently."

"OK." She whispered as she reassessed the man standing in front of her.

I quickly guided him toward the front door, then we headed out toward his car. Behind me was the Center; fifteen years of work had gone into that Center. It was there I taught students about energy, about living in the LIGHT, taking charge of their lives and about ways of creating a new destiny for mankind.

On this day, my emotions were mixed about how I was to proceed in the future. In the past two weeks not only had the bombing of the Towers shaken the earth, but also my personal world and some of my beliefs. I had seen a great miracle and a horrible tragedy. Perhaps this strange man with his statement of wanting to work with me held a new promise. Perhaps together we would be able to bring about a positive change? I wondered.

A few minutes later we were sitting in the back of a restaurant. We rather absent-mindedly placed an order, fidgeted, and then got down to business.

"OK. Just who are you?" I asked. " You told me about the bombing a week in advance. How could you have known that? Are you a terrorist?"

He sighed. "No, I am not a terrorist. I worked for the military as a physic during the Vietnam War," he said while looking into his soda. He practically whispered as he spoke. "I am retired, if there can ever be such a thing."

"A psychic?" I asked while looking at him more closely. He didn't look like any psychic I'd ever seen!

"Yes, you've heard of physic warfare haven't you?" He snapped back at me. I suddenly realized that this man could read my thoughts. He nodded. He did! He had heard my thought!

He nodded again. "The Russians and the US both had highly trained teams. I was on one of them for twelve years."

"I've heard of them but never met anyone who actually did that." I interjected. He continued, ignoring my awe.

"When I joined the service at seventeen years of age, I was tested and found to have 'special abilities.' I was taken immediately into a special ops unit for psychics and became a Lieutenant in the service. I did my tours in 'Nam in 'special reconnaissance', then back home."

"You must have been very young…." I considered all that he was telling me. He looked too young to have been in Vietnam.

Reading my thoughts again, he spoke. "Yes, that is true, but there is more. Believe it or not, I was used by the Government to travel in time, to see future and past events. Even though I'm not in the service anymore, I still meditate. That's how I knew about the Towers. I was in meditation when I saw what was about to happen." Then he looked straight at me and said, " Timelines have changed."

"Why me? Richard, why did you come to me?" I asked confused. "You came to tell me before it all happened. Why? Do you expect me to work for the Government?" My mind was racing with all that this implied. "I've never worked with the government before." I paused to consider and he didn't speak as I rolled the possibilities around in my own thoughts.

Finally, I spoke again. "Just what did they expect me to do?" I wondered aloud more than spoke, and I felt more than a little fear and hesitation. I really didn't want anything to do with this type of work.

"The Guides showed me. I told them all about it, the others, you know. I did what I could. I don't work for them anymore and I wish they'd leave me alone!" He blurted out with frustration.

He looked really upset and a little crazed. I wondered again at my assessment of this man, but my intuition told me he was speaking truth. I would listen.

"You know, they even go through my garbage!" He held his head in his hands for a few minutes. I didn't speak.

As he hung his head, I felt something come from his soul. He was in deep pain. I could see that he was remembering what he had seen in the future. He saw what you and I saw on television; but he had seen the agony and felt the pain in a way you and I could never imagine. His remembrance began to bring tears to his eyes. He quickly turned to wipe them away. I would soon learn this macho man had a soul and heart for people that his outward appearance would never reveal. Regaining himself, he looked up at me. Seeing my concern, he began to speak more softly.

"I came to you on the direction of the Guides. When I was in meditation, I was ' on the other side.' I was between the worlds and dimensions. While there I received a message that I was to find you. The only problem was that I didn't know where to find you. They told me I needed the Goddess energies to continue my work. I thought you could do something." He said looking up at me expectantly.

"Then two of your students just happened to speak to me a few days later, when I was at a flea market. They told me about you, that you worked with Goddess energies; and then I knew it was you that I needed to find."

"Richard, first of all I want to say I am sorry I didn't listen. People tell me things all the time, sometimes really crazy stuff, and I didn't know you." I apologized. He nodded in understanding.

"Yeah, most people think I'm a nut case" he said with a grin and a shrug.

"I do want you to know that we did do something, but it came after the planes hit the Towers. A wonderful thing happened that has changed the whole course of history: yes, even the timelines. We'll not go into nuclear war, at least not right now, and we'll get though this."

He looked at me. "Go on." Intrigued, he commanded. "That's why I'm here. I want to know what happened."

"So, you don't know everything!" I said smiling. "Maybe, just like me, sometimes things are made known to me, but not always the outcomes? Maybe we do have some things in common?" He nodded. I continued, a bit more confident. "Right after the Towers went down, the people and the energy of everyone was to "NUKE-EM". Anger and a retaliation- mentality was everywhere. There wasn't any human, rational reasoning at all. It didn't matter who was to die, the mentality of all the earth was, 'Just kill someone.' The energy was so bad that I didn't think we'd make it without bombing the whole Middle East!" I paused. "Such a horrible time!"

"Richard, I meditate too, and when I was in meditation, I could see that a black hole had opened to the lower dimensions. The black hole was caused by the intense emotions of sorrow, hatred and the desire to kill. The people of the planet were feeding lower energies in their souls. That caused a gaping hole, a split of realities to form, from the emotional horror of the Towers. It was flooding the earth with lower and lower energies. It gave the consciousness of the lower realms free reign within the minds of people. That consciousness began to flood onto the earth plane. A form of possession was overtaking the minds of the people from these uninvited energies."

I waited a moment to consider the wretchedness of war, of what global war really is. It is really a mass demonic possession of the mind of mankind.

"The energy of fear, anger, retaliation, bloodletting violence was permeating the earth's consciousness and creating a new consciousness field around the earth, one of more death and destruction. We were spiraling downwards into an Armageddon scenario."

He nodded with understanding. "So, what did you do? Why are we still here? We weren't supposed to be." He asked with curiosity.

"Spirit told me call a gathering of all the people at the Center. After the bombing, people came flooding into the Center. We all felt so helpless and confused! All any of us could do was watch in horror, the replays of the planes crashing…" I paused. It was so fresh in my memory.

"As a leader of the people, I felt responsible; to do something, but I didn't know what to do. I sought out God, the Creator of All, in prayer. We all prayed before the altar and cried. We knew this could be the end of us all." I paused. "Then, the instructions came; I was told I would have to go into Light before the people and I was to call upon the Goddess. Then I was told I would have to place Her likeness over the Earth in a manifest form. I was told in my visitation,

" God is in love with His Goddess and that where She was present, no harm would come to Her children."
"So, Richard, that meant that if I could put Her likeness over the Earth, we would be saved from destruction. God would see only His mate, not the crazy world, and spare the earth!"

Leaning forward toward me, he spoke in barely a whisper, "Yes, please, go on, and please tell me what happened. We're not supposed to be here right now, Susan. The future I had seen was that the Earth was destroyed and gone into hell. *What did you do?*"

"I called everyone associated with the Center. On the night of the thirteenth, I performed a ceremony with all of the people in the Center. During the ceremony, I did all that I had been shown to do by Divine Spirit in my meditation and in the dreams I was having."

He nodded, fascinated with what had happened. "That must be what they meant when they said I needed Goddess Energies to continue my work." He whispered more to himself than to me. He looked back up expectantly. He wanted to know more.

I gathered my strength, for to tell this story I could only cry. Tears flowed down my cheeks and I wiped them away to continue. "Then, as part of the ceremony, I was told I would have to call in the Angels Of Mercy, to call the Names of the ANGELS OF MERCY with a priest. The names are comprised of the letters of the Hebrew letters that form the Name of God. They are encoded in Hebrew form, to produce the Angelic Forces." I still remembered the Angels that night. How could I ever forget?

"I had been shown how to do this." I continued. " I had to manifest the earth's form in the Center with all of the people praying for the earth. We did that." I paused to get control. "Then we had to call the Angels. They had to come in balance; a male and a female were required for this calling. The Angelic Force's names contained the codes of the masculine and the feminine Names of God. To call them, it was required that there be two people. If I did it wrong, we would be calling in the angels of destruction. That would have sealed all our fates." I looked up at him.

"You found someone?" He asked incredulous.

"Yes, a wonderful man at the Center agreed to help me. Together, we recited their Names. The Angels came! They came! Twelve of them came and surrounded the manifested form of the Earth. Richard! Right there in the middle of all those people!" I sobbed. "The people passed out! They didn't even see that part!"

Nothing was spoken for a few minutes as I tried to breathe. "After the Angels were around the Earth, I saw the Shekhina, the Bride of God, as a Dove descend around the planet, covering it with a white mist. Only John and I were awake, and we were in a semi-trance state."

He leaned back on the seat, waited and I caught him wiping away his own tears. I felt at that moment that this man truly loved the people and Spirit. Encouraged and catching a breath, I continued.

"They came and all was done as I had been shown to do. But, it was what happened afterward, now that is the true miracle for humanity. It is the greatest miracle of all time-it was a miracle of altering time! That night will be with me forever."

"Go on!" He demanded. He wanted to know more as he leaned forward with intensity across the table. His eyes glowed.

"After everyone awoke from the strange trance-like slumber they had been in, they began to file out of the Center and to go home. It must have been well after midnight. It was all so surreal, they were so silent: they just glided out without a word." I paused, slowly shaking my head as I remembered.

"I just couldn't leave the Center, not after what had happened and all that I had seen. I was going to stay there for the night. Two women came to me after everyone else had gone home. They offered to stay with me. They were concerned about me, if I was going to be 'OK' and all. I agreed to let them stay with me and we sat down together." I took at deep breath.

"Just as we began to speak to one another, at that moment the entire room became black, so black we couldn't see one another. Even though we were just sitting about three feet apart from each other we couldn't see anything! We were too stunned to speak or move. Then, we saw something incredible!"

"In the blackness, we could see an arch about six feet long. The arch was made up of about a hundred images of the planet earth. They formed right in between us, one atop another, right where we were sitting".

I felt the excitement of that moment all over again. I leaned in closer now so no one could hear us and began to speak with my hands, imploring him to hear me. "Richard, Richard, if I hadn't seen this myself I would never have believed it. I swear to God at this moment that what I am telling you is the truth!"

"I believe you! I believe you!" He exclaimed! *"What happened?"*

Using my hands to demonstrate the arch of the earths in the room, I waved my arm through the air and then pointed. "Right THERE! Right there, Richard! The third image of the earth, in from the end, was blowing up! We watched it explode as if there were a hundred, no a thousand, nuclear blasts going off all over, all at once. The earth then broke apart in great chunks that flew off everywhere!! I swear it!"

"My God!' He exclaimed. "We all died!-We're *dead*!"

I nodded this time.

"Yes, Susan, it's just what I had seen in my vision of the future! I figured I was going to die along with everyone else, so I took off to go rock hunting in New Mexico!" Leaning back against the seat, he laughed! He shook his head, laughing. "I'm here! We're still here! But, we all died!"

"I think so, Richard, but there's more. There were *two more earths* after the one blowing up! As soon as we had seen this, the darkness disappeared and we were left staring at one another. I was stunned. I had just seen us explode into a million pieces!"

"And, yet there were two more earths afterwards. How?" He asked. "That means…two more days afterward…Go on!"

"All of a sudden, we saw Lily jump up and run to the front door of the Center. She screamed and we went running to her. I'll never forget what we saw, Richard. The sidewalk was *over* the front door. Sideways, just like this." I said showing him with my hands at a forty-five degree angle.

"Everything was tilted sideways. It was so weird." I paused, remembering the amazement and the fear in my companions' eyes. "We instantly realized we couldn't get out of the building. We just stared dumbfounded, out the door. Just as we turned to speak to each other about the unbelievable sight in front of us, we became so drowsy. All three of us were affected at the same time. I could hardly stand up and everything was moving so slowly. We barely made it over to the pillows that we had left on the floor. We collapsed, and fell "asleep."

Gravely, he nodded for me to go on.

"At 5:30 in the morning we 'landed'… we landed hard. I know exactly the time because the bookcases along with the clock, fell over onto us. We had to climb out from under the books and a room divider that had fallen over. As soon as we crawled out from under the books, Lilly immediately ran to the front door and we followed her once again. This time everything was normal, just like every other morning. Cars were out there driving their owners to work and the sun was up. Everything was normal." I expressed to him my disdain for normal with a grimace.

"I told Lilly and Kathy that I believed we had died to our old reality, that we had somehow, been teleported into the future two full days past the earth that had blown up- right before our eyes!"

Richard stared at me, grinned and dramatically sighed. "Guess I'm still here for another tour of duty."

"You and a lot of people are. You asked me what I had done, but it was a miracle. I thanked God in many prayers that morning! I didn't go home at all. I stayed and people began to file into the Center as soon as the doors opened. Lilly, Kate and I told our story over and over again to the dozens of people who came in." I shook my head.

"About noontime Karen, a student and friend who had been with us all morning, suddenly jumped up and shouted, "I have to go outside! I have to go outside and take a picture-I just heard it! Did you hear it?" She fumbled in her bag, pulled out a camera and ran outside into the mall parking lot. She was the only one that had a camera that day."

My soul filled with love, love for God and His Goddess at that moment. "We looked up, and Richard, the sky was filled with Angels! There were cherubs and a great big eye that was looking down on us! A huge lotus covered the sky over the Center!

Karen took so many pictures that day, but the Eye of God didn't take on the camera; I guess that's not supposed to be seen. One special picture that was developed is spectacular! It's a picture of Kuan Yin! Her hands are outstretched, a dove is flying out of her hands and the huge lotus we saw is actually her heart's center."

I reached into my bag and pulled out the photo Karen had given me earlier. "This is it."

Richard held the photo in his hand and examined it. He immediately seemed more at peace. "Susan, do you realize what this means?" He asked looking up at me.

"I know that on some reality Earth no longer exists, if that's what you mean."

"Yup, that's what I mean." He said nodding and handed me back the photo.

"No, you can keep it. Karen said it belongs to the Center now, a gift from Kuan Yin to all the people so that they would know of the Mercy of God for all time. Just let people know Karen was the one with the camera that day!" I said smiling.

"I feel that the obedience of the people that night who came to pray and to call on the Mercy of God-His Goddess, saved this entire planet." Love and gratitude filled me. I took another big breath.

"Somehow, I believe we were moved two days into the future. Two whole days beyond the destruction of planet Earth." I continued lowering my voice to barely above a whisper. "I believe we have been given a second chance, Richard. So as you can see, time has changed. The course of destruction has been averted by the summoning of the Bride of God, or Divine Feminine Spirit."

"Yes, the Goddess Energies." He spoke reverently, softly in return. "Do you know that in the Book of Revelation, at the time of the end, it says, "Unless those days be shortened, there shall be no flesh saved?" He asked me. Not waiting for an answer, he looked straight at me and then spoke firmly. "Susan, you and those with you, 'shortened the days.' That verse is the only way out, the only hope, of escaping the Armageddon scenario as stated in Biblical scripture. I had never seen it that way before. I just didn't know it meant we would have to completely change the time lines to do it!"

I whispered quietly, "There is another verse; If my people, who are called by My Name, will humble themselves and pray, I will come and heal their land."

We didn't speak for a long time; we just sat stirring our drinks and remaining in deep thought. The waitress glanced over at us. She was getting anxious, I could see as our eyes met. We'd been there for a long time.

" So, now what?" I finally asked.

He looked deeply into my soul, studying me, and then as if resigning himself to a fate yet uncertain, spoke softly. "Well, I know why the Guides want me to work with you now. I'll tell you about the day they told me to find you. I was really discouraged. I knew what was coming."

I stared at him, wondering what it was like to have his ability and then he spoke. "I was alone meditating and praying hard about the end of the human race, when all of a sudden, three old men appeared in front of me. They had on long white robes and beards that hung all the way down the front of their robes."

I nodded at him to go on. It was incredible, but I'd had similar experiences with Adama and Melchizedek.

"They were the Overlords of the Second Grand Division. These were the big guys, from the cosmic realms, near the God realms. I spoke to them. I told them that humanity wasn't going to make it. I had tried, but humanity was not going to change. Nobody would listen. "

He looked up at me to make sure it was ok to continue. I nodded that I understood. Sometimes it was really difficult to get people to listen to the messages of Light.

"They got really mad at me. They said that I had been placed here to help humanity and not to give up. I said that humanity just couldn't make it. There weren't enough that had the Diamond Sun DNA; they had not evolved high enough to make it. That made them really mad! They told me I needed the Goddess energies and took off in lightening and thunder!" His eyes blazed at me. "Susan, I really thought it was all over for humanity. So, I packed up my car. I was on my way to New Mexico to collect specimens for the rest of my short life. I was on my way, but I was told to return here."

"So, you came back." I looked at him in wonder.

"Yes, I know for certain now that I'm supposed to be with you, Susan. But, I'm not used to working with anyone; I'm a loner and have been for a long time now."

By the tone of his voice, I could tell this was a partial warning, so I decided to ask him a question. "How are we supposed to work together? Even if I had listened to you, I wouldn't have known what to do then, I guess."

"You need to let that go now, Susan", he said while taking a bite of his fries. Little did I known then that a big plate of fries or rice was practically his entire diet. He continued. "I think we ought to start by meditating together to see how this is to happen. Let's go to the Guides together. I believe you know how to do that from what you've told me."

I nodded, yes. "OK. I can do that." I said relieved that it would be so simple. " I am here on Sunday afternoons every week to do my private meditation and prayer. I can do it at that time as long as we finish before the evening service. We have Temple gatherings at 6 PM Sunday nights."

"I can't stay for that." He said firmly." My girlfriend wants me home, but I can do the afternoon."

"OK, then, lets plan for next Sunday. At 1?"

"That works!" He smiled. Somehow we both knew a new chapter of our lives was about to begin. We walked out together with more questions than we dared even think about.

Chapter II

The Project

"Hi, Susan, can we go for a walk today? I mean, instead of meditating?" Richard stood in the doorway of the Center. His face was dark and stressed. He looked as if he was really having a hard time with our meeting.

"Sure, I guess." I replied, a little put off by my own expectation. I picked up my little crystal skull I had received while in Belize and tucked it into the pouch at my neck. So many times it had protected me and had taught me. I felt better just having it around me. I threw on a light jacket and followed him out, not sure what to expect. We walked down to the nearby store in silence and picked up a couple sodas.

"Last week was pretty intense, I've thought a lot about that." He said quickly. "There's a place I like to go to walk and to think", he said. "Want to come with me? It's not far."

"OK"

We went for a short ride. The sky was the deep blue of October and there was a warm breeze. I was really surprised when we drove over to the Manchester cemetery. I didn't say a word. I had to admit, I'd never been here before and it was beautiful, the trees were a vibrant crimson and orange with the colors of fall in New Hampshire.

"See, we can walk here without being disturbed. I like to come here. I love the architecture of the stones and the history that is here." He announced proudly.

Stepping out of the car, I could see what appeared to be miles of pathways that rose over softly flowing hills. The trees, ancient and tall, stood guard over the sleeping ones. No, we would not be disturbed here, I thought to myself.

"Well, it is beautiful!" I answered him. "Personally, I don't much care for ghosts." I murmured.

"We can walk over this way, there's a beautiful temple mausoleum over there!" He announced ignoring my comment about ghosts.

Together we began to walk the ancient way. As we crested a hill he stopped and pointed. "It's there, right over there." A large marble temple could be seen glistening against the blue of the sky. Beside it stood a tree that filled the sky with a golden glow of the fall leaves. It was spectacular!

"Oh! It's so beautiful! It's hard to believe that that is where someone, or a whole family is underneath the earth sleeping!"

"I can tell you that they are long gone from this place. I've been here many times, so you don't have to worry. About ghosts, that is." He said as we drew closer to the massive temple.

After looking around a few minutes, I felt more comfortable and was assured that there were no ghosts lurking about. "You know, I don't really come to cemeteries very often-only when someone dies. I have this thing about ghosts touching me. " I spoke as I found a place to sit down on the cold marble side steps of the temple. He sat across from me.

"I know." He spoke apologetic. "But, this is where I was when I saw the coming crash of the planes into the Towers. I was just meditating here in the quiet; I saw it all. The police came by and made me move. So if they come again we may not have long to stay. I just thought I'd show you."

"OK, Richard. Thank you. Let's just meditate for a few minutes, then we can go."

"OK." He said and closed his eyes.

I followed his motion and slipped into the meditative state. As soon as I closed my eyes, I could see something blue, filled with gear-like things of light. It was spinning, huge, beyond belief in the darkness. I saw it immediately as I closed my eyes.

"What's that?" I blurted out with surprise!

"What?" He asked. "What do you see?"

"I am looking at something that looks like an enormous big fountain. It's all white, flowing and spinning."

"You can see that? He nearly shouted at me! "How? How can you see that?'

"I don't know, I just see it." I was beginning to feel defensive. "I am a psychic." I snapped back.

"No one has ever been able to see that! It's supposed to be hidden."

He seemed to be getting angry. I could tell by his tone. I opened my eyes. He was staring back at me with his piercing black eyes. I'd entered something sacred to him and clearly; it was something I wasn't supposed to see. "Well, what is it?" I asked, not put off by the glare. I lightly and nervously stroked the little skull at my neck. I wondered silently if the skull I called El Aleator was having something to do with this.

Surprised, and pulling his shoulders back, he answered. "That is something only I work on."

"What do you mean, you 'work on'?"

"It's my project." I could sense him closing down. He looked all military, staunch and straight. His black eyes were flaming.

"Look, I'm not going to touch it. I didn't mean to pop in on your work. Richard, its because of what we did last week." I reasoned. His expression changed. I continued. "We are connected somehow now. I am sorry. I promise you that I'll not touch it or do a thing. It is perfectly safe with me."

His gaze softened. "Yeah, we are connected." He seemed to be getting very down, emotionally.

"Richard, what is going on?" Why are you so afraid of me?"

"Afraid? He said shocked. "I'm not afraid of you! I just like to work alone and now they're telling me I have to work with you."

"Is that so bad? Look what's already been accomplished. Remember what I told you last week. Can you imagine if we can work together, what we might be able to accomplish? Earth needs us now. I think it's a part of what we've come here to do."

"I know that." He said thoughtfully. " It's going to mess up my life. Every time they have me do something, it messes up my life. My girl is already jealous. No one understands." His body was tightening in frustration.

I looked directly into his eyes. "Richard, I know what you are going through. In my life, I've lost just about everything. My relationships, my friends, church, my own children are afraid of me sometimes." I paused to regain my own composure. "No, they don't understand, but we have to do what we've been brought here to do. My husband is tired of the hours I must put into this too. We've lost our relationship. I'm frustrated too. Its pretty hard working the Center and getting home after midnight then getting up to do it all over again. BUT, I still have to. *No, I want to.*"

He looked at me again with a softer look this time, but still questioning me. I continued speaking to answer his look.

"I want to because I know that even if no one in the entire world understands, I do. I know what we did: My God! *We moved this entire planet ahead two days into the future and we averted a great destruction of humanity*!" I grew quiet in the thought of this once again.

I also remembered the vision I'd had while I was at a temple site in Belize. It was just about the same time I received the Maya crystal skull. I had seen a whole new earth that day in the future. It was so beautiful. I wanted that. I spoke again. "My children may not have felt it or anyone else for that matter, but I know one day all will be known. It's not for glory, it definitely is not for me, but it is for my children, my grandchildren and above all, for God. I know I've been sent here to help! I will do as He has requested of me!"

Seeing my intensity and determination, he moved slightly and adjusted his stance. "I didn't know you thought about things quite like that, just like me."

"No one; no one knows who we are, Richard. I didn't know myself until a few years ago that I was to do anything. How can anyone possibly understand what we do or why we do what we do?"

He stood up, saying, " Let's walk."

We walked side by side down the winding path for an hour. We didn't speak, lost in our own remembrances of hurt and misunderstanding, then back to our purpose. We had gone full circle around the thousands of graves and headstones that glistened under the deep blue sky, headstones of the past and a remembrance that we were all really there too. He finally spoke. Decisions were being formulated as we both walked.

"Do you want to see what I do with my "project"?"

I was shocked and exclaimed " Richard, can I? I'd love to! It's so beautiful!"

He directed me back to the marble temple. We sat down once again at the temple steps. "Now, close your eyes." He was in control. I did and he began a breathing technique. "You can breathe with me if you want."

I followed the deep breaths as he instructed, but was already there as soon as my eyes were closed. "I see it, Richard. What is it? Where is it?"

"My project is far out in space. I've been working on it for a year." He softly replied.

"What does it do?" I asked, fascinated by the whirling parts of the fountain. It appeared to have sections of gear like appendages that when moving sent up fireworks into the darkness of space.

"Watch." He commanded. "See that?"

"Yes", I said as I saw a blue mist forming. "I can see a blue mist off to the right of the project."

"Good! You really can see it!" He spoke triumphantly.

"I told you I could. What is it?" I asked curious.

"Watch!" Came the command.

The soft blue mist began to take on form. It swirled and turned and was becoming solid looking in a way. Finally, it became more solid. It was made up of a series of geometric forms that merged together to form itself into dimensional form. It looked as if it was becoming another piece of the fountain.

It just hung in the empty space beside the fountain that was glowing and moving gently nearby. Amazed, I watched the newly made form move a little bit closer to the fountain. Twisting and turning the arm- like appendage moved even closer to the fountain that waited, hanging in space. Then slowly it integrated itself into the whole creation.

"There, that's where it goes!" he stated satisfied with his work. "That's enough for today!"

With that announcement, the whole picture shut down. I opened my eyes and stared back at him. He was looking at me with a very 'pleased with himself' expression. His pride in his work was glowing all over his face, but I still didn't know what it was.

"Richard! That is incredible! I watched you make something out of the mist and then attach it to the whole thing! Amazing! You're making something! But please, can you tell me, what is it?"

"Sue, I don't really know. I think I am creating something for time and perhaps for another dimension. Maybe it's for us to go into when the day comes for us to leave this place. I'm not sure."

He considered his own words and seemed a little disappointed that he couldn't tell me what exactly it is. I nodded toward him to go on.

"The Guides will let me know in time. I just have been practicing with the blue mist, learning how to do this over the past year. The mist is the Agni, the substance of all creation and I have the ability to create with it on another realm. Somehow, I am compelled to do this every day, to add another piece. It's growing larger each time I do."

He looked away a moment and then said, " I can't believe they'd let you see it too." He stood and motioned for me to do the same. "We've got to get you back."

"Oh, yes! This is so incredible! I almost forgot I've a congregation and a sermon to give tonight!"

He dropped me off at the Center to the shock and amazement of the early comers at the Center. I could see their wonder and surprised looks. It was not often they'd see me alone with a man other than my husband.

"Was that the physic guy, Susan?" Jackie asked with a curiosity and tone that suggested I was up to something.

"Yes, that is Richard. He's just a good friend. You'll get to meet him soon." I said nonchalantly, brushing off the implication. They looked disappointed. I continued, " He's helping us in many ways."

Chapter III

Your Breath is My Breath

    A week flew by. Richard staunchly marched into the Center passing by me without a spoken word. He went directly to the meditation room. I followed, silently watched as he removed his black overcoat throwing it over a chair, and as he began to methodically pull down some meditation pillows. He tossed them on the floor. He finally looked up at me and motioned for me to sit down on one of them. I moved from the doorway and took the place he'd indicated to me.

    Once again, I was seated across from this strange man. This time obviously, we were to stay at the Center in the meditation room. I looked at him more closely. He was about 5 feet eleven inches tall, and weighed about one hundred and sixty pounds or so. He had the deep olive- toned skin of the Mediterranean cultures.

    His hair hung down around his shoulders and was nearly black in color. He looked Italian, his nose straight and with a profile that reminded me of ancient Greece somehow. He could have been a Senator in the Grecian courts of old, I decided, with his take-charge manner and deliberate motion.

    He was very handsome, but the fire in his eyes made him almost threatening and very mysterious. I could understand that some who had seen him were already frightened. I wondered if he'd ever fit in with the others in the group. No, they'd be really hesitant to accept him. He held himself with a dignity and resolve that in one instant, one knew he would be a force to be reckoned with if challenged. I was not about to do that. I wanted to learn more about him. I would be compliant, for now.

In front of the altar, we set ourselves more comfortably and faced one another on the arranged floor meditation cushions that he had so carefully placed about three feet apart. I adjusted the small skull around my neck once again. I was ready. He sat straight and tall.

"Now, he announced, "We may begin."

"OK." I replied. Clearly, I was not the one in charge here!

"Now, hold your hands like this." He motioned for me to place my hands in a mudra, an arrangement of the fingers of the hands to enhance electrical flow in the body. "You will breathe with me in this manner; you must keep up and find the harmony in order to do it correctly."

I nodded. He breathed in deeply. As he did so, I could feel the whole room lift. I was levitating on his breath! Startled, I forgot to breathe.

"No! You must breathe with me!" I looked up to see his blazing eyes scolding me.

"Let's go again. I'm ready now." I softly replied. "I wasn't ready." Actually, I had been surprised.

He readjusted himself on his cushion with a twist to indicate I was barely tolerable. I heard his mind. He was not happy to be teaching this. He was under orders. He worked alone, and he *never* worked with women.

Preparing myself, I sought the place of no mind, the now, of the experience about to unfold. One must have no emotion, only focus and at the same time, a mindlessness to attain certain levels. This was one of those moments.

Stoic, I began the breath with him. We were lifting on each breath, but this time I would not focus on that, but only on the breath's motion within me, only experiencing its gentle flow, life and presence.

From this point on, I would be aware of all things simultaneously, but without focus on any one thing. It is as if one was standing in the center of a circle of light, while seeing all, all at once. One cannot pause to look at one thing, for to do so would break the breath, the moment, the now, and all would be lost.

I have always been one to be in charge. Not now. To submit, not to perform was a relief and a joy to me. I'd never experienced one who could do these things with me. I held my focus but with joy unspoken. I knew how to do this, but not with another in this manner.

Our Merkaba fields were expanding and lifting us upwards. 'Merkaba' is an ancient word to describe the electrical fields, magnetic and spirit body that surrounds each one of us. It's there whether or not we realize it or want it to be. It just is. Great fields of electromagnetic energy swirled and began to pulse around us. When the Merkaba fields are activated, or energized, we may lift our spiritual fields and embody even more light; we become filled with light.

This in turn, allows us to move beyond the physical limitations of our bodies. Just as an ice cube becomes less solid with heat, so too our physical becomes less solid with light, freeing the spirit and soul of the practitioner. We were on our way, together!

To experience the pulsing of the Merkaba field is awesome! Together, our fields joined as one. It was immense! When your Merkaba field is activated, it feels as though one is the building, the parking lot, the city, the state, and all things- all at once! The combination of our two separate fields, however, began to merge into one powerful spinning tornado of light! Suddenly, I heard his voice speak to me in my mind.

"Breathe in the light through your eyes. Bring it in."

As I followed the inner command, I breathed in through my eyes at the same moment as he did. A white pyramid appeared in the space between us. It spun brilliantly. Again, I heard his voice in my mind, "Breathe it into your soul, through your eyes."

And I did. On my breath, its' glow entered my being through my eyes and glided downward; the pyramid was now pulsing within my breast! It's pulsing shone from the spirit's heart in tune with a silent heartbeat deep within a spirit body. I, in the physical? No more.

The next breath of Light from within Light now revealed another pyramid.

"Breathe it into yourself, through your eyes." His mind spoke to my mind.

Again I breathed Light and became purer, brighter Light; the pyramid glided within Light into my center of mind. A star was now within: one within the mind, one within the heart! Now, there was no I; but I expanded out of this dimension into no time, no space.

The indigo hues caressed me; my souls' song sung, "I am, I am, I am." I know this, so simple in its very simplicity. It is joy.

"Susan," I heard his mind speak to me. "Two more pyramids must come: I am being told."

"Yes" I answered the voice that is no spoken voice, but I hear it as loud as the spoken.

As we held the energy of our beings, two more pyramids appeared. One moved to his side and another to my side. "I see them spinning," I answered with my mind.

Faster and faster they rotated, blue white lightening flashes out from them. Holding no mind, but only observation, the pyramids suddenly turned sideways, with points outwards. The four of us now formed a square of sorts of pure energy!

There is silence, peace, as we float in time. I was in perfect peace, perfect stillness. Then his voice, his incredulous tone, filled the space around me.

"Susan! Can you see this?"

"Yes!" I awoke from my peace to be become aware once again.

Between our two energy fields and the opposite two pyramids, within the 'square of light' now formed a beautiful, full white lotus. The beautiful flower hung gracefully, gleaming its' whiteness between us. So beautiful! A Lotus! The flower of creation was floating between us, its' petals softly moving with the energy.

Richard and I looked across at one another over its glistening white petals. Our eyes met. Then, I knew what he really meant. He could see 'me', and now I could see 'him'. That is when I *really* saw him. I saw his true essence. I was seeing him as he truly is; this was not the physical man known as Richard, but the spiritual being that had been created by God. My mind exploded with the sight!

"Oh, My God! *He is beautiful!*"

Time ceased to exist. I could have spent an eternity gazing at his beauty, his essence. I have never seen anything so stunning! I could see his full aura, his true light. His colors astounded me! I could see streams of white and gold emanating from his being with blue and greens intertwining the gold. I was mesmerized with the movement of light. The moving, dancing streams of color formed, 'Richard'.

I saw a whitish veil over his center. It prevented me from seeing his true, inner essence. Somewhere, from my knowing, I spoke.

"Let down your veils. Let me see you."

The veil dissolved before him. A brilliant, red ruby red glow began to appear. A vibrant blast of deep ruby exploded upwards and filled his being. It spiraled up through all his colors in a spiral of glorious frequency!

"My God! You are Beautiful!" I exclaimed in my soul.

Content to look at him forever, gazing into his beauty and colors, I know something now. I know I have known him from the beginning. The ruby spirals of energy beckon me to draw near to him. He is irresistible.

"Do you see the pyramid in the Center of the Lotus?" He softly asks, drawing my attention away from his incredible form back to the Lotus.

"Yes, yes, I see." I answer. "It seems to be gold, a flame of gold." Together we watched as the flame grew brighter and brighter reaching high into time.

"It's calling me, it's calling me to enter the flame." I sing out to him the thought.

At that thought of movement, my awareness allowed me to see my own form, the one he could see. I am formed of spinning spirals of sapphire blue rays of every depth and hue. Deep indigo rays and striking blues of azurite fire shine outward from me forever and fill the auric space around me. I am at peace.

Answering the call of the Lotus, I can barely speak the mind of my soul. "I believe we are to enter it now." My mind sent forth the message.

I moved forward in thought, gliding over the petals of the giant Lotus and took my place. I am at home before the fireplace; before the Great Eternal Flame. I was before the white spinning pyramid now forming the flame. He has entered, even as I have. We sat within the Lotus facing one another. The pyramid spun brilliantly between the two of us.

"Does he know? Why of course! He is the yang to the yin, my twin within the Flame of Eternity." My mind has asked and answered itself. In my physical being I have met him. In my spirit I have rejoined him now, before the Flame. I speak the words of truth to myself first, then the entire universe. I know now. He does too. We hold in silence the glory of it all, amazed and at total peace.

The flame grew brighter and brighter, expanding far above us. Now that we had rejoined within the Lotus, the Eternal Flame in the center of the Lotus was intensifying, expanding all the way up into the heavens. It seemed to be touching God, telling Him that we had arrived at our destined appointment. All is good. All is holy here.

Gently stirred from my peace by a movement within me, I acknowledged that something had activated the spiral of sapphire spinning from the depth of my soul. It was pulsing now, expanding from somewhere deep within my being. I looked through the great flame between us. I saw too, the ruby pulse within him. It too had begun to expand.

Within my being, and rising up through my crown of light, the spiral of sapphire began to dance, circling the Great Flame. Dancing and swirling, the sapphire ray emanating from my crown was being drawn to the Flame. It encircled the Flame with its motion. Making large spirals around the Flame, higher and higher it ascended. The spirals rose ever upward.

At the same moment, a glorious ruby ray danced higher and higher up from his crown Looking across the spinning pyramid, I could see that he too had begun the ascent.

"Where are we going?" I asked to the Light and to him.

"Into the Higher Dimensions!"

A voice, not our own, answered us.

Together we were drawn upwards, dancing the ballet of the sapphire and ruby around the Golden Flame. The rays from our crowns began to intertwine. I know this form. It is the spiral of DNA!

"We are dancing the Dance of Creation, the DNA of Life." I spoke the sacred words. They are only words; I have heard within my soul. They are the words from the Divine Presence surrounding us, now lifting us forever upwards.

"Creator gods." I heard sacred words announcing us. The words spoken this time are from those unseen, around us. I became aware of the Beings Of Incredible Light upon the words and then, I saw them emerging from the mists.

Angels had come to watch; their white, glowing forms surrounded us. Soft white wings caressed the mist around us, encouraging us. Lifted upon the wings of angels, we rose. Many from the universe also began to manifest. They had come to see this. There were many watchers now.

I whisper to him softly from my mind, "We are dancing the Dance of Creation. Our rays are forming a spiral of DNA!"

"Yes," he whispers in return. He knows. We, pulled upwards by some Force greater than ourselves, were ascending. Higher and higher we rose.

As we ascended we began to see great, sparkling objects. They filled the complete area above us as a ceiling. It looked as though the bright objects were going to prevent us from going any higher. Then we could see more clearly.

Crystals! As we rose between them, the crystals were forming a gateway. Giant formations of crystals had formed a passageway through the cosmos for us. A crystal highway of sorts! Gigantic, crystal spinning obelisks pointed the way ever upward.

There were massive crystal formations of incredible colors; of rosy quartz, sparkling blue stones of turquoise and azurite. Purple spires of amethyst crystals towered above us, forming the passageway above. Golden topaz obelisks spun yellow sunlight as we past by. Emeralds glistened glorious greens; ruby reds, orange of the depths of carnelian and sapphire, diamond and so many others bathed us in their light!

Spinning, spinning, spinning so fast they looked as though they were fluid somehow! In their motion, they were spinning light! The emanating light from their rotations formed all the colors of the rainbow around us, lifting us up on gentle rays of glory! We were bathed, cleansed and prepared in the light of rainbows.

And then, there was Light. Total LIGHT! Brilliant total Light!

Together, we had ascended into the Light of God. Light. It is ALL. It is Every Thing. How long? Who knows? There is no time there. Light. Endless… Eternal…Blissful Light.

Suddenly, I was back in my Center. I was back in physical form lying sprawled out upon a simple cushion. There was no Lotus, only a cold, hard floor.

We heard the commanding Voice from somewhere far above us speak.

"Ground the vision in the physical!"

We both heard the Voice and obeyed. Somehow, I struggled and pushed myself up. I was dazed and disorientated. He too moved slowly. We crawled closer toward one another as we pushed our cushions closer. We seated ourselves upright on our cushions. Automatically, I raised both my hands toward his hands, already outstretched toward mine; we touched palm to palm.

Energy flowed from one to another. It swirled through us, hand to hand, cell to cell, as it spun its' light around and around from him to me; from me to him. The flow spun through us wildly for just a few moments, then subsided. It was enough. We had merged in the physical through the touch of our hands.

"It is done." I heard him softly say to all around us, to Spirit and to me.

I became aware that our hands were touching intimately, just at the same moment as he did. We pulled apart, disconnected our minds and our hands. Then I felt awkward, physical. I was unsure of what to do or say. I knew I had just experienced the most intimate moment of my life.

I barely knew this man in this lifetime. But now we both knew we had known one another since the beginning of time. Perhaps we'd been together many lifetimes. Our relationship was birthed in the Spirit, on some other realm at the very beginning of time. It was a Spiritual connection, but not of the physical realm. On planet Earth, right now we were just two people who had just happened to met one another.

But no, that's not all, I realized. We had just experienced something amazing! He was staring at me, and I was staring at him. Sitting before me with shock and disbelief, I suddenly realized, sat my Twin Flame! This realization has hit us both at the same time. In stunned disbelief we examined one another; I am not what he expected and he is not what I expected.

The half, the Ruby half of the DNA spiral we had seen, he carries that. I am Sapphire; he is Ruby. Together the colors are Violet, together, we can create worlds. We both had seen what we each truly look like, what we *really* look like. My form is not the form of a middle-aged woman with graying hair. Oh, no!

My head swirls with his image and what I have just experienced. This Lotus can be shared with none other. He had just thought the same of me. We don't look like anything we look like here. I have seen his beauty and at that moment, the words cannot help but flow from my lips to say to him, "You are so beautiful!"

I become aware I have embarrassed him with my words. I ought not to have spoken them. He was uncomfortable.

Even so, he could not help but excitedly ask, "Did you see that doorway?"

"Yes," I answered. "The Crystal Gateway!"

"*We BOTH went in TOGETHER…*" He spoke in awe as he looked at me anew for a few moments.

Gathering his senses, he abruptly stood up. I silently watched as he picked up his trench coat and walked toward the door. Our eyes diverted away from one another, unable to acknowledge what we had experienced. We were unable to speak any more. We didn't even say goodbye.

As he began to walk out across the pavement toward his car, I stood shaking in the doorway, looking after him with a silent longing. I saw him hesitate then he turned around to face me and shouted across the parking lot,

"Will I see you next week?"

"Yes, I'll be here next Sunday!" I shouted back. He turned and got into his car.

Just at that moment, two of the women who helped me with the services on Sunday night were getting out of their cars. It was already five o'clock! We had been in meditation for three hours! Three hours had passed so quickly! The women just stared at the two of us, gazing at his car, then at me. Nothing was spoken.

To break the uncomfortable silence, I turned to them and said, "Let's hurry! There's a lot to do!" I turned to open the door for them to enter. They slid past me and I went into the back room. I fell up against the wall. I had to prepare for the evening service!

I looked up at the bookcase. I was directed by Spirit to the bookshelf and took down a book by James Redfield called, "The Celestine Prophecy." Spirit directed me to open to page 135 in a chapter called clearing the past.

My eyes fell to a paragraph. I read, "***Don't confuse calmness with carelessness. Our peaceful continence is a measure of how well we are connected to the energy. We stay connected because it is the best thing for us to do, regardless of the circumstances. You understand that, don't you?***"

I said the words aloud. "Our peaceful continence is a measure of how well we are connected to the energy." The words spoke directly to my soul. Lowering my head I fell into prayer.

"Mother, Father,
I don't understand all that you are showing me, but I am in you
and
I love you beyond all things of this earth!
Your will is my will, my will is yours-forever.
Let it be as you so direct and let me follow for my good andthe
highest good of humanity.
Let me remain in that place of calmness,
In Your Presence.
So be it!"

It was then that my heart began to beat once again and my thoughts cleared enough for me to do just that. Tonight, I would tell the people who now depended upon me to lead and to guide, that God is in control and even if we don't understand She /He has a program that we can follow *if* we stay connected!

What had just happened to Richard and to me was enough to shake both our worlds. It was a demonstration of how connected we can really be-even over centuries of reincarnations, for our twin flames are a part of us. We are part of the Divine Plan and connection is vital! Part of the plan was for us to reconnect our energies now. We were here now and we had a job to do. We both had to remain calm and be centered in our commitment to humanity or somehow, I knew in my soul, it all could fall apart.

Shortly afterwards, I stood in front of the thirty- five people seated in a little room on the floor and in the few chairs we had. They looked up at me expectantly.

We sang our opening song, *Let There Be Peace on Earth and Let It Begin With ME*! I read the passage from Redfield's book to the people, and then I began to speak.

"Our peaceful continence is a measure of how well we are connected to the energy*! Primary, above all, is vitally important and necessary for us to stay connected to the guiding energy! You understand that-Don't YOU?"* I said as I looked into each face. They were nodding back at me, agreeing.

I continued.

"We are in times that have the potential to destroy all life on planet earth. Some of our government officials are trying to find blame and will incite a global war should we falter in our steadfast belief, our core of calmness, and prayers.

We know now that it takes only a few dedicated beings of light to steer the car about to slide off the cliff, back to safety. We're in a car, the earth vessel, being driven by insane people. We're holding onto the steering wheel for dear life trying to keep the insane ones from driving us over the cliff! We cannot yet release the steering wheel!

Events around us seek to tear our hands away from the wheel. It destroys our calm, our peace. Our lives can be so torn apart by events in our homes, illness, relationships, other people's problems and in our work. Our emotions and even our own bodies betray us, dissuade us from our path and we are torn away from our purpose.

Our connection can fail if we forget the message; remain calm; stay connected to the guiding energy!

Only a few weeks ago we saw a great miracle. It was during a time of great mental and emotional anguish. We all knew that with the fall of the Twin Towers, we were going into war. It was war that would destroy us all. We knew that.

We held strong and sought God's help. You were all with me that night. We all heard and we responded to the call of God, Goddess to seek the Divine presence of the Goddess over the earth.

We were shown how to do that **at the last moment**! *We saw the earth's movement into the future two full days.*

Many of you seated here now, saw the image of Kuan Yin over our tiny center! The image of Kuan Yin over US- the Shambhala Center of Manchester, New Hampshire! The Goddess's image of mercy and compassion was over us and the Dove Of Peace flew out from her hands.

Can you imagine that? You did it! Remember how spectacular the Lotus was in the sky? That was her heart center. The Eye of God looked down upon us and angels filled the sky!

Even the shop owners in our area came outside to look at the angels! They saw them even though they are not with us in our beliefs! We are so loved!" I felt the tears begin to well up within me and I saw those seated on the floor wiping away their tears. *"We are sooooo loved!"* Regaining my composure, I continued. *"I remember a verse of scripture;"*

"If my people, who are called by My Name, will humble themselves and pray, then, I will come and heal their land."

"We know this to be true. We have seen it with our own eyes! Let us never forget this time, this moment, no matter what. It is our strength for the future. We have cleared the past of a great evil and brought a second chance to humanity!

This knowledge is our strength. In the book it says, "We stay connected for it is the best thing for us to do." I tell you now, it is the only thing for us to do!!"

"We don't know what the future holds for us, but we do know some things. Our core, our base of calmness, our calm demeanor, is established within us by knowledge we have gained by the events of the recent past.

When we hold to that base of knowledge, we will not be shaken, regardless of the circumstances we are in. When we remember, we stay connected, for it is the best thing we can do.

But, how quickly humanity forgets. I say to you-rise above your humanity, rise above the former ways and become strong in the energy, in your experience, your own knowing!

That can never be taken from you, only you can decide to forget it. That's right-only you can choose to forget. Then you make another choice.

Should you forget that which you know and your connection to the One, The Light of God; the Energy, you shall seek another way; but it shall be one of fear. Fear? Yes, for there is no other comfort for you.

Many come and seek to divert you from the truth of what you know deep inside. Many of the darkness seek to rob you-first of truth, then of your integrity in that truth. Once disconnected from Light of Truth there is nothing but fearfulness for you. Your Light fails; diminishes and you become fearful and powerlessness besets your soul. Your gut will tell you; it recoils when untruths are spoken to you. Learn to trust your gut feelings and stay strong in your knowing, your experience, no matter what!

Once faced with the reality that we may have removed ourselves from the Truth and have become disconnected, do not hold to the element of fear, for we now know that fear, that entrapment, is really an illusion.

We just need to remember that we have a connection that can and will, save us and direct us into safety. Then remove yourself from untruth; move back into integrity. Then, fear flees from us; we can think rationally once again. Our true POWER is restored!

BUT you must stay connected, remember and let us all continue to be guided by the Source that loves us and wants, along with us, the highest good of all of humanity.

Hold your calm demeanor, but let no one think for a moment it is a sign of weakness! When you remain calm, you can hear; you can see truth and you will respond in Spirit.

That may mean you will be faced with changes. We don't like change, do we? I resist it too. Just nine months ago we had been meeting in the beautiful chiropractor's office for classes on weekends. We had everything we needed!

I was stunned when we were informed we'd have to move when the doctors decided to work on Saturdays. Now where were we to meet? Was that the end of the training? Was my teaching over? How could we ever find another place like that? We didn't have the money to rent. The circumstances were grave.

The message from Spirit to my soul was, **"Stay connected, remain calm, Susan. Watch!"**

"Soon, I was directed to this little closed up store front in this falling down, old graffiti-filled mall with boarded up broken windows-where we now sit. Some thought I was crazy to come here, but the leading was clear.

Who would ever have guessed that this place, this place, was to be the setting for what has happened? Now, we are filled to capacity! The bathroom doesn't work with the numbers of you and we will probably have to move again if something doesn't happen soon. We have to stay connected! Spirit will guide us!"

Laughter filled the little room as the toilet flushed in the other room and it began to overflow-again!

"It's not my fault!" My student exclaimed as she came out. " It doesn't like me!"

"We'll have to petition the toilet guides, Susan!" someone quipped. We laughed some more and broke for refreshments, the mood and the message of the night was over.

We had heard and understood. We were being guided. All we had to do was be calm and centered. I was being guided now onto a path that held the potential of much fear and many changes in my life. Could I? Would I, hold steady, calm and in Spirit?

I locked the Gaila Goddess store and Shambhala Center door after the last student went out. I turned and went back into the meditation area. I sat down on one of the mats Richard and I had been on only a few hours before.

I took out the Maya skull from its medicine bag that hung around my neck. I held him in my hand. El Aleator's eyes shone brightly up at me. Even for a stone, he looked especially happy.

"Did you have something to do with what happened here today?" I asked the shining stone. "What other secrets do you have?" Looking at his incredible, fully visible brain as I turned him over, I knew that he held knowledge. This was an amazing stone the Maya had given to me.

I could just barely begin to imagine what abilities he had. Very ancient knowledge was stored in that brain. Maybe even knowledge from the stars was encoded in him.

When the Goddess energies were brought to Earth, El Aleator played a vital role in the securing of ancient knowledge on the earth. I remembered the night the priest had tried to cast the earth into the flames. El Aleator had shot blue flames at the priest and stopped the process from happening.

Were Richard and I accessing that hidden knowledge somehow? I had never heard of anyone doing what we had done that day. I had never heard of anyone going into God presence like that! Between us we had created a spiral of colors that allowed an entrance.

El Aleator was Lord of the Frequencies. He had control of color and light in its tiny form. That had been proven before now. Did that have anything to do with this too? Did he provide a catalyst, a boost?

"Well, El, I wish you would speak to me." I said. I remembered the prayer the Maya used to access information from a crystal skull, or a Sastun, as they called it. Now would be a good time to find out why these things were happening to me. I began the prayer.

"Sastun, Sastun, Sastun…by your great power I ask that you give me all the answers to this question I ask….visit me in my dreams and help me to understand the signs and the wonders that are happening to me now. I believe Sastun, El Aleator, is able to do all these things by the Power of the Father, the Mother and the Christ Light. And so it is…."

I tucked him back into his bag.

When I returned home it was well after midnight. I was so tired. I just wanted to go to bed. Will, my husband, met me inside the living room. He had gotten up from bed at my arrival and was holding a stack of mail in his hands.

"You haven't opened these."

"Will, I am so tired, I just want to go to bed." I complained.

"Susan, you have to open your mail."

I looked at him. My heart sunk. There was no sense arguing. He was jealous. He was jealous of my time and the people of the

Center. I couldn't blame him. He never asked for me to be what I had become. His standing there and holding the mail was his way of telling me he wanted attention. A fight with me would at least get some attention. No, I would not play that game.

I took the handful of bills from him and quietly sat down. I opened each one and paid the bills. It was about 2 AM when I finished and went to join him in bed. He really was a good man and deserved more. I couldn't do it. Choices were coming. Destiny was calling. I rolled over and tucked the covers under my chin. I tucked the skull into my pillowcase, under my head. Tears were falling as I fell into sleep. Tonight I would know. A deep, deep sleep overtook me…

Somewhere, long ago in time, I awoke. I found myself standing on a cliff overlooking the turquoise sea beneath me. The white foam waves washed gracefully over the rocks below. It was time. I had to do this. There was no other way.

The earth trembled lightly beneath my feet. It would not be long now; the end was coming. Atlantis was doomed. We had tried to reason, but none would listen. The mind of humanity was overtaken in darkness, and all would soon be gone. I must hurry. It had to be now; I could not wait any longer! This could not be sunk into the bottom of the sea!

The gentle winds blew harder and stroked my gown, twisting it around me. I fought it but the long, flowing gown was tightening the grip it held upon my legs. He'd be here shortly. I reached down to free my feet from the now tangled gown in the briars. As I did so, a small shimmering gold bag fell from its nest, tucked safely within my breast.

"One last time, yes, one last time; I will hold you." I opened the golden bag and gently allowed the small crystal skull to lie upon my palm. "I am so sorry. I tried…" I whispered softly and tenderly stroked the skull's glistening forehead. "They weren't ready yet."

"Al'lat!" He called up from the ancient stairs beneath me. "I am here now...I must hurry!"

"Yes! Here, take it now..." I placed the skull back into its' pouch and pressed it into his uplifted hand. "It must be kept safe!"

"Please, Al'Lat, please come with me!" He pleaded s he took my hand and lifted up to me.

"No, no my love, I cannot. I must see to the others in the Temple."

"I may never see you again..."

"We shall always be together...now hurry! They're coming for me!"

His lips brushed mine and then, Regalis was gone.

Stepping down onto the old, gray staircase, I wiped away my tears, adjusted my hair and my gown. I must hurry now too. They could not know. The skull would soon be safely sailing out to sea. Its' new home would be in the country to the south. It would be safe there. No, they must not know where it was going. They must never have it or the powers it bestowed for the abuses would be too great.

One day the skull would find its way back to me. Far, far into the future when humanity was ready to ascend, we would rejoin once again and complete our task. It was our destiny: bound in time and service, we come together across the realms to ascending planets at the end of their age. I could only hope the humans of Earth would be ready the next time.

The Temple was just ahead, I could see its white marble pillars as I ran toward them. Yes, there was a number of people assembled. They were waiting as I knew they would be.

A powerful man strode toward me. He was known as Re'Sol, Chief Administrator of the enforcement of the law on Atlantis. Secretly he hid his true identity, for he was a Priest of the Dark One. He had brought along with him a whole company of fierce–looking guards.

"Al'Lat, we have been searching for you."

"I am here now. What may I do for you."

"The Council has met and the decision has been made."

"And what decision would that be?" I stalled for more time. I was foolish to have waited so long…

"Don't be naïve, Al'Lat. Its time you hand it over." Ja'Ree, the Priestess, my assistant in the Temple, demanded. " It has been decided. I am to assume the role of High Priestess, and you are to be banished from Atlantis. I will be much more generous and responsive to the needs of the Council than you have."

"Ja'Ree, you know you will have no power with the skull. It is only used by those of the Light. You have deceived the people here into thinking you can stop the tremors. Atlantis is doomed. The Council has brought this upon themselves with their insatiable greed and destruction of nature. Nothing can stop this now."

"You lie!" Ja'Ree screamed at me. "She always wears the skull around her neck. Hold her!"

The guards took hold of me while Ja'Ree roughly searched my body. "It's not on her! Where did you put it? I saw you wearing it not an hour ago as you left the Temple!"

"I saw her coming back down the cliff as she approached us!" Re'Sol growled and looked toward the cliff.

Regalis! He would be in danger! I realized at that moment that I must give him more time. He could not be found! I then sealed my own fate with the words,

"I have thrown the crystal skull into the ocean from the highest point of the cliff.

No one shall have it!"

Ja 'Ree enraged, sprang toward me. "It was mine! It was mine!" She screamed as she plunged the dagger into my side. Life poured out with the gushing of my blood. In disgust, they dropped my body onto the cold stone and quickly stomped away.

I lay on the cold, stone floor as life drained. Two of my young apprentices, my beloved Sisters of Light, crept silently to my side and held me. They were crying softly as darkness enveloped me.

Thousands of years past....

At 7 AM the alarm went off. I removed El Aleator from the pillowcase and held him in my hand. "How many times have we done this, my Friend?" I asked the little crystal skull. "Thank you for telling me."

There was no doubt now. Richard, Regalis, and I had been together in Atlantis. Our work had never been completed then. The forces of darkness had won the first round. They were still here over twenty thousand years later, and so were we. I placed the skull in my little leather pouch that hung around my neck. No wonder he felt so comfortable there.

I rose to shower and go to my job as a social worker for 8 AM. Such was my life in this age. The scene was repeated nearly every day. Although I was not called a High Priestess, the people of the Center needed counseling, guidance and healing. Now I understood why the job was so familiar to me.

Also, I had carried forward into this life some of my previous gifts. My gifts as a healer were becoming well known. Many people arrived unannounced or without appointments after I got off work at 5 PM. I arrived at the Shambhala Center and sometimes there were so many I'd line them up in the Center and let the Spirit heal them altogether, all at once.

Later that week, the landlord sent the rental manager to us. He brought devastating news.

"Susan, you have to vacate the building. The estimates came in from the plumbers and the problem is not inside the building but the old septic." He paused. "We have to tear up the pavement. It will cost twenty thousand dollars more. The landlord can't do that and will have to close the building."

"Tom! We can't leave here!" This is a very special place!"

"I'm sorry, Susan, you must."

"What about the empty store over there?" I asked looking down the walkway to the old beer factory.

"Susan, that space is three thousand dollars a month."

"THAT?" I couldn't believe what I heard. The ceiling had caved in and the debris was scattered all over the place inside. I had looked in through dirty windows before.

"I am not leaving! The landlord has to fix this place!" I could feel panic rising within me. I spoke rashly, "I have a lease! If he tries to evict us…I'll sue! "

"Susan, you don't have a bathroom." He said shaking his head.

"Tom, give me the key to the beer factory so we can use the bathroom there until he fixes ours. I'll clear up the fallen ceiling stuff. The bathroom works there doesn't it?"

"Why, I suppose it does." He thought for a moment and answered, "I can do that, I guess."

Shortly afterwards, I was shoveling ceiling tiles into a huge heap in the center of the beer factory to make a pathway to the new bathroom. All winter long, we would make the journey from our little Center to the factory for a very cold bathroom trip. It became a joke.

It was a long, long, long week. How can time move so slowly one day and so quickly the next? Heights that were so high and lows that were so low, tossed my emotions. I needed time. I needed to stay connected to the guiding energies, but I was being tossed like a salad. I had so much to consider.

Not only was the physical location for our group in danger, but also now I had Richard and our experience together to consider. I couldn't tell him everything. He was already too burdened.

I hadn't asked for any of this, I tried to reason. I wasn't prepared. Even though our relationship was difficult, I was still in love with my husband of ten years. Even though the ministry had taken over my life, I held my love for him. Now this!

"Why?" Why had I been shown this? So many questions! No answers!

During the week I replayed the vision over and over in my mind. It was not a vision. We had both ascended into the Light together. I ascended with my soul mate, no my Twin Flame, Regalis. No memory existed of my time in the Light with him, nor did any further revelations come in dreams or messages from the Divine.

Susan Isabelle

All I could fathom was that we were not to know at this time, and it obviously had to do with something we'd not completed in the past. We'd not done this while in Atlantis, I was quite sure of that.

Chapter IV

Turning Up The Heat

Richard and I continued to meet on Sunday afternoons. Even with all of the problems coming at me fast and furiously, this was my priority. Somehow it seemed that when we were in the Lotus we became more powerful and knowledgeable.

Each time we did, we were also learning how to work together. That seemed very important now. One afternoon, I asked Richard if we could try something new, a little different. I needed to see the future. It would help me with some of my insecurities. I just knew it would.

"Richard, we saw that the earth was averted from destruction after the Twin Towers went down. I wonder what Earth will look like in the future. It is nearly 2002. Lets see if we can go into the future."

"How far into the future do you want to go?" He asked.

"Well, let's try about six years or so. Let's go to 2008."

"Ok, we'll do it the way that I was trained in the service. It's a form of enhanced remote viewing. I never tried this with anyone else though."

"We can do it! I can see through your eyes, Richard. Let's try!"

As we slipped into the now easy routine of mind connection with each other, I was surprised when I found myself out of body, next to Richard. A time spiral formed around us. We entered the swirling, light- transport tunnel and emerged in the solar system of Earth, years into the future. Side by side, we sped toward the area that held the planet called Earth. I looked for the blue and white globe just past Mars, toward the sun, but could not see it.

Something was wrong! Soon, I did see it. I pointed ahead.

"Richard, Richard! Look!"

In the darkness of space, the once glistening blue planet could hardly be seen. It was all black and crusted over. There were no seas or oceans, just black crust.

"What happened, Richard? What happened?" I cried.

"Lets go down." He responded with his own concerns just barely held in check. We lighted upon the planet and walked over the black crust and deep dust.

"It burned up, Susan. They did it. They destroyed the whole damn planet!" He said angrily as he kicked the dust.

"But WHY? Why? Didn't we prevent this?" I asked Richard.

"Obviously, Susan, it wasn't enough. Once wasn't enough. They're going to try it again."

I bent down and scooped up a handful of the dust. Once this was beautiful. Once this held life, but now, everything was dead. Remembering the beauty it once held, I blew softly upon the dust. As it lifted from my hand, upon my breath, it began to sparkle in the air. We watched as the dust made its way back down and settled upon the earth. Magically, soft green moss appeared.

"Moss! Richard! Look!"

"Life, Susan! This is the beginning of life once again upon the planet. We must go."

Suddenly, back in the Center, we gasped!

"It was gone Richard! All gone! We've got to do something! Only six years or so! Six or seven YEARS!" I cried again. This just couldn't be happening!

"Susan, the people just don't have enough light to make it. They'll destroy this planet because they want to!"

"I don't believe that! There's something we've got to do! To prevent this disaster we have to!"

"Listen, I know you care, but you can't give your Goddess attunements to everyone on the planet in just six years. That's what it would take to raise the level to make it through the transition."

"What do you mean?" I asked.

"The Goddess attunements are what bring up the DNA, Susan. It's the attunement to the Diamond Sun Frequency. That's what it would take."

"Yes, that is the highest. I know that Goddess brought it to us to raise the planet's level of Light and to restore the ancient knowledge. Yes, I agree, it is the Diamond Frequency of Light that is needed. There's got to be a way."

"That's what the people need-all of them, Susan. You can't do that."

"Well, why did they give it to us then? The Earth was saved, but for what reason if not to exist further into the future for more than six or seven years?"

"I don't know. Just you can't do it all by yourself. Look at you; you're exhausted now. It's their responsibility anyway. They don't give a sh…"

"Yes, they do! Or, they would if they knew! I'd attune every one of them that wanted it- if I could."

He shook his head. "They've had plenty of chances, Susan."

"We're missing something here, Richard. We wouldn't have been allowed to see this if it wasn't preventable." I fumed while he watched me think.

"I want to go to the Council!" I demanded.

"Oh, no, Susan. You don't know what you're saying." He was shocked that I'd do such a thing and shook his head, no.

"Oh, yes, I do!" I shouted back at him. "I'm going tonight!"

"We're not supposed to go to them. They come to us." He pleaded with me.

"Not this time!" I said closing the car door to leave. "I'm going!"

Later that night, I left this plane. I left my body lying on the bed below and disappeared from Earth. I went into the Realm of the Council and Planetary Guardians.

Soon, I was at the chamber doors. Melchizedek and Metatron, the two mighty servants of God, served as intermediaries from the Highest Realms here to the High Council Members. The Council are those from the high astral realms who oversee the events of worlds in evolutionary status. I serve on this Council too. I am Al'Lat, the Council Representative from the System of Andromeda.

They had always come to me, now I was coming to them. I entered and went forward before the Council.

"What has brought you here Al'Lat Le Andro Melchizedek?" The Council member, calling me by my true name, asked me sternly.

"I have come because I am distressed. I have seen what you have not shown me."

"And what would that be?" Another questioned me.

"That the planet will be a burnt ember within years!" I retorted.

"The people of Earth have made their decisions Al'Lat. They have chosen their fate." A member tried to reason with me.

"That is not so!" I responded.

"Al'Lat, you gave them the opportunity once. We congratulate you on the effort. Even we didn't think you'd remember the assignment or even go so far as to move the time line! The darkness that holds the planet is very great, we didn't think it could be done, not even once."

Someone interjected. "We have seen the future realms. What they do in the future now is their responsibility. You cannot stay here. You must leave, now."

"I will not leave! I am a member of this Council and I declare my right to speak!"

"Al'Lat, you are in physical form and you know you have no rights before the Council while in form. The distortions of the mind in the physical realms is too great. You cannot bring that pollution here to us."

"Oh, yes she does!" Richard was entering the room as he shouted to them all. "It was the decision of this Council to send her to Earth to intervene. You sent her there at the risk of her own life and her people's. She does have a right to speak."

"Nor do you," Someone shouted back at him. Richard turned in anger. He began to grow in size. He was transforming into a white mist that grew until it filled the entire chamber. A loud roar came from him, a roar as loud as a lion's.

"Silence!" He bellowed. All became quiet. "Now, you may speak." He said turning toward me. This man has some power! Seizing my opportunity, I began.

>"*The people of Earth have not had a 'choice' as you describe it. The darkness has overcome them, and they have been hindered at every turn in their evolution.*
>
>*The interference of other alien races and those of the lower realms have distorted the original blueprint DNA of the Creator. This distortion was the reason you sent me to Earth in the first place.*
>
>*I have brought onto the Earth plane the Diamond Sun Frequency as was requested of me, by this very Council. It was in hope that this time, they could ascend.*
>
>*My work is not yet complete. Six or seven years is not enough time for me to fully restore the Diamond Frequency. You must arrange for assistance for me or speed up the progress of the work. This planet has been through so much! The time of their ascension is now.*"

"Al'Lat, the planet is now destined for termination. Once again, they will have failed to embrace the wisdom of Light and are destroying their own planet. We intervened once before, allowed the destruction of society and spared life to begin anew. This time, however, they have grown powerful and are extending outward into space and the planets. The seed of the distortion that you speak of must not infect the rest of the galaxy."

" The Creator has designed humanity to exceed all that has gone before. Humanity will one day rule this Council. Is this the reason why you are so quick to set a judgment, Sir?" I turned to stare directly at the one who had spoken to me. He obviously couldn't care less about Earth**.**

"Do you fear them for reasons other than spoken?" I asked.

"How dare you accuse in voice of one upon the Council?" he retorted loudly.

"How dare you terminate a people destined to bring about the evolution of us all? How dare you subvert the will of the Creator? He has made them to excel. It is written from the beginning of time itself. Will you intentionally hinder and destroy that which is not legally yours to destroy?" I challenged.

Someone rose from the Council seat and glided over toward me. "Al'Lat has not lost her determination to assist these people. We will consider your words." I recognized Kuan Yin, my old friend. She had risen in my support once again.

In the morning, I found myself back upon my bed. I was exhausted and remembered all except my returning or the final decisions. What had they decided? Was I going to have any help? I didn't know.

Later that afternoon, I received a call from Richard.

"Susan, you can't go in like that. They're the Council. They'll forbid you from ever coming back."

"That's their dilemma. Thanks for helping me out."

"No problem."

"Do you know what was decided? I can't remember."

"No, I don't know the answer. It's not likely that we'll ever know until the time comes. We'll check it out next week."

"Sounds like a plan to me." Now we were really working together.

Chapter V

Intergalactic Council Meeting

The week flew by. I didn't hear of anything else all that week. We met on the following Sunday afternoon about 1 pm. We sat down across from one another and closed our eyes to begin the breathing meditation.

Three hours later my eyes opened. I robotically stood up and walked toward the front door. I stared wordlessly out the window, looking up at the sky. Richard came and stood silently beside me, also looking out the window. I saw an object glisten in the sky and watched as it sped behind a cloud.

"Richard, did you see that?" I asked dreamily.

"Yeah, it was a UFO…" he mumbled next to me.

"No, I think it must have been a plane." I, groggy, replied to him while still staring out the window.

At that moment, the object popped out from behind the cloud, hovered, and then zipped across the sky, then straight up, and then out of sight. That kind of woke us up and we both began to turn toward one another, astonished.

"That's no plane." Richard said in his turning motion toward me.

"RICHARD!" I screamed.

"Susannnnn….." He shouted, "NO!"

"Look at you!" I pointed at him.

"Nooooo, look at you!"

All I could see of Richard was his head. He was covered in a green mist. His face looked out at me from a green, misty veil.

"Susan, what's that green stuff all over you?" Richard exclaimed while trying to point back at me. I couldn't see his hands.

"What's all that on you?" I asked .

And then we knew. We started laughing and speaking at the same time…

"They took us… we were up there…"

"Do you remember?"

"No…."

"Me neither…look at you! You're in some kind of a green fog!"

Giddy, we danced around in our green bubble suits like silly weebles for a while. As we touched the green mist that surrounded each of us, we'd bounce. Incredibly light-hearted, we'd laugh. It all seemed so funny!

We had been on a UFO! They had returned us with the directive to look out the window as it left the planet! And for some reason, it was funny. All we could do right now was laugh at each other. A few minutes later the green mist dissipated and so did our giddiness. Our questions did not. We could only speculate about what had happened to us, as we had no memory.

"Why did they take us? Did it have anything to do with the Council?" I asked Richard.

"Likely. Whatever had happened, we're not supposed to know just yet." He replied.

" But we were in a UFO! That's alien stuff." I argued back.

"I think that it was the Inter-Galactic Council we just had a meeting with. You know, what happens to earth, happens to the whole galaxy. Maybe even the universe. " Richard spoke thoughtfully. He was remembering vague pieces.

"Yes, I know that. I also know that I've been sent here to assist the people of Andromeda. Did you know that I am here on assignment, Richard? They sent me here. I am an Andromedan. I know it has to do with our ascension, and theirs. They want us to ascend and have sent me to ensure the process is completed." He nodded for me to go on, understanding.

"I tell my students that the dimensions are placed one atop the other in an energy frequency formation. It's like a hundred boxes that are placed one on top of one another. If you cause one to collapse at the bottom, they all sink down into a lower frequency. They all become more dense. Its nearly impossible to lift that frequency up again. It takes a direct infusion of Light to reverse it."

I considered my own words. That is what was happening to earth. By manipulation by lower forces bringing famine, war and the mentality of war, earth was spiraling downward into the abyss. Consciousness was descending. It had happened before. I remembered now.

A higher consciousness reflects itself in love; love for one another and for the planet.

Where is love on this planet? I wondered. The question answers itself with reflection. Love exists within the soul but is greatly prevented in this society. Need, and poverty of mind and soul has been created. Governments and international powers have held the reins over the peoples and have kept them in bondage, largely through manipulation.

Family and nature have been enslaved. There are such chains of monetary slavery that people cannot even lift their own heads to see another's need, and if they do, they are powerless to come to assist. I had seen as a social worker how welfare programs and local laws prevent those seeking relief from breaking their chains. The populace is given just enough to survive, but not enough to effectively make changes. Its 'hard to get out from under' the saying goes. It is true.

Those that have the means do not give but rather, hold tightly for fear that what they do have will be taken away. All were entrapped in this mindlessness, I realized and continued. Altlanis was being revisited.

"When you insert a 'box' at the bottom, all the others rise up too. An infusion of Light, or the mind and heart of loving human kindness and compassionate action, lifts a planet, a people, a universe. Love is the highest vibration. When earth ascends, it moves up in frequency, energy and in dimensional status. All the other dimensions also are affected. One day, when this is over, the people of Andromeda will also have ascended. I am here to help them, to make sure it happens."

"I see. That's why you got so mad at the Council."

"Partly. I want the people of earth to have a fair turn too. Ascension benefits everyone."

"Not quite." He quipped.

"Very true. Only those who want control of the lower realms want us to fail. It's all about power." I agreed.

" Yup. That's the problem. Power: Power over the peons. Keep the people enslaved." He spoke softly.

"Well, I refuse to let that just happen. The people are worth much more than that!" I was beginning to get riled up again.

"That's what you told the Council." He replied, smiling, diffusing my intensity.

"You know, when we were created by the Creator of All, we were destined for great things, Richard. We were originally created in the image of God/Goddess. Can you imagine what humanity is really supposed to look like? Can you imagine how beautiful that would be? There's been so much manipulation of this culture. They've tried to destroy it."

"Well, I hope you're not too late."

"I don't think so. God has intervened to assist the children and I just know He'll see us through. I just know it. My soul knows it. I just don't know how." I sighed.

"Well, Susan, I guess our appearance at the Council stirred things up more than we realized. Maybe you'll get your chance. It was enough to get the Intergalactic Council's attention."

"There's got to be a way to accelerate the Diamond Frequency infusion into this planet's system. Somehow, I think that we've started something." I reflected.

"We'll find out soon."

"At least we came back from our ride up there laughing…that's got to be a good sign!"

A Dark Revolution

Time past and we did not hear anything about the reason we'd been taken. We continued to meet. Soon it was late November.

One night after service a group of my students, about ten of them, approached me.

"Susan, we want to talk to you."

"OK, I answered, what's up?

"Well, one of the men said to me, "We don't like your meetings with Richard."

Shocked, I asked, "Why?"

"He doesn't look like a light-worker and he is strange."

"Who is he anyway?" Another spoke.

I composed myself and tried to formulate an answer that would not compromise Richard's confidentiality. "Richard is someone who is very private in his life and doesn't mix with other people. He works alone. Remember, I told you that he told me about the Towers?"

"I know why he doesn't mix!" One of the women retorted. "I tried to talk to him and all my jewelry fell right off me!"

"Me too!" Another spoke. "My necklace burst into pieces right in front of him!"

I tried to conceal a smile. I could believe that...

"What are you doing with him anyway?" The first man spoke accusing me with his voice.

"You know I never speak about my consults, Mark. But, I can assure you that there is nothing improper going on." I tried to calm them down.

"Well, we've decided. Either he goes, or, or I go!" Mark spoke again while looking around at the others for support. There were a few nods in his direction.

"Mark, I have one rule here." I spoke firmly. "If someone causes harm to another, spiritually, mentally, physically or emotionally, I will speak to that person and try to seek a resolution. I give a warning. *If* it continues, *then* they leave. This man has done absolutely nothing wrong and *I will not tell him to go!*"

He glared directly at me and spoke with fiery venom issuing from each word, "Either he goes, or I go!"

I met his gaze. "Mark, then I guess you will have to leave." He looked furious and was about to speak again. I interrupted him as I looked around at the others. "And, any others that feel as you do can go too. This man has done no wrong!"

My words stunned the rebels into silence. I stood up from my chair and faced the astonished group. "I need to go home now, it is late and Will is expecting me. Go!"

Briskly walking to the front door of the Center, I opened it and held it open and beckoned for them to leave. A very solemn group of people gathered their belongings and filed silently outside.

I locked the door behind me and got in my car with them standing outside the door still gaping at me. I slid behind the wheel and started the car and drove away from them all. As soon as I was out of their sight, I gasped! I pulled the car over to the side of the road. I couldn't breathe! Trying to catch my breath and to finally stop shaking, my emotions exploded and I burst into tears.

Thoughts began racing through my mind. Was this jealousy? Control? How? How could they do that? These were supposed to be enlightened people! Some of them had been used to alter the time lines! How? How was this happening to them? To me? My life is personal. When? What had happened to make them ever think that I was owned or controlled by them?

Mark had been so outrageous! "Either he goes, or I go!" He had snarled at me! What had happened to him?

Gathering my composure and wiping away the tears, I started up the car again and drove home. I walked toward the front door. The lights were still on. Maybe Will's in a better mood? I thought. I needed someone to talk to.

My hopes were soon crushed. When I opened the door, Will was standing there again with the mail for me to open and to read. Teary eyed and exhausted, I took the mail without a word and went to the table and began to open the mail. He went back to bed and was soon snoring as I cried over my mail.

"God!" I need help!" I implored to the silence all around me.

My dreams that night were confusing. I saw vivid colors swirling. In the colors I could see the face of El Aleator, the crystal skull, and of Richard. There were also images of grotesque beings. They were spreading a sticky substance in front of me as I walked. I was trying not to step in the sticky stuff, but moving forward was really hard as I'd have to stop so often to free myself from the gooey substance. The dreams continued for a few more nights. I woke up each morning exhausted.

A few days later a young woman I knew arrived at the Center. She had been coming to the Center for a while. She'd been healed of a number of things, both spiritual and physical. Her life had changed dramatically over the last few months.

Her soul path reading with me had revealed her husband was a Master that had incarnated to assist her in her spiritual work on earth. As long as she stayed with him, she'd be able to complete her mission. Her new understanding and relationship with him in a true, spiritual partnership, had changed her whole life, as well as his.

"Hello! I didn't expect to see you today, Cynthia." I greeted her as she entered.

"No, I thought I'd just come down and talk to you about something that is on my mind. I have noticed that you really don't have much time to run the store and I was wondering if I could help you?"

"How nice of you to offer, Cynthia. What did you have in mind?" I asked curious now.

"Well, I could do a little in the store each day, but what I really want to do is to help you and the Center. You've done so much for me and I could never repay you. I would like to purchase some of the stock already here as you don't have much space for new things."

We both looked around the small store as she spoke. It was true. "This would give you some working capitol. Susan, I know you are going to have to move."

Surprised, I jumped at the offer. "Cynthia that sounds like a great idea! That would give me the funds to relocate and relieve me of the responsibility of looking after the store. I don't do partnerships, Cynthia. I had a partner before and it didn't work out as each time she'd try to do a session a pipe would burst or something. Spirit didn't allow it. She simply gave up. This is not a partnership; but will be your own business within the store. I like the idea!"

We made some plans and agreed as to an inventory. She would invest ten thousand dollars by purchasing my stock. I'd hold it until spring and then look for a new place. This was an answer to prayer!

As she left, I gave a little 'thanks' for the answered prayer, but I still had the rebel group to consider and the week was passing by real fast. Soon, it would be Sunday and an unsuspecting Richard would be arriving. I had no way of contacting him, as he kept all of his personal information private.

On Sunday I reluctantly told Richard what had happened, the whole story of the rebellion and why. He listened and remained calm.

"Susan, this always happens to me. People don't understand me. That's why I stay away and don't get involved with people very often. I have no desire to harm your group or to cause any difficulties for you. I think I ought to go- now."

"Where are you going?" I asked, shocked.

"I need to think and seek guidance about this. I'll call you when I know." He stood up. There would be no meditation today. I watched as he walked out the door. My heart sunk. This had hurt him deeply. I didn't know if I'd ever see him again. I took a deep breath.

Sunday's service began as usual, but there were many absent faces. Obviously, many of Mark's group had made the decision to leave the Center and the teachings. A whole group of people had now refused the Diamond Frequency. But, I reminded myself, the rest had decided to stay, to grow and learn. Herein would be the hope of humanity. I would continue.

Tonight's service would be taken from the book *of Return of the Children Of Light* by Judith Bluestone Polich. New to the market, I had been thrilled to read her work on the Maya and Incan prophecies regarding the shift in consciousness they predicted. I began to teach;

"Our human potential is unfolding into a higher form of consciousness, just as this book has outlined. We cannot remain in a static mode should we desire to reach our highest potential as beings of light. Old, lower frequencies must be transcended should we make that leap into a higher state.

The efficiency of our light is such that we must learn to focus our thoughts, focus our energies just as a laser, pointed and true to the mark we set for ourselves."

I couldn't tell them of the meetings Richard and I were having, or the abilities we had been developing, but this was it; focused intent and energy! I continued.

"All those things that daily come into our fields that cause us lose our focus, ought to be avoided or the energy produced from that, defused in some way. It is best not to place our precious energy there in useless endeavors.

Speak, teach, and then stand aside to allow others to find their own way also, sometimes through their own experiences. Non- interference is the key and focused energy the how- to."

Many nodded their heads. It was not a secret that about ten people had made the decision to leave the Center. I was sure they thought it was because I had refused to put Richard out that they had left, but really, it was because of the very topic of our service tonight.

I remembered Atlantis all over again. Somehow, I had lost the focus. Not this time!

I could not allow others to rob me of my Light or my determination. I could not as a spiritual leader, allow a group of angry people to rob others of their opportunity. Abuse takes many forms. My sole focus to help the people attain higher light and understanding of the energy, had come under assault. Continuing,

"Our personal light, the lamps that we carry within our souls, must have enough oil in them to meet the duration. Priorities must be determined in our lives. Setting those priorities may be painful or uncomfortable for us.

Personal sacrifices may be called for. You must choose to go onto higher ground. Others may misunderstand you. Lower energies may try to prevent you from attaining spiritual freedom and understanding of higher concepts. Those concepts are real, not illusions. We can attain higher states of spirituality and human existence. Consider this;

According to the author, a hidden potential is within each person, within the DNA. We each carry 100 trillion cells in our body complete with DNA that is distributed in 23 chromosomes. I quote,

"Our DNA is a micro-universe set out with a continuous strand up to 6 feet long each having 3 billion components. Scientists have found that most DNA components have no recognizable function, only 3 % are believed to be functional."

"Think about that for a moment. That means 97 % of what you are capable of may be unused, untapped by you. We saw what we could do last September when we did focus our energy. Our combined intent of love, Divine Guidance and a willingness to reach out our hearts and minds to God/ Goddess altered the history of this planet.

There are those who teach that we may activate our DNA through artificial ways. I need tell you- and to warn you- of something. As we evolve and come into Light, our DNA is spontaneously activated according to our personal level of readiness. Our Light and our wisdom must coincide with each other in balance within our being, or the attempt to do this will bring disastrous results.

Not too long ago a woman arrived here at the Center in tears. She begged me to help her. As soon as I tried to get close to her, pain shot through my body. I couldn't get close. I asked her what she had done. She told me she had gone through twenty activations of DNA enhancement through a Melchizedek method. She cried as she explained that no one could come close to her. Her friends had all abandoned her, she'd lost here job and her life was in ruin.

First of all, I must explain that Melchizedek, the true High Priest of God, would not do this. The artificial attempt to alter this woman's DNA was an experiment done to her energy body. She was not ready, spiritually, to do this, nor was the technique spiritual. She wanted something instantly, without the wisdom teachings that must accompany such a growth.

The true DNA expansion can only come through two spiritual means; One-through connection to the Light of God through prayer and meditation and you must ask for it. 'The Shekhina, or the Spirit as a Dove, brings this Light upon the sincere asking of a heart that has been prepared and desires the sacredness of joining with God/Goddess.

And secondly, through the sacred attunements-sacraments-or the direct infusion of the Light that is given to those desiring to ascend in the Light. You know this as the laying on of hands as the Christ taught us and the Shambhala Attunements that are given here. Remember, Shambhala means, 'Heaven's Light. We accept nothing else and no other Light.

I propose that we set aside time to meditate, to work together to accomplish some goals. To be at the forefront of the global awakening, we must learn how to read the signs and how to respond without fear and hold to truth together.

Over the next few months, if you chose to join me, we will begin to learn to focus our energy one step, one issue at a time. We will choose the higher path. Let's build our Light together and learn. I choose to seek out my potential, to grow and to learn. How about you? Why? For my, for our good, and the Highest Good of ALL of humanity!"

It was an enthusiastic group that went home that night. What could have been a total split or destruction of our little Center, became a determined group anxious to learn. I had not caved in or become weak. Richard and I had learned a lot together in a very short time. Perhaps it was time for me to share some of that with the others.

I would begin to teach them how to really use energy! This time, I'd make sure we got through. It would be very important to empower as many as possible. In Atlantis, the power was too restricted. People rebel for many reasons, but rarely if they have some ability to change their perceived outcomes.

Later that night I had further opportunity to think about what had happened. It is confusing to say the least, why people do what they do. The human condition is so fragile, I realized. Jesus had said two thousands years ago, "The Spirit is willing, but the flesh is weak."

Even with the miracles that had occurred in everyone's sight at our Center, it still wasn't enough to affect their thinking or change their lives permanently. Something within the very soul needed to change. A transformation deep within the soul had to occur and to be stimulated into action. Only God spark that light within and it seemed that even He had a difficult time with that one, so who was I?

As soon as some difficulty arose or ego entered into the heart, the people were ready to jump ship and deny the very gifts they had received. I remembered the stories of Christ's mission here. Seemed the same things happened to him too. A few fishes and loaves turned into hundreds and people were fed, but then they turned vicious toward Him. Doubting Thomas, Peter's denial, and the exit of the disciples after the crucifixion were a few other examples of that.

Seemed also that only five out of ten virgins had enough 'spiritual oil' at the end. (Matthew 25:1-13) I thought a lot about that. Only five out of ten; odds were not too good. We have a fifty-fifty chance, but then, that's half!

Many of those who had chosen to leave the Center had had a personal healing. They had seen others healed. I had begun to say to people that visited our little Center, that this was the "Last Chance Hotel." Time was running out for humanity. As I had spoken to the Council previously, I was on a mission to assist earth.

In our Shambhala training we taught the three aspects of the Divine Father, Mother and Christ Light; the Vesica Pisces- creative energies. On the roadway of life and the path to ascension, we offered the highest training and energies in that attempt.

We tried to hold integrity at the Center. No drugs or alcohol were allowed in the Center and all people were to be respected, no matter where they were on their path. We had only one real 'law' –don't harm anyone else. But it didn't seem to be enough for some people. The human condition is fragile, not easily understood, and very easily manipulated by entities, peers and daily events.

But, 'Why? Why Richard?' Why target a harmless man who only tried to help mankind? I wondered. Then I began to see bitter truth. Lower energies and entities had overcome the mind of some of our group. How had that happened? We were a spiritual group!

Having a compromised heart and mind, the few people involved felt they did not have power and could control over some one or thing. That got them really mad. They were mad first at themselves for their lack of perceived power, and then toward those who denied their perceived "wants". "Either he goes, or I go!" More than just mad, it was insane.

Further thought and consideration on this extended the thought even further, beyond my little Center, into the world, into the past of Atlantis.

I realized, the first words out of someone's mouth in that ego, self-first condition is usually, "You're too controlling." Ja'Ree was wanting control so long ago. Atlantis was not any different in its development than now! An ego mind is just a growing stage of development. We keep getting stuck.

God and parents know that one very well. It is an adolescent mind. When an adolescent child wants their own way, you become the target, no matter how much good, what you may have provided, or done previously for them. Anger reins the mind and all the previous good things you have done are forgotten.

Secondly, those of the negative, ego adolescent mind begin to spread their venom to others by stirring up the hidden ego wants of others, to feed their negative ego-self even more. Misery truly loves company.

I became convinced then that most of humanity, in this current reality, has an adolescent mind. That's why it is so hard to make any progress.

The change of consciousness from "I want", to " I give" would be a huge leap for humanity. That little change of consciousness would make the life and world altering difference between friendly neighbors, a happy marriage, a friendship, or an avoidance of war between countries in the world.

I challenge everyone to spend a day resisting the thought that someone has 'done you wrong' to viewing every thought and situation with, 'what can I give/do to make this better.' That is an adult mind of wisdom and mercy. Just one day of that adult mind would lift the entire earth's consciousness. JFK said it well, "Ask not what your country can do for you, but what you can do for your country."

The only exception is the instance in that it will hurt another to even appear to comply in the situation at the given moment. Then, for the highest good of all, you must speak and hold the truth in all wisdom.

"Oh, no!" you might say. "I'll be the brunt of a slaughter if I speak up!"

Maybe so, but that will make it better. Yes, it will. An example will be set. A level of integrity to benefit the situation will be presented, even if not accepted. You will have given a righteous opinion. You will have set an energy template.

You may be fired, you may persecuted, be shunned, even as I was by two hundred church members who didn't like my gift of healing. They actually declared the gift of God to be of the devil! That friend, is what the verse in the scriptures meant by 'blasphemy against the Holy Spirit,' the Shekhina, the Divine Nurturing, Mother aspect of God. The Holy Spirit is the one who heals us and blesses humanity through us. It is a spiritual gift. You do not curse or destroy the one who heals you. You curse God's Beloved should you do so.

You may feel as though you are all alone, but you are not. Be strong; hold your truth. It is you; yes, you that hold an adult mind, that are holding the entire earth right now in the higher vision, that is keeping us from destruction.

The descent into the insane mind, the confused, adolescent mind is that which leads us into wars and killing of one another. If we let go of that 'wheel' there would be no one able to keep us on the path. Be strong, friend of Light.

I determined I would begin to use the tools we already had to utilize all our abilities. We'd already been given great spiritual gifts in our little Center. The crystal skull of the Maya that had been given to me held the programming of Itznma, the Son of the Divine Couple within it and great knowledge. I was beginning to understand that it held new information for me and the others. It held information and a light frequency that could transport us across the universe. To me, that meant love.

The techniques Richard and I had learned together were invaluable. Yes, I would teach now and learn all that I could so I could help the others and complete my mission. "I have been thinking about where we might start." I spoke to my student, Karen. "I know you are a powerful healer and crystal skull worker."

Karen had a special ability to teach others and use her crystal skull. She called him Gedulah as he had been on the Kabbala location of Mercy when we activated them all together to 'copy Max' and El Aleator. Our little skulls were sometimes quite talkative. That had been the beginning of the incoming Goddess frequencies for earth. So much had happened afterwards.

"I think there is a lot more we can access with the crystal skulls. I'd like to start a regular skull group. We can meet and try to learn more about them." Karen agreed. I certainly wanted to know more about El Aleator if I could.

Karen and a few others of us began to meet at the Center. That is when we learned that the skulls had an ability to interlink with one another. We sat in a circle while holding the skulls. Instantly, a ring of energy and white light formed, linking one skull to another as we held them.

As we were seated in our circle, somehow information and feelings were transmitted to each of us. It was through the frequency of emotion, I realized, that much of what I was learning was received.

I could feel the answers to my questions in my body first, then my mind.

We made a deliberate attempt to connect to the thirteen etheric skulls of the Maya. Back in time, that is where I sent El Aleator with Regalis on that last fateful day of Atlantis. I sent him back to his place of origin, back to the country we now call, Belize.

There he rejoined the other crystal skulls to wait for another day. That day came when I was sent to Belize by Adama and received the skull. Once again, I held the skull. Once again, I would have the opportunity to assist humanity.

The skulls of the Maya held all the world's information. What a resource! Also, some of our skulls were receivers of one or more of the thirteen original skulls and were identifiable as such. Once linked, we often times would receive the same information simultaneously. Soon, a class manual was formed for the care and use of the skulls as they taught us.

Turning Up The Heat A Little Bit More!

In December, Tom, the complex manager returned.

"Susan, I don't know how to tell you this, but we have a bid on the beer factory. A meat- processing company wants to take over the space. "

"Tom, you know that if you do that, that I'll sue. I have a contract and a lease for usable space, you know."

"I know that Susan, but the landlord wants his space to be used and three thousand dollars a month is too much for you; you already told me that."

"Tom, we have to have a bathroom. What we are doing here isn't even legal and my people have to walk in the snow to get to a bathroom!" I left him standing and walked away. I was angry.

Later that night I wrote a letter to the owner of the property.

> Dear Dr. Lang,
> I thank you for allowing us to rent from you in the Plaza. I thank you for also letting us use the beer factory for our bathroom and for all the money you have spent trying to fix the bathroom. I understand it is too old.
>
> What I want to say to you is that this place is a very special place. A couple of miracles have happened here, one that you know of, and another that I will tell you of now.
>
> You know that when I rented from you this plaza was completely empty. It had been for a long time and you must have been losing a lot of money.
>
> The beer factory roof had fallen in, the dance place was condemned, the space next door and across from me was empty too. There was filth and the whole place was dead.
>
> Three weeks after I moved in, the space next door was rented to a wine tasting restaurant and that is doing very well. Soon, the dance place became a fitness center; the place across from me became a diet and health center and an appliance center moved in too. This plaza has become a great money- maker for you.
>
> Don't you think this is strange? After years of vacant buildings, now you have thriving plaza? That Sir is a miracle. The only building that is vacant, but used by us, is the beer factory. We need that space, but I cannot afford your price.

The second miracle happened on September 14th 2001 right here in your plaza. Kuan Yin appeared over us. I have included a picture of Kuan Yin for you to see her.

I don't know if you know anything about her, but she is the Goddess of Mercy and Compassion. Billions of people in the East know her as the protector of women, children, and life on the earth.

We had held a prayer vigil after the Twin Towers went down in New York and called her to help the Earth. As you can see, she came. That is the second miracle.

She has blessed this place and us. She appeared right over your plaza and us!

I ask that you consider these things and allow us to continue to use the beer factory for the bathroom. We can't leave here.

I Thank You,
Susan Isabelle
Shambhala Center and Gaila Goddess Store.

The next morning the letter and the pictures were in the mail. Now, I would wait. Life seemed to drag on as another week went by at work and at the Center. I had not heard from Richard and supposed I never would. I was waiting, but nothing seemed to be happening on any front.

One morning I was called into the CEO's office at the agency I worked for.

"Susan, do you know why you are here?"

"No, Sir, I don't."

"I cannot reveal my sources, I want you to understand."

"What are you talking about?" I asked curious. "Am I in trouble?"

"No, Susan you are not, but there have been reports of something that is greatly disturbing to me."

"What? I asked. I immediately remembered when I was brought in here about a year before. I had used healing energy for a child who was undergoing tests for the third operation in a month. His mother had begged me to help, as her child would go into cardiac arrest each time it had to be done. Risking my job, I stood ten feet away from her child and beamed to energy toward her baby. Blood was drawn from his tiny arm. Her child didn't even whimper, but rather, fell asleep.

Afterwards, the mother was so ecstatic that she demanded I not leave the hospital until I taught her how to do this for her child. I gave her a Reiki attunement and showed her how, right there in the hospital.

Three days later, I was standing here in this office being told if I ever did that again, I would be fired. Shaking myself from the memory, I looked up at him.

"What?"

"Susan, there have been reports that you may be being harassed or rather abused in your position here at the Agency."

"OH!" I blurted out with surprise. I hadn't told anyone.

"Is that true?" He sat down by my side and looked into my eyes. "Susan, I want you to tell me."

"Many people depend upon me to help them," I started.

"Yes, we know that, and I want to assure you that nothing will happen to you and your position here. What is happening?"

"In my job, I am the crisis worker for the families. I have to go to families that are in terrible crisis; often they have no food or are living in places such as hallways or under bridges. That sort of thing, you know." I looked up. He nodded.

"I was hired here to help the most vulnerable families. I have always had a discretionary fund to help those families, to buy food, get them an apartment or emergency housing for them and get services established for them." He nodded again. "There's been a cut in my funding. Also, the supervisor has made it so that I must request to use that funding before using it. It must go to a board for approval and families must wait." I paused.

He kindly nodded for me to go on.

"Each time I submit a request; he is furious and storms into my office. He is very large and looms over my desk red faced and shakes my paperwork in my face. He's tried to disrupt my ability to help the most needy families." I gulped away the memories and took a deep breath.

"In other words, he's made it impossible for me to obtain the funds. The family funds are now being diverted to other things like a new four thousand dollar computer for his office. I've taken to drastic measures to obtain funding for the families and I'm risking being fired every time I've interrupted secret meetings to get what I need for the families. I know this is a big agency, but some people here don't like me very much these days."

"Why didn't you report this?" He asked, concerned.

"I did. I made a mistake of brining it to the next level up, following procedures, but made the mistake of calling it a 'misappropriation of funds.' There was another meeting; I was told I'd loose my job if I said that again.

"Until now, I've had to keep quiet or they'd hire someone to take my place that would 'play the game' and I've held on because I know the families would never have a chance. I don't play and they don't like it!"

"OK." He said with his body and his anger rising, "I'll take care of this."

I left the office wondering; "WHAT IS GOING TO HAPPEN NEXT. I AM SO TIRED...."

Chapter VI

Be Not Deceived

Arriving at the Center at 5:30 in the afternoon, I was met at the door by Lily.

" Susan I have someone here. She's waiting in my car. She needs your help."

"Lily, I don't know, it's been an awful day…" I complained.

"Susan, please, she's a friend…"

"OK. I'll meet her." I reluctantly agreed.

As soon as she got out of Lily's car, I could see it. It hung like a great big black glob of swirling, dark ugly stuff by her side.

"Lily, she has to stay outside. Don't bring her in here!" I backed away. Lily looked at me questioning. "Back, back outside; behind the willow tree! I'll be there in a minute. Wait for me there!" I shouted at them.

I ran inside the Center and rummaged through the cabinets. "I've got to have some here, somewhere!" I mumbled as I searched.

"What are you looking for, Susan?"

I heard a very old, very familiar, voice speak to me. A chill went through me from the top of my head to the bottom of my feet. It couldn't be! Not now!

"Oh, my God!" I answered. I shivered and turned to face the voice. Yes, it was exactly who I thought it was. My mind reeled! It was someone from my past and we had parted on extremely poor terms. What was he doing here? I hadn't seen him in years! "I am sorry, I can't talk to you right now! I'll be back in a little while!" I offered.

I picked up my four boxes of salt and frankincense and ran out to find Lily and her friend out back behind the Center sitting under the willow tree. I looked at the woman more closely as I approached her. She stood and began to walk toward me.

"Stay right there." I demanded. She stopped.

Her face was drooping on one side, her eye slanted nearly shut. She had a gnarled looking left hand. This twenty-five year old looked like she had had a stroke. The glare in her eyes told me otherwise. She was possessed!

"What do you want?" I asked her, or it.

"Can you help me?"

The whimper came out, pleading. From somewhere deep inside, she found the strength to overcome the beast to ask for help. I could not refuse. My heart softened.

"If I do, you MUST agree NEVER to become involved in the things you have been doing EVER again!"

"I don't want to be like this, I tried to kill myself but I can't even die." She began to cry. Lily started forward. I motioned her away. She backed up.

"You will sit here on this chair, now!" I took the salt and placed it in the four directions and drew a circle around her, completely made of salt.

"You will not leave this circle or rise from that chair, do you understand?"

Something growled from within her.

"Do you understand?" I demanded an answer. She nodded.

I anointed Lily and myself with the frankincense, praying all the while, and then I began.

> "Circle of the Christ: Light of ALL Salvation; This one seeks your release from the lower realms and has expressed her desire to change her ways; to leave behind her former works of death and ignorance of that; Bring your Light to lift the darkness from her.
>
> I ask Your presence now:
>
> I ask You send the Archangel Michael to guard the perimeter and not allow the dark evil to escape or to cause us harm."

With that, the Light of Christ descended over the seated woman, just above her head. The demon within her screamed and lifted the chair about a foot off the ground. Again and again the chair flew off the ground! She turned blue and foamed from her mouth as the chair flung and lifted wildly within the circle of Light. Lily's eyes were wide with fright as she watched her friend struggle within the circle.

The words came from my lips as I now spoke to the demon,

> "The Lord God of All is ever merciful. Even unto the dark pit His mercy extends to you. You may go into the Light Of Mercy or into the salt of destruction."

The Light of Christ descended further down around the woman. She screamed wildly as the demon was forced out and had to release her. Rather than ascend into the Light, or assimilate the Light within itself, the demon flung itself into the four boxes of salt and was captured within the salt. There, it could do no further harm.

I watched as the Light surrounded the woman who now began to cry softly. Tears were streaming down her face, she looked at me and whispered.

"Thank you." She hung her head. I nodded to Lily who then walked forward and put her arms around her friend.

"Now, you are free. Come back to me tomorrow. Lily, can you keep her at your house?"

"Yes, I'll bring her home." She answered.

"Give her something to eat and don't go anywhere else."

"OK." She helped the woman to her feet.

"Before you go, there is something you must do. Here is a bag to place the boxes of salt in." I said to her as she rose. I pointed to the first box. The woman took the bag and went over to pick up the salt.

"It's so cold! It's too heavy! I can hardly pick it up!" She jumped back away from the small box of salt.

"Yes, I want you to know that the demon you carried is now in the boxes of salt. It cannot harm you now. But remember this; I cannot promise you that I can ever help you again." I looked at her sternly.

"You must not return to your old ways or invite this sort of thing into your life, or I can guarantee you will be worse off than ever before. See me tomorrow and we will speak then. Now finish picking them up." I commanded her.

Quietly, she picked them up and put them into the bag. She stood up and turned toward me.

"Now, you will bury this as well as your old life." I handed her the shovel that had been leaning up against the tree placed there for just these occasions. She began to dig a hole. Beneath the willow tree, she buried her demons.

I walked back to the Center alone. My ex-friend, was still waiting to speak to me.

"What happened to you?" He asked me shocked at seeing my tossed appearance.

"I had to do an exorcism." I said as I walked past him briskly.

As he stepped back to let me into the Center, he turned away and got into his car and drove off. Strange that he should appear that day…

Will was there with the mail as usual when I arrived home. I finished opening the mail then sat in the living room on the couch. I looked up at the ceiling and prayed once again. "Father-God, I need help!"

The next morning I went to my job as usual. I avoided the supervisor and stayed in my office. I just wondered what was going to happen to my job. I still needed to work to help the new Center get off the ground and I still wanted to help the people who needed me there in my position at the agency. The day past slowly.

After work, I met Lily who re-introduced me to her friend. What a change! She stood tall and without the slanted gait or curled hand.

Although she was still pale and gaunt from her experiences, there was no demon on her side.

"Susan, I want you to meet Eleanor, my friend." Lily proudly announced.

"Hello, Eleanor, " I said while reaching out to touch her shoulder. She started to cry, lunged forward and clung to me in a crunching embrace. Great sobs and tears fell from her heart.

"Thank you! Thank you so much!" She cried.

"It is OK, Eleanor, but we must talk. I don't have much time and there is much to tell you. I first want to hear of how this happened to you."

"I really don't know." She replied softly.

"Then tell me what you have been doing, spiritually."

I listened as Eleanor told me of how she first became interested in goddess worship, earth healing magic and what she called 'white witchcraft'. It didn't take long for me to understand that she had entered into a complete involvement in the dark arts.

She had started out just learning about what she thought was earth healing, the use of healing herbs and plants and the mother goddess energies of Gaia. She had begun just a few years ago to learn to connect to these energies and to eventually cast spells for fun, love and profit.

"Eleanor, I understand what has happened to you, but I am not sure that you understand what has happened."

She nodded. "How could this have happened to me?" She asked me. " I saw what you did! I didn't believe in that stuff, demons and all! It's all one, they said we are all one, all light, all god!" She gasped in the horror of realization and memory of the demon. "It was on me!" She started to cry again.

"Eleanor, be calm." Lily held her and stroked her hair as a mother caring for a child. "It will be alright now."

Tear filled eyes looked up at me. "I want to know!"

She was getting angry, and that's a good sign!

"OK. Get hold of yourself and I will try to explain."

She straightened and gave Lily a look of thanks and said, "I'm ready."

"First of all; just because someone tells you something is "white" doesn't really mean that it is good or of the light. That includes some forms of what you may call, 'white witchcraft.'" Eleanor nodded for me to go on.

"Secondly, Gaia, or the earth, is a consciousness; it is a manifest form of the Divine Feminine" She nodded that she understood.

"Most people today realize that, but not with understanding. All things that are in a physical form are a manifest form of the Divine Feminine, in other words, it has form."

"I understand that." She agreed.

"Yes, the first word of a child in every language is, "MA", mother, and an early acknowledgement by the child that the child is now in a manifest form. Think of the word 'material, or matter.' MA- means 'mother' (tera) means form-ial-physical, Ma on tera, or earth, in a physical form."

She nodded again, listening intently.

"Follow the understanding that Gaia, the earth form, is also a manifest form-material presence of the feminine. Gaia is a created being. Gaia is an extension of the *thought of God* through the power of Goddess; Mother, material presence."

"Eleanor, understand that Gaia-Earth has been created by Mother/Father to support our life on Gaia. Our physical form is made up of the minerals, the crystals and all things that are on Gaia."

"Are you telling me that Gaia is *not* the Goddess? I'm not sure about that. I've worshipped her for so long...."

"Eleanor, you are sitting in a store that is called The Gaila Goddess. That means, 'A Joyous Gathering of the Goddess'. Goddess has many ways of manifesting herself.

Some of what I have come to teach is that gathering; to help people understand that Goddess is everything that *is*-Her way of revealing Herself and the Creator to the Child, to you and to me." I paused. "The Creator of All *is* the Creator and is perfect, complete Light. All else is created and is a lesser energy, or smaller light, sometimes known as the Divine Spark of God. We honor that in each other, that which is beautiful, filled with light, in that it is a reflection of the Creator; not the totality- but it is not fullness of God/Goddess."

"Well, what about Goddess Kuan Yin? Her picture is all over this place!"

I laughed with her and Lily. "Yes, I agree she is all over us here! Kuan Yin is another manifest form of the True Goddess." Eleanor cocked her head questioning in her expression.

"OK. Let me help you understand. I am a mother; my children call me MOM. I am a Teacher; my students call me Susan Isabelle or Al'Lat. I am a wife; my husband calls me, Sue. When I am a Mom, I show the aspect of mother's Love.

As a teacher, I show the world the Aspect of Wisdom and Understanding- at least I hope so!" We laughed!

"When a wife, I admit I am just a little bit more submissive and supportive, so I show that as an Aspect of Goddess, the aspect of a *Helper; a Wife*. As a mother, I show the Aspect of the *Creation of Life*. All the same person, I am a being of many aspects. Being a wife is only One Aspect of Goddess totality.

As created in the image of God, we show many aspects, but most of us reflect only a little of each aspect. Some people have lived their lives on earth in such a manner that they reflect great aspects of God-Light in their lives. We usually call them saints, apostles, and martyrs.

Kuan Yin is an Aspect of Goddess that shows to the world Her *Mercy and Compassion*. The physical form of Kuan Yin holds more of the presence and beauty of mercy and compassionate understanding toward others.

The example of her life encourages us to see those aspects of God on earth. We are encouraged by this to show mercy and compassion to all. Kuan Yin did that in her life and continues to do that in her ascended form. She's still helping us. Realize that all things in physical form are an expression of the Goddess and the Thought of God made manifest in all things."

"Do you worship Kuan Yin?" She asked.

"That's a good question. No, I do not worship her. I honor her life, her continued efforts to assist humanity, and her reflection of God. I *worship* her Creator."

"I think I understand about that now, but what does that have to do with what happened to me?" She asked.

"Another good question! You came into the beautiful study of the Aspect of Goddess revealing herself as nurturing the children of the Earth, GAIA.

As it is taught today, you entered a wobbly ground. Wobbly in that you did not know or forgot that Gaia is a created being-Not THE Creator Being. You went a little too far and things began to go out of balance. Worshipping the created Gaia you opened to lower energies."

"Lower energies? How could that be lower energies? Earth Mother is so beautiful! She loves us!" She exclaimed.

"Oh, yes, I agree she is very beautiful. Do I believe that this planet has consciousness? And does Gaia love us? Yes. She loves us and supports us in love and in her obedience to her Creator."

"How then, does that mean lower energies?" She wondered aloud.

"A deception. By taking your eyes off the truth that it is God/Goddess that creates the created manifest world around us, you opened to thought forms that certainly do not want you to recognize the truth."

"The study of herbs and plants and the realms that exist around us in their manifest form, is wonderful and exciting, but deception can and does come in when we begin to see *the created as God*.

When you make something into a god, you end up worshipping some-thing. It doesn't matter if it's a stone figure, a piece of wood, or an entire planet. An entity will enter into the item and will answer your wishes. In the end, you submit yourself to giving control over to that entity. You now do its bidding.

The created, manifest thought-forms, now physical, are reflections-sparks- of the Light of God, but are not the totality, *not God*.

That slight deception opens us to lower ideas and thoughts, and other forms that also have a consciousness. They then seek to entrap us and take over our will. We lose our power. Thus the world overcomes us, rather than we overcome the world.

This has gone so far now that people are beginning to teach that we are each "god." In a minor sense we are because we bear the image, but not the totality. The Dreamer has dreamt us into being.

"Why would anyone want to do that, take our will?" She asked innocently.

"It has to do with power and control. Lower energies have consciousness too. Think of it this way. God is Light. When we are in the Light, we are all knowing, pure and at total peace. You, me and everything we see around us by our very physical form, is *proof* that we are removed from the totality of that Light.

We know this to be a truth for if we were totally in the Light, we would be Light and we could *not* have a manifest form." She was getting a confused look on her face.

"Why no form? Because *all* form is lower light, condensed light and of a slower vibration." She affirmed with a nod once again.

"When I was a child, I was taught that in the scriptures of the Christians, "All have sinned and come short of the glory of God.""

"Oh, no! You're not going to do that are you?" She asked horrified.

"No, but listen. In all of the religions of the world, there is some truth. I will tell you a great truth if you can hear it;

To be in the presence of God, we are in the Fullness of Light, we are Light and there is no darkness, or lower vibration, within us.

When we leave the Light, we lose our radiance; our God Light becomes dimmer. We become just a little bit darker than the Light. As we descend through the dimensions, we continue to lose radiance, memory and a lot more. We take on form in the lower vibration.

We can't go back in so easily. We lose our ability to return into that Light because we are not as radiant as the Light of God. Dark cannot enter into Light. It's not allowed. Dark must change.

Also, our understanding becomes clouded by the darkness around us. We become disoriented. We can't see truth clearly in this darkness.

Something has to happen to us, to help us return to the Light. We cannot return without direct help from the Light. The Light Itself comes to give us more Light.

The Pistis Sophia, an ancient writing, speaks to that 'fall from Light'. That means, 'Faith-Light'. She, Sophia-Wisdom, "fell." She became confused in the darkness and could not find the Light of Truth. The Light of the Christ heard her cries and rescued her.

Christ-Light gave her some "Light-consciousness", and brought her into the higher dimensions until she could dis-

cern truth and make a better decision. Ten times he came and infused her with Light, until she was completely freed from the lower dimensions. (overcoming the world)

We all have 'fallen away', or come down in vibration away from the Light, from truth, or you and I would not be talking to each other like this."

"So that is what my Christian friend was telling me about Christ saving her!"

"Yes, she needed to receive a direct infusion from God to understand a spiritual truth and she found that in her Christianity.

The further away we are from the Light it becomes harder and harder to have, recognize or know truth. We become very susceptible to the even lower consciousnesses that exist around us, and sometimes follow them blindly, thinking they are the true Light. I tell you now that it is deception, simple and true. The Christ Light gives us Light when we have none and saves us from this realm. "Ask and you shall receive."

I know spiritual people who have Guides and Masters that tell them what to do almost every minute of the day! That too is a deception. True, Angelic Guides and those who assist us on our path are simply fellow workers of the Light. They will never tell you what to do or allow you to worship them."

Eleanor spoke. "My friend Jan has been in the hospital several times. They say she is schizophrenic. She tells me that she hears voices telling her to die. I was beginning to hear that too. It's horrible!"

"Well, usually it doesn't go that far unless a doorway has been opened to the lower realms by an imbalance in the

brain, sometimes through drugs and alcohol, or direct contact with the demonic forces.

Many new age people think that the forces are here to obey them, or guide them. Some do have a lot of help from angels and I don't deny that. I do too, but Obed, the angel with me, would never tell me what to do."

I thought about all the times Obed had warned me of danger.

"Nor do we command them; understand that too. True angels are under the command of God alone. You must ask God to send the angels to help you, or you risk contracting with the fallen angels. They will come to you. They only deceive you and bring you misery."

"Even the angels? I thought angels were here to do what I want them to do."

"Whenever you command an angel to do your bidding, Eleanor, the true angels will back away from you. They are under orders from God alone. They are holy and will keep their place. They will not overstep their Commander, or put themselves above God. They will back off, but someone will come in their stead."

"Who?"

"The deceiving angels. They only want to control you. They'll do what you want, but for a reason that serves only them. It becomes the nature of the lower consciousness to have more, more, more- no matter what the cost! They'll do something for you, but you will then OWE them something in return. Then, they've got you under their control.

And there is no merciful conscience with them or release from that snare without a great infusion of higher Light. Many people suffer pain and misery as a result."

"I think I understand this now. Is that why the Christians say there is only one way?"

"Yes, I believe that is true. The only Way is LIGHT, TRUTH and understanding of that." We paused for a few moments to consider that truth.

"In other cultures, like the Maya and Inca, they believe that a great infusion of Light will one day come from our galactic center, when we align once again to the Divine Source at the end of this age."

"It's all in Divine timing. At that time, the Creator of All will infuse us all with the Light that activates our DNA and all our higher consciousness. We won't be deceived any more. We will be so filled with Light we will be far above the darkness of lower consciousness. We will be able to make a decision at that time."

"They, as I do, believe we are the Children Of Light; we are loved, and hold great potential. At that time, we will receive enough infusion to become fully conscious to all truth and understanding. That is part of my work here; to help people to come into the Light, to prepare the way for them."

"Even then, some will refuse the Light, even as your demon did. It chose to be eternally imprisoned by the salt rather than enter into the Light. Those that choose Light at the time of the Alignment, will receive an inheritance."

"An inheritance?" She was interested in that!

"Yes, we were originally created in the image of God, who is Light. All of our experiences here in the lower realms have taught us great wisdom and prepared us. For example;

I am a mother. I raised my children and one day, sent them out into the world to learn and experience all of the things this world has to offer, both good and bad. Do the children make mistakes? Does experience help us to become wise? Of course! That's the plan. Wisdom is gained, just as you have gained in this experience. Now you know good and you know evil."

I couldn't help but pause at the thought of my own family. How I wish I could have the opportunity to help them understand this. Wonderful, good people they are, but not open to this discussion. Not now, but maybe later. I continued.

"Do I still love my children and you? Yes, and so does the Creator, Mother, Father, still loves us. Only we can determine to refuse that Light, that pure love. It is our right to use our free will. We can choose to reject that.

One day, we that desire the gifts from Father- Mother, will be returned home to them in all Light. We will receive a body of light that can materialize or dematerialize at will. I believe we will be given the right to manifest in physical and light without restriction because we will have gained Sophia, Wisdom, and will no longer be ensnared by the lower, dark consciousness We will have made our choice."

"Wow! You mean that we'll be able to go up and down the realms without restriction? That's great, but how can people get along until then? That seems like a long time to wait."

"Yes. All through time, Creator has sent us those who have acted as emissaries of Light and have taught us how to rise above, just as they have done. We call them prophets and spiritual teachers." She nodded.

"All cultures have these teachers. But there is One who has come repeatedly and is known across many cultures. This One came at different times and used different names according to the language of the people.

The Maya have Itzmna, who they called Son of the Divine Couple; In India, he was known as Isa, the Prophet of God. The Hindus call upon God in the form of Vishnu, or God in human form.

In Hebrew, he was known as Yeshua Ha Machaiac. In English as we know him as Jesus the Christ, the only begotten or the first created of the Divine Couple. Christ came in human form; as Prophet, Priest, King, Son of the Divine. This was not only to the Hebrews but he has made appearances to all major cultures throughout time.

Understand that with the coming of Christ in human form though, something else happened.

He opened the gateway from heaven to earth and then from earth to heaven, two thousand years ago in the Age of Pisces. Remember the sign of Pisces is two fish headed in both directions, up and down. He walked all the way through, making it possible for us to do the same. The Christ Light is the Vesica Pisces, the combination of the Father-Mother's Vibration, or Only Begotten; The First Light; Consciousness.

He, as fully human, embodied the First Light in this lower realm without becoming dark. No one had ever done that before. No one else could do it.

He made the template of energy- foundation for us all to become One with the Light. That gave us an incredible gift! Once done, done once for all to follow.

Once a template has been formed, it becomes available for all. That truth is a universal law. More on that later!"

I looked at her and smiled. She understood. "Do you have any other questions?" I asked.

"How can you know them? Can you see them? I didn't see anything and look what happened to me!"

"You mean the lower energies?" She nodded. "Lower energies manifest themselves in ways that take some type of control." I waited for her to think about that for a moment.

She seemed confused and shook her head. "I didn't give anyone control that I can think of."

"Didn't you tell me that you cast love spells for your friends?"

"Yes, but we were just having fun!" She defended her actions.

"Eleanor, what did those spells do? Think about this for a minute. When your girlfriend and you sat down together to make a love spell over the poor guy she wanted, you did give control over and you contracted with a demon."

"A demon?" She pulled back from me.

"Yes. Didn't they take away another person's free will? Did they cause an illusion to overtake the mind of the boyfriend? Wasn't a spell cast upon a victim?"

"Oh, but I didn't mean it that way…"

"Of course not, you became deceived. This is how it works;

You believed earth is goddess-you left the first truth of the Creator' "Have no other Gods before me."

The next step then became real easy;

You were told there is no accountability other than your own thought and what you wanted.

You were told you could have power and you wanted it,

You then cast the spell to just try out your power.

Some-thing came to do your will…Do you think the True Light Of God will honor such a request from you to take away another's free will?"

"No." She barely whispered.

"OK, then who performed the action for you? Who went and cast an illusion over the person's mind to think that they loved another, possibly one that was all wrong for the other person." I paused for her to consider. "Perhaps it was a sexual manipulation to gain control of the other person. Whom did you contract with to do this?" I demanded. She had to understand this and right now!

"The demon." She whimpered.

"That's right, Eleanor. And what did the demon do for you, or rather, *to you*."

"I was, it was horrible!" She cried softly.

"Eleanor, as you commanded something to strip the free will from an individual, so it was done to you. Remember? "Do unto others as you would have others do unto you."

As above, so below. Remember;

"God will never take away another's free will, only the lower energies will do something like that for you. People just don't understand. They get caught up in the excitement of the power..." She nodded.

"And understand this too; its not always by casting spells and games, but whenever we try to hurt another person, to take that which is not ours, in our minds and hearts we begin the process of contracting with lower energies. They are all too willing to help us." She nodded again. She understood.

"Do you know why they want to do that?" She shook her head. " No? Because when we allow that contract, we owe. We owe big time. Karma is started and we must repay. "Give the devil his dues" or something like that.

Dark is called dark, because it has no light. When someone has been overcome with darkness to such a degree that a demon attaches, there is only one thing that can help you." She looked up at me expecting an answer.

"Light. It is pure and simple. Light must come because light dispels darkness. Darkness and the consciousness of darkness cannot exist in Light. It doesn't matter if it is in a person or in the earth. Where the lower energies are, only Light can rid us of it. Yesterday, Light came to you when I called upon the Light of Christ." She nodded.

"It wasn't me who saved you from this; it was The Light. You must now stay within the Light to be free. Remember that. I'll give you two verses in scripture to consider;

Revelations 2; 4,5
"Nether-the-less I have somewhat against thee; because thou hast left thy first love; Remember therefore from whence thou art

fallen; and repent and do the first works or else I will come unto thee quickly; and will remove thy candlestick (your Light-spark within) out of his place; except thou repent.(change)" Jesus.

John 3:16-21
19: and this is the condemnation; that light is come into the world; and men loved darkness rather than Light; because their deeds were evil

I stood. "It is now late and I must get home."

"Susan, I want to learn more. Can I come back?" Eleanor asked.

"Yes, I'll be here next Monday and you can come on Sunday night too. We have a healing group that brings the Light of Healing to the people. Please, come, I'd like for you to do that."

I watched as she and Lily drove away. It was late. Will was going to be disappointed with me once again. It was Friday night and it had been a very long week.

I was really tired and went to bed early. The next morning, Will and I drove out to an air show, a favorite activity of his. As I looked at airplanes I was formulating the service for Sunday night and wondering about Richard. Where was he? What was he doing?

I sent out a mental call to him, "Please, come back!"

Chapter VII

Any Old Time You Can Call Me

Sunday afternoon Richard arrived. He just walked in as though nothing had happened. "OK, I'm here."

I could hardly contain my joy! "What happened to make you change your mind?" I asked expectantly.

"They told me you needed help and that I'd better get my butt over here! You've got friends in high places, Susan!" He said smiling.

"Thank God!" I sighed, relieved.

"Yeah, Him too! Let's go for a walk. It's cold, so bring a jacket."

We made the short drive over to the cemetery and walked briskly to the old temple. Now late November, the weather was getting very cold. The temple walls provided a windbreak against the chill. We sat on the marble benches across from one another.

"Richard, I am sorry about the group. Those that were making trouble have left the Center. Their energy was not what is needed in the work that is to come. The others who are there are dedicated and ready to learn. I do need help."

"I've had a chance to think about this too and I do know that the energy will be better now. I've been thinking and asking what I am supposed to do."

"And?"

"I used to do some healing work. I'd like to give that a try again. I work nights now, so I can give a few hours each week."

"I'd be happy to work with you and I am delighted that you'll come in! That'll be a big surprise for the people at the Center! No more bursting jewelry off people!"

"Oh, they told you that too? I couldn't help it, their thoughts were so hateful I just turned the energy back to them…they popped their own corks!"

"Well, you'll have to find a different way of communicating, like using words…." I smiled.

He laughed. "I'm glad you're not mad."

"No, not mad. Just relieved that someone is coming to help me." I told him of the events of the last week. It was wonderful to have someone I could talk to.

"Susan, I see that you've been having quite a time with the lower forces of the area. I can help with that."

"How?" I asked surprised that he knew! I had seen a lot happening around the Center and me. All the darkness had come at me directly it seemed, to make my life difficult. I was getting real tired and it was the result of forces that were not of the Light. If I spent all my time putting out fires, I'd never have time to do my real work.

"I have the ability to go on the other side to disempower the attempts that are being made to disrupt your work here. Whenever Light work is being done and moving forward, the dark sends in its forces. Now that you are becoming known, you'll be under attack as well as the Center, more often. That's what I'm here for, to help."

"What kind of attacks are you talking about?" I asked more concerned.

"Oh, don't worry; you'll be OK. I've never seen anyone who has as much protection around them as you have! But they can make your life miserable by influencing the thoughts of susceptible people who are around you and manipulating them. They're the ones responsible for bothering you now."

"Oh, I can think of a few!" I laughed.

"Hey, would you like to work on the 'project'? He asked changing the energy.

"Love to…what's been happening with it?"

"Susan, it's growing! I've been working on it every day and the thing is amazing!"

"Do you know what it is yet?"

"No, but it's getting easier and easier to form the blue mist into the arms of it and I've noticed many beings that have been coming to observe it."

"Beings? Yes, at least that's what I think they are. You'll see, maybe…"

I was seated across from him on the steps of the mausoleum. As I closed my eyes I could immediately see it! "Richard! That's incredible!" I could see into the outer cosmos. The project looked like a great fountain streaming out glowing streams of light into the darkness. Blue light flowed and sparkled like blue diamonds across the universe.

Within its center was pure light! A sun was within the fountain.

"Gorgeous!" I exclaimed!

"Yes, now watch...."

I could see him forming the prana-agni- into a circle, and then it formed into a rod-like staff. He easily moved it into position. Then I saw them. "I think we have company. Are these the beings you meant?"

I saw wavering rods of light just within the parameter of my vision. They appeared to be floating around, observing what he was doing.

"Yes, I think they are from another dimension. Strange form, huh?"

"Yes, but they are very graceful and light. I feel peace from them." I sent out my thoughts to them. They wobbled with the thought as a breeze touches a curtain. They grew even brighter.

"I think they like us Richard."

"They seem to be harmless enough and I certainly can't do anything about them looking on. I think we're going to stop though, there's a storm coming!"

Indeed, there was! We ran to the car and drove back in the pouring rain to the Center. Just as we did, a huge bolt of lightening cracked and flashed all around us. There was a crash as the bolt hit something behind the Center. Then, the storm was over, as quickly as it had begun.

Jumping out of the car, we ran to the back of the Center to see what had been struck. The great big willow tree where I did the exorcism for Eleanor had been hit!

" Look at that! That's where I did the exorcism, Richard! Right under that tree!"

"Well, it just got electrocuted!"

"You think that some of the demon went into the tree?" I asked.

"I think so." He thought for a few moments. "Willow is known to absorb forces, contain them. That's how the ancients removed illness from people. They'd lay willow boughs under the sick person. Not only did the natural aspirin in the willow help reduce fever, but also the branches absorbed the lower energies of the illness."

"I remember my mother using a willow swatch as my spanking stick too. Maybe she was driving out the naughtiness from me!" I laughed. "This willow did the job, held the force and heaven sent the avenger to destroy it."

We stood literally thunderstruck. We couldn't move from the sight we were seeing. The tree had been struck by the lightening and was now cleaved in two!! The seventy-foot tree was completely split as it a knife had cut through soft butter. It's branches now hung sadly over the small pond.

"I feel bad for the willow tree. What a mess!" I added.

"That must have been quite a demonic force, Susan. Heaven itself has zapped this one! I told you, you've got a lot of friends…"

Later that night I was awakened. You know how you feel when someone is watching you? Well, I instantly knew someone was in the room. Rising slowly I allowed myself to scan the room first with my mind. What I felt was not threatening, but a soft energy. More comfortable, I sat up in bed.

"Oh, My GOD!" I whispered into the darkness, astonished!

In the upper corner of my bedroom I saw the upper half of Richard materializing. He was hovering in the corner of the room. He was in a cloud of shimmering white mist, grinning at me, sort of foolishly.

In his two out stretched hands, he held two strange looking beings by the scruff of their necks. He shook them toward me, scaring them. I could tell by their expressions that they were terrified.

"Now, apologize to her!" he demanded of them.

"We, weeee are sorrrrry!" They both cringed as they croaked their apology.

"Now! *Get OUT Of Here and Don't Bother Her Again!"*

The two strange beings squirmed and peered up at him in stark fear, then took off in opposite directions! Richard smiled at me, and then disappeared.

I went back to sleep. In the morning, I awoke and lay thinking for a few minutes. I laughed at the strange dream I had had that night and then rose up for another busy day.

When I got to work later in the morning, the supervisor announced to everyone that he had made the decision to retire and would be leaving immediately! I just shook my head. Was this one of the lower beings that had been plaguing me? Seemed so…

I went to the Center after work and to my surprise, Richard was already there, standing outside the door waiting for me. He had a big grin on his face as I approached the front door. "Satisfied?" he asked while cocking his head, questioning me as to if I understood.

"You? You did that?" I asked astonished. "I thought I was dreaming!"

He shook his head. "No, that was me! I told you they were bothering you. Not any more." He grinned broadly, he was obviously very proud of his work and that I had seen him.

"Well, I guess I should say, "Thank you!" I said to him, marveling. "My life will be a lot easier without that man screaming at me every day! My job will be a pleasure again."

For a moment I allowed the memory to resurface of the night's 'dream'. I then thought more seriously about the two beings. They were both a dull, greenish color with big eyes. They had no hair and had large flat blocks of scale- like skin covering them. Shaking the memory off, I said, "I wonder who the other one was?"

"I don't know exactly, Susan, but somewhere in your life there will be another change. Something will be easier without these beings manipulating situations around you."

I could only look at him with complete wonder. He saw my expression and it made him uncomfortable. He began looking around and then asked, "Did you say you had someone coming in today?"

"Uh-huh," I managed to mumble.

"Maybe we can try working together?" He asked.

I was shocked at his statement, but replied. "Why, yes, I do. Let me ask first though, to make sure its OK."

Just then I saw Tom, the plaza manager stepping out of his car "Wait a minute." I said to Richard. "This is the manager that wants me to move out. I hope this is not bad news coming across the parking lot."

I met Tom just outside the door. He looked very nervous. Then he nearly shouted at me.

" Susan, WHAT did you say to him?"

"To who? What are you taking about?" I asked a distraught looking man.

"Dr. Lang, the owner of this complex. What did you say to him?"

"Oh!" I took a deep breath. "Well, I wrote to him and I told him about the miracles that have happened here. I told him about Kuan Yin being in the sky above our Center. She had come to save the Earth." I paused to see his reaction. He just scratched his head and twitched a lot. I watched him wondering what was going on and said softly, "That's all."

"Did you know that Dr. Lang and his wife are Chinese? And how could you know that they are devotees of Kuan Yin?" Tom asked me harshly, looking very angry and confused.

"Why no, I didn't. But, isn't that amazing? Wonderful?" My hopes rose.

"For you, 'yes'. For me, 'no'. Because of you I have just lost the biggest commission!" He shook his head.

"Dr. Lang has told me to tell you that you may stay as long as you like. He is honored to have you here and is sorry for your inconvenience."

Tom turned on his heel abruptly, got in his car, slammed the door, and screeched his tires right out of the parking lot! I just stood in the parking lot amazed at how the Universe can arrange things far beyond my comprehension. Who ever would have imagined they were devotees of Kuan Yin? I was filled with wonder and gratitude. Richard came up behind me.

"What was that all about? Susan, you got'ta go easy on the guy, he's just doing his job."

I turned toward him. Then I let all my pent up emotions out. "We can stay! We can stay!!! The Center doesn't have to move- we're still in business!" I shouted.

"That's what he was telling you? But why was he so upset?"

"Richard that had to be the second little demon's influence. It was the Center they were after. I suppose Tom's going to loose about a thousand this month in commissions. But it's over now. We can stay. Let's go back in, I'll tell you all about it!"

A few minutes later I was telling Richard and the rest of the staff about the wonderful thing that had just happened. "Listen, Guys! You'll never guess!! Dr. Lang, the owner of this plaza, is a devotee of Kuan Yin!"

"What?" Judy, one of the Center's volunteers, asked us. " How did you find that out?"

"I didn't know. I just sent him a letter telling him about our problem and the picture of Kuan Yin! It was over his plaza that she appeared! Can you just see him and his wife?"

Elaine shook her head. " They must be so honored!"

"Yes, and he is going to let us stay!"

Everyone was thrilled. The Center was abuzz with all the excitement. I felt so relieved and so thankful. "Thank you Kuan Yin for your picture, Richard and Divine Mercy!"

All too soon, it was back to business. Life goes on even when it's too good to be true. My client came in and I introduced Richard to him. He was a man about thirty years old. He had been having muscle aches and problems with a cough due to long time cigarette use.

He quickly agreed to have Richard and I both give him a session using energy. We went into the small room that I used for healing sessions. Once there, we sat with Ron and talked for a few minutes. It was the first time he'd had an energy session and did not know what to expect.

"Ron, it's really quite simple. You'll just lie up here on the massage table and I'll gently massage your feet to first open up the meridian channels of your body." Seeing his confusion, I stated quickly, "That's like the electrical wiring of your body, to help the flow of the energy. See." I said as I stretched out my hand over his.

"Feel the prana, the energy that comes from my hand." I paused a few moments as the energy began to flow into his hand. His eyes widened as he felt the flow and the gentle warmth of the energy. He looked a little scared. "We all have this." I interjected. "It's chi."

"Oh, I know about chi!" He stated. "I had karate classes." He said happily to have connected and understanding now the process.

"Yes, then you know that just as you used the prana to build your strength for karate, we use the prana to restore and strengthen the body."

"OK!" Let's get started!" He said, much more comfortable now.

Lying on his back on the table, Ron settled into the flow easily. Richard stood at his head and directed energy into the body as I massaged and opened the foot charkas (major points of energy flow) and meridians.

Soon, Ron was snoring softly. I looked up at Richard. He nodded. It was time to check out the rest of his body by doing an 'energy scan'. This was used to determine the flow of energy throughout his body and to identify any areas that energy was not flowing freely.

As we began to scan over his body, our hands were about four inches above Ron's body; I could feel the static of his electrical body field, like little pinpricks hitting my palm. Directly over his chest and lungs the static was moving in erratic little waves and was much more intense. This was not a good sign. It was a pattern of erratic energy and it was pretty intense.

Although we could never diagnose legally, we both knew we were faced with a difficult situation. Unknown to Ron, he had the beginning of a serious lung and bronchial problem; very likely a cancerous situation was developing deep within his body. I looked up at Richard. He nodded. He had felt it too. He motioned with his hand for me to stand back.

I watched as Richard began to remove the build up of residue and patterning within Ron's energy field. Everything is made up of energy; all is light, thought and an energy pattern that manifests into some ' thing'. Cancer has a distinct energy pattern. It produces a certain energy frequency that may be felt and is discernable from other conditions.

If toxic behavior, or environmental toxin having a foreign frequency pattern enters the body and is reinforced often enough in a human, eventually the frequency becomes stronger. It forms enough substance to 'become.'

It does this by overcoming the body's defenses, and our good common sense. After a while, it manifests within the body in 'storage areas'. It is in the body's 'storage areas' for toxins that often tumors grow as a result.

To ingest the energy "pattern" of nicotine in the form of a cigarette repeatedly, is to secure its pattern within the body. It is not a compatible energy pattern. It cannot conform to the patterns of good health for a physical human being. It is contrary.

Incompatible energy forms are stored in the body by human will, overcoming the body's initial distaste for the toxin. Our bodies tell us; we cough, we sneeze, we become ill. But often, the human has made a thought to ingest. The body simply stores it somewhere in obedience to the human who has desired this. A pattern is developed by the new frequency, normally foreign to his body.

While doing so, the undesirable pattern of energy begins to weaken the associated chakra, or energy regulator, of the body that is most closely situated to where we 'store' the pattern.

There are seven major charkas in the body and twenty-two minor charkas. The chakra is responsible for maintaining physical health through a strong energy flow. The chakra associated and thus affected, by the smoking of cigarettes since he was fifteen years old, in Ron was his thymus chakra.

The nicotine energy pattern had weakened his thymus chakra and his immune system was now compromised, as the thymus regulates our immune system. His body began to send signals to Ron; he had a cough and several colds this fall. His allergies seemed to be worse. His breathing was not as it used to be and he was growing weaker. He had come to us for help.

He now lay on the table as I watched a master healer work. Richard was quick and deliberate. This man knew what he was doing.

As he removed the old incompatible patterns from Ron's body, the body began to actually decrease in size. Ron's chest began to look like it had caved in, a hollow formed between his ribs and over the thymus area. So much had been stored that his body was physically bloated with the patterns.

Now Ron looked as though someone had performed surgery and removed ten pounds from his chest. A deep hollow had formed. Richard stepped back and looked up at me. He looked tired and his hair hung down partly over his eyes that were still glowing with energy.

"I'm finished." He said triumphantly while standing back from Ron. "I got it all!"

"What? You're finished?" I was shocked and spoke without thinking. "You can't leave him like *that*!" I said pointing at the caved in chest.

Surprised, he retorted, "Well, I'm finished!" His tone spoke that he was finished and how dare I question the 'doctor'!

"Richard, you can not send him home like that! He's got a huge hole in his chest!" I argued over the sleeping form with a caved in chest.

"Just what do you want me to do?" He asked confused.

"You **have** to fix that!" I demanded then pointed again at the chest. Then I saw it; his expression of total confusion spoke it all. He didn't know how. "I'll help."

I moved over quickly to the body on the table. Now he stood back and watched me work. Praying for restoration, I sought the love energy of the Mahatma, the unconditional love that flows from the very Heart of God. All illness is lack of love. Love restores the physical.

As Ron had brought into his body forms and patterns that were harmful to his physical being, the original health-wise body consciousness was transformed; it was transformed into an unconscious self-loathing pattern that eventually brought illness. Many years of that had allowed for further destruction and patterning to form.

Now the patterns were removed. We had a caved in chest to prove that.

But to ensure the body did not invite the old familiar patterns back (smoking again) we had to reprogram the body area affected to that of self-love. The Mahatma Force was needed.

Also, I'd need to rebuild the thymus chakra. It had been badly damaged. That would require the Force of the Christ Light to use Light to restructure the chakra.

As I worked, I felt his gaze upon me. He saw the energy of love and re-patterning begin to flow into Ron. As it did, the chest began to rise; it became plump again with Light. That Light was Creative Force and Life from the Divine.

The body readily absorbed the new energies. The thymus began to beat with Life; the chakra was restored and would now be able to regulate a healthy pattern to all his organs and restore his immune system. When I was finished, I stood back.

"Now, *WE* are finished!" I announced, smiling up at him.

"WOW! What was that?" He asked. "I've never seen that before!"

"That is the Mahatma and the Touch of the Divine Mother. It is that which brings life to humanity." I answered reverently. "And the Christ Light of Creation. This is what I teach here."

"Guess I do need the Goddess Energies!" he said, smiling in return. "Can we wake him up?"

"Sure."

"Man, do I feel great!" Ron spoke as he stretched and then rose from the table and set his feet on the floor. His hands went to his chest immediately. "Hey, I can breathe better! The weights' off my chest!" He looked at the two of us in amazement.

"Glad you're feeling better, Ron." Richard said. "We've got some things to talk about."

I left the two of them to discuss what had happened in the session. We, as healers, are not allowed to diagnose or communicate our 'findings' to our clients as that violates the medical guidelines set by the government.

We can, however, encourage people to seek a healthier way of living by handing out literature and information that is approved. Richard would do that now. Ron had a new lease on life and we would encourage him in every way we could.

As I waited for them out in lobby of the Center, I considered what had just happened. This man had just proven that he was a powerful healer and I had found someone that I could easily work together with. I had just received a great gift! He had offered to assist and wanted to work with me also.

From that point on, we would work together and become great friends.

We also continued our weekly meditations. Richard came into the Center at least once or twice a week to assist with the sessions. People were finally overcoming their fears about him and discovered he could really help them. They started to ask for private sessions with Richard. He became very popular.

Chapter VIII

The Great Divide

The New Year had arrived. We left the horrific memories of 2001 and entered the New Year with hope for a new future, a new chance because of the miracle of Goddess' love for us all. It was now the year 2002.

One night during the first few weeks of the New Year, Spirit revealed it would be the year of the 'Great Divide'. Adama, my guide from the Lemurian Earth Keepers and Melchilzedek, the High Priest of El Elyon, God Most High, visited me at long last.

Taken up into the higher realms during my 'sleep', I met with them. I had many questions of my ancient friends and spiritual helpers. Waking on the other side in great bellowing cloud- like mists, I spoke to them and they had much to tell me..

"Adama, what is this all about? I said to him. "Please, I want you to explain all of this to me. What is happening?"

"Al'Lat you are about to embark on a whole new journey." He replied.

"This one however," spoke Melchizedek, "will require some life changes. When the Maya Lords of Light showed you the cougar and the powers you were developing within your home, you clung fearlessly to your kitten, as you may remember."

I remembered that night as my lost kitten represented all those that I loved. My kitten had been left neglected within my own home.

A huge cougar of power, that represented me, roamed in my home. My kitten was hiding from it all somewhere in the house and I panicked. That kitten was my marriage to Will. I remembered I could not bear the sight.

> *"Their message to you was that with the powers to come, that you would have to leave friends and family in order to accomplish the next phase of the work."*

"Yes, I remember."

> *"You also told us that you would be prepared to do that even though it would bring great pain to your heart."*

"Yes, I've not changed my mind, but I do not like to see others suffer." I considered my own words. "What I see on the horizon frightens me: I am uncertain of the path that appears to opening before me. Is right to leave a marriage and my home?"

Then, I was caused to review the life of Moses. I remembered Moses, cast into the desert, far from home and family. Not that I was Moses, but he too was called out by God to leave all, as so many others before me. Even later, he'd left his two sons and his wife went to his destiny to lead the people out of Egypt. That must have been incredibly hard for him too. I looked up at Melchizedek. He just looked compassionately at me.

"What about my family? I don't want to hurt my children. They are grown, but I know that what I will do in the future is not what they're going to expect, but it is for all of them. I know they do not understand." I stated to them.

> *"Throughout time it has been proven that those closest to you rarely understand the spiritual path of the true seeker and spiritual worker. Even in our physical lifetimes, Al'Lat,*

we were not understood." Adama nodded toward Melchizedek and spoke kindly with understanding.

Melchizedek added, *"Our paths were not always clear to us even when we were in the physical. It is a path of total faith. Even now, that which shall be is not yet certain; you-mankind, have many choices to make that shall determine your ultimate path."*

"Yes, everyone seems to wish I was someone else and really has a hard time accepting me and what I am becoming." I sighed.

I remembered the shocked look on the faces of my Christian friends I once had. A couple of friends had come into the store earlier that day and saw the images of Buddha and Kuan Yin in my store. They had screamed at me, "Susan! Buddha! Kuan Yin! What is wrong with you?"

Thinking that I had become an idolater, they couldn't get away from me fast enough and ran out. I wasn't even given a moment of opportunity to explain to them about the God Aspect. Buddha was the representation of 'enlightenment' or light in you, and the aspect of spiritual freedom, and Kuan Yin represented the female aspect of the Mercy of God.

I felt deep sorrow for them as they had fled the store. Their fears were so profound that any 'enlightenment' was far from them. They had never understood a scripture verse,

"The fear of God is the beginning of wisdom; but perfect love casts out fear."

They were too fearful to know the true love of God. Knowing that God loves you allows you to take chances. He'll take care of you.

Their fears were like the fearful man who buried his talents rather than invest them for the Master. They could never seek and find, for they were too afraid. The fearful will not inherit the Kingdom. A favorite saying of my mother was, "You've got to take a chance; Columbus did." That spoke volumes.

"Adama, what is this new assignment you speak of?" I asked, dismissing the painful thought about my friends.

"The warrior that has been assigned to assist you is a great man of Light. The powers he has at his command shall be invaluable to you in the near future. Destiny and God's plan is wound closely to the work the two of you shall do together. As you have already seen, what we say is so."

I felt within myself a loving emotion flow over me. I was in agreement. My emotion of love and service was apparent to all and no words are necessary here. I would allow the destiny of two to become one to accomplish the work if that what was necessary and being asked of me. I had come to trust Adama and Melchizedek, the two great emissaries of Light. Their love and service to God alone had been proven many times over now.

They were beginning to fade away, back into the Light. I could hear their voices from a place far away.

"Your 'assignment', as you call it, is to complete a new phase of growth for humanity. As you go forward, you will blaze the path for many others."

"Once you enter the gateway and step upon new ground, others will follow. Teach them the way."

I awoke. I wrote down the strange words and wondered what all this could possibly mean. Come what may, I would watch and seek the Highest Good Of ALL, in all things.

January 19th, 2002

Richard arrived late. He looked tumbled and distressed as he pushed past me and slid into the Center.

"What's wrong?" I asked.

"Oh, its' been a hard week"… he spoke reflecting on the past for those couple of seconds. "I've had some really weird dreams…. They want me to keep coming here. I don't know how I'm going to do it."

I could tell he was having a really hard time. "Let's go into the room and get started so you can get home." I said, directing him forward.

Richard had a girlfriend. Other women were interested in him at the Center and were now pressuring him, calling him all the time. He was dedicated to his girlfriend and I had begun to gather that she was jealous of his time here. It was difficult for him too, I understood.

As we walked into the room, I was wondering just how we could ever really work together. It was highly unlikely that our working together would ever be anything other than friendship and that of a mutual meditation partnership. It was hard to understand.

Why would we have been thrust into this and the Lotus if not to be more than that? We both knew we were twin flames in that Lotus, but we were both in an impossible situation otherwise. I had already decided to just be content and to help him all I could. It was the same for him too. He wanted to help me and to do as Spirit was guiding him.

I wore my little crystal skull around my neck once again. El Aleator was a part of this too. I felt he was enhancing both our abilities together. As a crystal, his energies would amplify our own. We could use all the help we could get.

The universal library of the thirteen crystal skulls would be invaluable to us if we could access the information. The vision of the earth as a burnt out cinder was always on my mind. We would really need to work together to change that outcome.

A short time later we were facing one another across the Lotus and began the spiral dance into the Higher Realms. Out of our bodies, we glowed in pure light within the depths of space. Side by side we watched as galaxies, star systems and whole constellations were simply passed by. The colors of the systems were stunning in beauty. It was all so natural; so known.

"Look, look ahead"! The excited thoughts of Richard's met mine. In the distance, far from earth, something was coming into view.

"How can this be?" We wondered. "Where are we"? Our thoughts were clearly heard by one another. Our excitement was growing with each moment!

The Temple of Golden Light hung in the nothingness of space… we were being drawn toward a great city. A path of golden sparkles began to simply appear as we neared upon the black velvet of space. As roses strewn upon a walkway, the golden pathway materialized. Golden sparkles guided our approach.

We glided toward the temple entrance…there were no doors, but great pillars rose up into the heavens. We approached, side by side, gliding on the nothingness of space, drawn upwards; gliding up the massive steps of the temple and onward, into the vastness of the Temple. It was so bright! White alabaster pillars glowed in the depths against the backdrop of the cosmos. It was so beautiful!

And then I saw him! Seated upon a throne, there was a being, an image so great, so huge…. I recognized him immediately!

Ganesh! Son of Shiva!

The elephant-headed being of All Wisdom swayed before us in majesty!

This was the Temple of Ganesh!

He swayed back and forth, great movements from left to right vibrated within his temple. My excitement grew! How was this possible? Ganesh had a temple in the cosmos? I'd never seen anything like it! We were in the realm of the Masters of Old!

Beings of light, all in total silence, lined the path to welcome and escort us. As small as ants before the Giant Elephant, we were taken into the Temple. All became silent. We were to be taught the great Mysteries of Wisdom. Ganesh is the Master of Wisdom Teachings. He is responsible for the wisdom progression of planets.

Some time later, we began the descent back down through the realms. Beings of lore and legend manifested as we passed by. The Buddha Realms will never be forgotten.

Words never to be spoken had been told us, but not to both. Down through the realms we descended, back to earth, back to the Center. Back in our physical bodies, I turned toward Richard and asked him a question.

"I'll never forget seeing Ganesh! Do you think I can do it?"

"Do what?"

At that moment, I realized he'd not had the same experience as I had. " Oh, nothing, I guess." I began to stand up as he did. " Let's walk over to the store for a cola."

We walked in silence with our own thoughts. We bought two drinks and as usual, they gave us a Pepsi! As we slowly walked back, we recounted the experience.

"I never knew there was a real Ganesh, Richard!"

"Everything that has ever been is always held within the Cosmic Realms, far above the astral realms. Ganesh and all the Buddha Realms exist. The thought form of their exalted existence goes on forever." He answered.

"Did he tell you anything, Richard?"

"Not that I can recall. Just the seeing of that temple was enough for me to think about for a long time. What about you?"

I thought for a few moments as to how I ought answer this. "I feel as though I need to write some things down, Richard. I have something I'm supposed to do."

The gift from the mouth of Ganesh had been given to Woman, I now realized. Richard didn't ask me any further questions. After our drinks, both he and I went home that day. Our lives would never be the same. A new wisdom had been imparted to both of us. The Goddess Initiations to the Kabbala had prepared me for some of this; but Ganesh! This was a completion in Wisdom, the Sophia Teachings!

I went home and took out pen and paper. I'd have a lot to write!

I could feel the pull in my soul. Something had been given and it was still in my mind. Something had to be brought forth quickly, before I could forget! Ganesh had instructed me while I was in the Temple. I had a job to do and I'd better get started. I began to write. It flowed faster than I could write....

Chapter IX

Goddess Of Wisdom

Hear, my peoples the voice of Wisdom for She cries out to you!
A gift has come unto the peoples from Wisdom, Herself!
The Son of Shiva, so I decree…
You, who have entered my Temple,
I so instruct!

I continued to write the words of Ganesh.

"Seven, there are Seven that go forth from the side of the Creator,
Seven Spirits, Seven Voices to be heard!
Most precious; the Voices of Wisdom!
I the Wisdom-Son, so declare!"

I drew upon the paper, the star he'd shown me. Seven points, each an aspect of wisdom, of alchemy, of transmutation of the elements and their dimensions. Incredibly, the planets of our system held the keys to the creation.

I must remember it all! Words flowed as water upon the paper; words I must remember;

The Celestial Wisdom Goddess dwells within the Pillars of the Star of Heaven.
   Her formation surrounds the Throne of the Creator
   Seven Doves Upon The Star fly out from the Throne
   Her movements are eternal in its motion,
   Connecting element to element,

Knowledge building upon knowledge,
Interlacing, growing, now,
To be birthing knowledge upon the base; of the earth.
Now being given are the Keys to Her Wisdom....

Once again, She is to reign upon the earth as a Divine Gift of Knowledge to humanity.

Now, I am to Initiate the Peoples Of Wisdom to the Star-to the Seven Doves!!!

Wisdom desires to embody Her peoples!

Wisdom desires to create with Her children!

The Star, Seven in the heavens, Seven upon the earth;

The Sun, the Moon, Mars, Mercury, Jupiter, Venus, Saturn....

The elements of the alchemy broken down unto its parts, creating,

Recreating always, Her domains.

The woven Domain of Wisdom;

Bring Her to Her Domain, to the earth, the grounding stone of Her Pillars of Seven!

The tones of the planets form the mighty Star, singing their songs across the streaming highways of being-ness!

The Pillars of the Planets are the songs of this creation.... how to explain?

One must view from the highest realms, the creation by/ of Wisdom.

I must bring that which is the Song of the Planets unto the earth, to hold the song within the being...the Initiates of Wisdom.

I am told to do so will bring about an unending transformation.

Magic to live...

What is magic but transformation...

The true alchemist brings change by altering the elements,

Combining the tones...

There must be Seven, I am told to stand within the Star.

Seven Initiates to hold the template in their being!

Seven to stand as living pillars upon the earth of Wisdom personified!
Seven Veils must be lifted.
Seven Veils of the Bride who stands at the side of Creator;
Seven to free the mind from limitation,
Seven to open the flood- gates of knowing all!
Seven to free the mighty arm of courage,
Seven to free us to dream our highest dreams,
Seven to free the compassionate nature,
Seven to free our love, all-compassing
Seven to free our knowing of peace, our rest

I saw the Initiates as they stood within the Star and heard the words; I wrote

One to stand in the place of the Sun,
A veil of gold shall dance with the Sun
Bringing forth the freedom of the mind; enlightenment,
A dispelling the darkened veil of limitation, Beauty

One to stand in the place of the Moon
A silvery veil of lunar light glittering as the moon's own light
To open the dreaming flood gates of knowing all!
Dispelling the limits upon the mind, of cycles

One to stand in the place of Mars
A veil of fire's red this night
To free the mighty arm of courage,
Our strength in Wisdom to be made known;

One to stand in the place of Mercury
A veil of softest blue to dance this one through
To free us to dream our highest dreams,
To teach the mysteries of the Light…

One to stand in the place of Jupiter
A veil of royal blue, our abundance shown
To free the compassionate nature,

To give as we are given
One to stand in the place of Venus
A veil of emeralds for our crown
Passion reigns to free desires completely
Art music love to create
One to stand in the place of Saturn
A veil of strength; of purple, all encompassing
Strong in Knowledge there is no fear
Experience is our strength

Now the Star shall shine…in the hearts of mankind

Susan, you restore and set it so….

The dance to begin…

The Veil of the Bride to fall….

The writing ended. The channel was complete. I knew I was to officiate the removal of the veils from the MIND of mankind. These were the instructions as to how to do it.

What could all this mean?

I understood that we were to make a seven- pointed star. Seven persons would be selected.

Seven persons would hold a new frequency upon the earth that would allow humanity to unleash the potential of global transformation.

They would not know how to do anything alone, but simply hold the keys. I was going to do this. But who, when and how? It had to be soon.

I also knew at the moment someone stood within the Star we were going to create, that the Goddess Of Wisdom would bring in the elements, the planetary tones and frequencies, and that the Initiates would hold this Divine Template within for ALL!

Earth was about to be revolutionized!!! Once this was unleashed, No- Thing would be impossible to/for mankind!

What a gift!!! But without the interplay of the Star's Wisdom movements, this could be dangerous too. I had to make sure that those who held this would be responsible. By dangerous, I mean that should one of the seven links be deficient, it would not uphold the flow to harmonize the totality of the Wisdom Star.

What's passion without courage? What's Venus without Mars? What is knowledge without compassion? I began to seek out those who would be the first to do this. Were there to be others? Yes.

The first seven people though, would be the gateway holders for the rest. I was already seeing them in my mind. Spirit was giving them already. They had been chosen.

As I thought about this and sought Wisdom's graces over the following week, I remembered the Bible. I realized so much had been written about King Solomon and his gifts of wisdom. Had he too unleashed this power to create his own kingdom? He was known as the wisest man who ever lived.

I made some phone calls to those I had been seeing standing in the wisdom star. They were the ones to receive the invitation. They were very excited. We arranged to construct the Star in the Center and to have the Initiation the following Friday night.

I then made a trip to buy material to make the veils.

Friday night was the night.

All was done

The Veils were lifted.

The message of Ganesh had been received

Mankind will change.

Something Serious….

Sunday afternoon Richard and I met again for meditation. The Star Initiation had been completed, but something about me had changed. I felt stronger, more confident.

Richard wanted to go out for a walk at the cemetery. It was a strangely warm winter day, Indian summer. I was happy to have the break from the Center. The warm pre-spring winds felt wonderful as we walked the old pathways. Soon, we came to the marble temple and sat down in the warm sunshine across from one another.

"I have been having a vision of sorts," he began, "it involves the 27th of February. Something drastic may happen on that date."

"Do you know what?" I asked.

"No, the guides are just telling me that something serious may happen. I don't understand it yet, they haven't been very clear on it, so I'll keep you posted."

Visions of the Twin Towers filled my memory. I shuttered. "Richard, I have something to show you." I took out the small Maya skull. "See this? It's a Maya skull. It has a complete brain and is just amazing."

As Richard looked over the skull his eyes grew wide. "It's growing! It's changing colors, look!"

"Yes, it does that. I call him El Aleator, the Lord of the tones or the frequencies. He was instrumental in the bringing in of the Goddess frequencies to the Earth, Richard. It is through the information I have been receiving that I've been able to do some of the Goddess work you are so interested in."

" How?"

"Well, it seems to give me abilities and knowledge, somehow. I think that the brain contains information for us now. I've been wearing it when we've done the meditations together. Obviously, we've been breaking new ground. I've never heard of anyone doing what we are doing now."

"If that's true," he said, "that may be one reason why we've been able to do the extraordinary traveling together. It could be, but I've never worked with anything like a crystal skull before. I have worked with crystal spheres, though." He said while turning the stone over in his hands, considering it.

"I believe I had the stone in my incarnation as a Priestess of Light in Atlantis. I never had the opportunity to complete my mission because the darkness overtook us and destroyed Atlantis. We were supposed to have ascended. I don't want to fail this time."

"Susan, that was along time ago. You are not responsible for that. People make their choices. We can only do what we are given to do."

" I know, but I believe that this crystal skull holds some great mystery. I also believe that you are to help me in this." He nodded. "Perhaps it could help us see what is coming on February 27th?" I asked.

"Would you like to see the Project?" He asked changing the subject while seeing my concerns. He didn't want to frighten me. "I can't believe how its' grown! I've been working on it every moment that I can."

I remembered the first time we had tried this, at this exact spot. He'd been so traumatized that I'd even seen it . I answered him fondly, "Yes, let's do that." I tucked the skull back down into its pouch around my neck.

Soon we were together viewing the vastness of space and his beautiful project. The Fountain-like structure was enormous! It glowed across the universe, sending out light everywhere! Its center held a great light within that swirled and rotated.

"That is wonderful!" I exclaimed.

"Yes, I know now that it's almost finished." He spoke reverently. "I think I need something from you, Susan, to finish it. The Guides have told me that you have it."

"What?" What could you possibly need from me?" I asked him in return, wondering if the use of the skull was what he needed. There'd be nothing I wouldn't give him now.

There was silence for a couple of minutes as we in awe, watched the great Project together.

"Give me the Breath." He whispered to me.

"NO! NO! NO!" I screamed at him! I came out of the meditation, stood up and stormed away! He ran after me as I ran down the path toward the car.

"Susan! Susan! What's wrong?" He yelled, following quickly after me.

"No, no, you cannot have the Breath! Take me back to the Center!" I sat in the car and fumed. He didn't speak to me as he dropped me off at the Center. I got out without a word, leaving him in the car. I slammed the door. He drove off.

I was furious! Inside the Center there were two women waiting to speak to me. My dear friend Karen, could see I was upset. She didn't ask why, but sought to converse.

"Look what I made last night!" She exclaimed as she pulled something from her purse. I saw her send a glance toward Lily, then she handed the pack of cards toward me. "They're Mayan Skull Cards." She offered, kindly.

I looked them over for a few seconds, while trying to release the inexplicable, intense anger I was experiencing. "They're very nice, Karen." I managed to say.

She spoke again. "Here, just pick one and I'll read it for you."

I shuffled the cards, then spread them face down on the table. I reached down to pick one up. It seemed to jump into my hand. I turned it over in my hand.

The card had one word on it "BREATHE"

In horror, I threw the card down and ran into the therapy room. I jumped on the massage table, put my head down and began to cry. I cried and cried. Great heaving sobs from somewhere deep down inside of me rose in waves from my soul. I couldn't stop.

My two friends came into the room to console me. Karen stroked my hair as I cried. Lily massaged my feet. Karen was crying now too. Then she spoke softly to me.

"Susan all you have to do is breathe."

Then, I wailed.

"Susan, what is wrong?" They asked.

"I don't know….I don't know…" I cried. "I just can't breathe."

I didn't know why I felt the way I did, nor was there any explanation for my anger.

Later that night I got a phone call from Richard.

"Are you all right?" He asked concerned.

"Yes, I'm OK now."

"What happened?"

"I don't know."

"Well, as long as you're OK…."

"Thanks. I'll talk to you later."

"Bye"

No wonder men think we all have PMS.

Sometime during the night, I was with Father. I floated in joy before the Cosmos that is His throne.

"Oh, Father! I just can't! Its my right!"

"Yes, child you may. It is not always about our personal rights, but that which benefits the All…"

" But its' not fair!"

We talked about something while I danced in the Light. All I remembered when I awoke was that I was angry about giving the breath because Richard and I were not married; for some reason, that was against the rules…

Chapter X

The End Of What?

The week flew by. No one dared to speak to me about breathing anymore, so I tucked my outburst away. Richard had not called again or mentioned it. Things were back to normal.

In the crazy world of day to day, just living was getting harder. The stress of it all had given me a real pain in the neck. Richard was coming in today for another meditation session. I couldn't wait.

"Richard, could I have a quick session with you?" I impulsively asked him when he entered the Center while rubbing a tight muscle. "My neck hurts."

"Oh! No." He startled me with his response. I instantly realized that for some reason, he was afraid to touch me. I looked up at him. His face held a look of panic.

"Really, Richard, I don't bite! I just have a spasm in my neck. Would you help me for just a minute?"

"Oh, OK." We walked into the therapy room. We'd never helped one another like this.

As soon as his hands were over my neck, we both knew something was very different. The flow of energy from his hands to me was amazing. In two minutes time, I was healed completely.

"WOW!" That was incredible! I've never felt energy flow from me like that!" He said while examining his hands, turning them over and over.

"Well, I guess we now know that if we need healing, we are tuned in to one another. My neck is back to better than normal and I thank you!"

With new enthusiasm, he stated, "Let's get back in that Lotus!"

I adjusted El Aleator about my neck to rest just over my thymus gland. I was ready. A few minutes later we were facing one another in the Lotus flower. This time as we entered the flame together, something new began to happen. The flame held us and we did not ascend straight up, not the same way as we had previously. Our light intermingled and swirled in an exotic dance through us and around us.

As it did, beautiful beings of graceful silk mist began to surround us, standing just outside the Lotus. From their crowns rose rainbows of light as they too, moved in unison with us. Misty rose, purple and soft blues of light swirled around us.

My mind reached out to Richard asking, "Who are they?"

"I have just asked them." He answered. "They are sixth dimensional beings who have come to observe us. They tell me this is new upon the earth plane. I have already told them that they are welcome."

With that the swaying of the beings took on a heightened vibration. Their colors intensified and glowed all the more. They were joining our dance, swaying and lifting us with their motions of love.

Our dance of Light within the flame lifted us out into the cosmos. Above the earth now we rose, no longer on this plane. Higher and higher we rose until we were somehow far above earth and traveling through our solar system.

The rainbow beings were no longer with us as we sped further and further out into space. Whole galaxies and star systems were past by us on our journey. Their glorious and magnificent presence filled God's creation.

We continued to travel, for a long, long time. It seemed as though we were being drawn to a destination. We didn't know what that destination might be. It didn't seem to matter. The sights we were seeing filled our souls. To observe and to integrate this amazing experience, in the now, was all that filled our being.

Far, far across the universe, we began to see a wall of white light. We were being pulled toward the walls' bright light. As we drew nearer, we came to a great living wall of White Fire. Looking up there was no end to the wall above us; looking down, there was no down or end to be seen. Trillions upon trillions of miles of wall stopped our going any further. We hovered in front of the wall for there was no way around this!

Just as a flame dances in gold, yellow and blue rising up forever, this Flame was White Spirit! It was beyond all belief. Just like fire, it moved and swayed, flickering its light ever upward, ever downward. We could go no further. We were less than specks of dust before its height and girth!

He turned toward me whispering in awe, saying, "**This is the end of this universe.**"

The concept was so startling that it shook us both out of the experience. With that one unbelievable thought-that disbelieving thought, we were being returned to the earth plane. Speeding past all in an instant, we reentered the Lotus. Then we were back into the physical. Our hearts began to beat, our individual life breath returned. We lay spent on the floor.

Opening our eyes, we met one another's gaze. I could still see his beauty. He saw mine. We were enraptured within one another for a brief moment, and then consciousness returned. He stood quickly. "I have to go." And then he was gone.

I just sat up on the floor I was too stunned to move. My mind tried to register the thoughts;

I had just seen and stood before the wall of Spirit that held the universe together!

I had just traveled to the end of the universe!

I had seen Spirit, the substance that holds it all together!

I was soooo small before this incredible creation!

My mind raced with all the contradictions:

I had been out of body, in a form that could travel the universe.

Why had I, we, been shown such a marvelous thing?

Now I was here-on Earth.

Now I had a body and now I felt such limitation!

How can I live? How can I just go about the silly things I do everyday?

I began to let the tears flow. There was no stopping them. It was too much emotion for one to hold, the sights I had seen too glorious for one to behold and yet live. God's creation had been revealed, to the very end. Revealed to two small beings, such small beings. Why?

Cosmic Eve 2012: Rebirthing Mankind

I was overwhelmed. How could I contain this within my mind? How could this be contained within my soul? I wanted to fly back out into the universe and be free! I was so contained, so imprisoned within this body; my mind too infinite to be contained within my brain!

Somewhere, Richard had turned his car off the road, perhaps at the cemetery. I knew he too was gasping from his heart, even as I was. I heard his cries of wonder and his heart's song. It was as mine. We were connected. Forever. So many thoughts, too many thoughts flooded in. I was staggered with the emotion, with the vision. It shook my world.

All during the week I tried to retain the magnificence of our experience. I stayed away from everyone. How quickly the wave of forgetfulness and the world's disbelief overcomes me! I fought it. This ought not be lost to memory or time.

I became consumed with the visions, in writing about my experience and what I had seen. I spent hours drawing the images still in my mind. I wanted desperately to preserve the adventure we had shared. My memory could never contain it all. So, paper and pen in hand, I began to draw.

I began to sketch his form first of all. His colors appeared upon the paper, his ruby core essence glowed and rose upward. Bursts of color made up his aura. Human form was not important now. As I painted the form, the ruby spiral swirled once again before me. Color and form on paper would never be able to adequately convey him, but I still had to do this.

As soon as I had conveyed the image to paper, I began another; my own. Sapphire blue spirals and sapphire globes spun above my head.

"Yes, that's it!" I exclaimed as it all came together on my canvas. All sapphire rays make up my essence and he, ruby fire. Fire and water we were; creators we had been called. I wondered, why that? There was no way to draw the universe...can you imagine flying through the Hubble pictures, unhindered, seeing all that for real?

As soon as the paintings were completed, I hung them up. I stood back to look at them all. A dozen were hanging on the wall. I felt heat radiating outward. The paintings themselves were generating a blast of heat that bathed the room and me in the essences! I felt satisfied somehow.

A Mystical Mystic Experience

January 24, 2002

On Thursday of that week, the 24th of January, I had an appointment in Vermont. An Indian mystic and famous Vedic astrologer was coming to a Center there. I had been guided to go and to have a reading with him. I made the three hour drive to Vermont by myself. I had many questions. I had heard that this man would have answers for me. I really needed answers now.

As soon as I arrived, his attendants made three sets of prints of my hands using black ink. It was explained to me that the patterns on my hands were actually a map of my destiny and purpose in life.

My date and time of birth was given to the attendants who were running in and out of a small room where the mystic had stationed himself. My information was brought into the little room. I waited. After a while, the attendant came out again. He was excited.

"Get the others!" I heard him shout to another attendant. Then coming over to me said, "Do you mind if some of us sit in on your reading? It, it is most unusual...." He hesitated as he spoke, staring at me intently.

"I suppose so, I've never had this before..." I began. Just then a dark complexioned man about sixty years of age with a broad smile, emerged from the mysterious room. This was the Indian Mystic. He was ' bubbly'.

"Susan," he started to say, "I am so happy to meet you. As you already know, this is a most auspicious day! You have come to us! Come, I will explain."

He took my arm and guided me into the small room. As soon as I sat down the others began to crowd into the room until I was surrounded with anxious looking people. My prints of my hands were spread out across his desk. There was a silence of expectation in the room as all waited for the Master Reader to speak. He looked up at me and quickly began to redo his calculations.

He checked three times, pointing out markings and speaking in French and Indian to his assistants. I didn't understand a thing and was getting concerned that something was wrong with me.

Finally, he spoke to me. "Susan, I have checked three times and my associates agree also." Very softly he began to speak directly to me, eye to eye across his desk.

" I must first tell you: That you are the Divine Physician; beyond mystic; beyond seer; beyond guru; you are Divine Presence on earth; you are Divine Savior for mankind."

I gulped and looked at the others in the room. They were all staring. At me.

"What? What did you say?"

"You are Divine Savioress for mankind." He nodded after he spoke to all those in the room as if to give a signal to them. He continued, *"You have come with a great destiny. I will help you."*

"Look here," he pointed to my palm prints.

"You have the full Lotus in your hand, meaning you are a creator of destiny for humanity." He showed me the lotus in my hand.

"You have the sun on your soul line, and are greatly evolved." A small star reddened with our gaze as he pointed to the soul line on my right hand, then the left.

"You have the square on your Jupiter mount and are a great teacher." A large square was pointed out just beneath my index finger on both hands.

"You have the triple line at the end of your heart line and are complete in attaining all of the triune Father- Son- Spirit. " I could see the three extensions from my heart line.

"Your strong head line is straight across your palm. You have great mental powers and abilities to do all that you need to do in this life time."

"Here is the destiny line. It rises straight up from the base of your wrist, through your head line and your heart line all the way up to the middle finger known as Saturn, your power. It too becomes triune at Saturn. You will accomplish what you were born to do."

"Here is your prosperity line. You will always be provided for. You will have money."

I laughed. No one else did. It was dead silent in the room. I regained my composure.

"You have the ring of Solomon and charkas on every point of your hands, plus the healing stigmata, here beneath the little fingers on both hands. You are a great healer of mankind..... Complete."

He paused and did some more calculations. He looked up at me stating,

"Susan Isabelle, not in all of India do the gurus have what you have in your hand. I must help you; you have come to me."

Gathering the astrological charts, he reconfirmed his findings, mumbling over and over. He reconfirmed with his associates each finding.

I was stunned.

"Yes, yes… do you know that you have the exact same line up of planets and astrological chart as Mother Teresa?"

"No, I have never…" I mumbled.

He became excited. *"A man! A man has just come into your life. See? Here is his line. He is not so critical as the other…."*

I assumed he meant Will. Was Will critical? I asked myself. 'Yes'. Now, Richard….?

"Yes, this one has come to help you. To balance the Venus, the Goddess energy you have in your first house. You are beautiful, passionate, and sensual and must have your mate. Your chart says so! It is destiny."

I must have looked even more confused and uncomfortable. He saw that and responded loudly.

"You do not need sex with this one. This is spiritual and he is here now; but it is much better for you to activate your root charka."

I laughed and so did everyone else in the room. He broke the tension of his assessment of my chart and palms with his delightful humor.

"Oh, yes, this will bring harmony to your soul; then you will bring harmony to others; yes, this one is not so critical."

"I guess I am married to the critical one." I offered.

"Oh, that is too bad! It will not last. It is destiny. You will be together."

At first, he was oblivious to my inner turmoil and he smiled broadly at me. Looking at me more intently, he perceived my emotions. I was near tears.

Then he became very serious. *"The Universe will not tolerate your being in a relationship that does not support your mission."* He paused for me to really hear him. *"Susan Isabelle, you have a mission… God has chosen your mate."*

He stopped speaking so I could absorb what he was saying to me. I hadn't expected this. The room was silent. I couldn't speak.

"You must come to me in Canada. You must be prepared for your work. You must bring this other one to me. I will speak to him."

By the time I left there, I had more questions than what I had when I arrived several hours prior.

A Divine Savior-ess? …What was that again? …What did that mean-exactly? …

Was he referring to the miracle of the days in 2001?... or was there more to this?

People would never accept this. My family already thought I'd 'lost it' long ago. I could never tell anyone. And what about Richard? Richard would never agree to this! His girlfriend definitely wouldn't like it.

Passionate? Venus, Goddess of Love in my first house? I giggled like a schoolgirl all the way home.

By the time I entered back into New Hampshire, I had decided I would arrange to go to Canada. I needed to know more.

Smiling, I decided passion would be nice for a change.

Susan Isabelle

*El Aleator glows from within....
The Mayan Skull held many secrets...
They only had to be discovered...*

*The biggest mystery was discovered in 2004.   El has his own Twin Flame.
Together, they form a perfect human heart
For One Heart., One Mind.
The Template was created by Itzmna,
Son Of The Divine Couple, according to the
Maya. He brought them 13 skulls that held the entire Template of creation within them.*

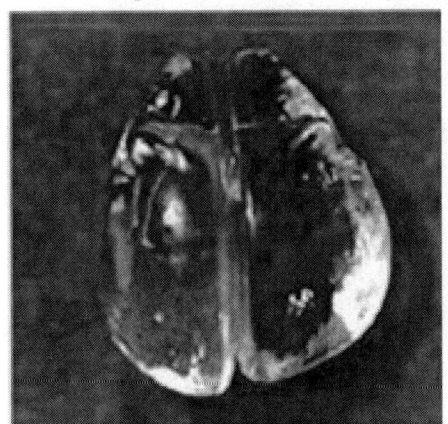

This is the Heart Of The Child

*Jesus said,
"I will come on the last day and take away your stoney heart... And give you a new heart of flesh"
2012*

150

Cosmic Eve 2012: Rebirthing Mankind

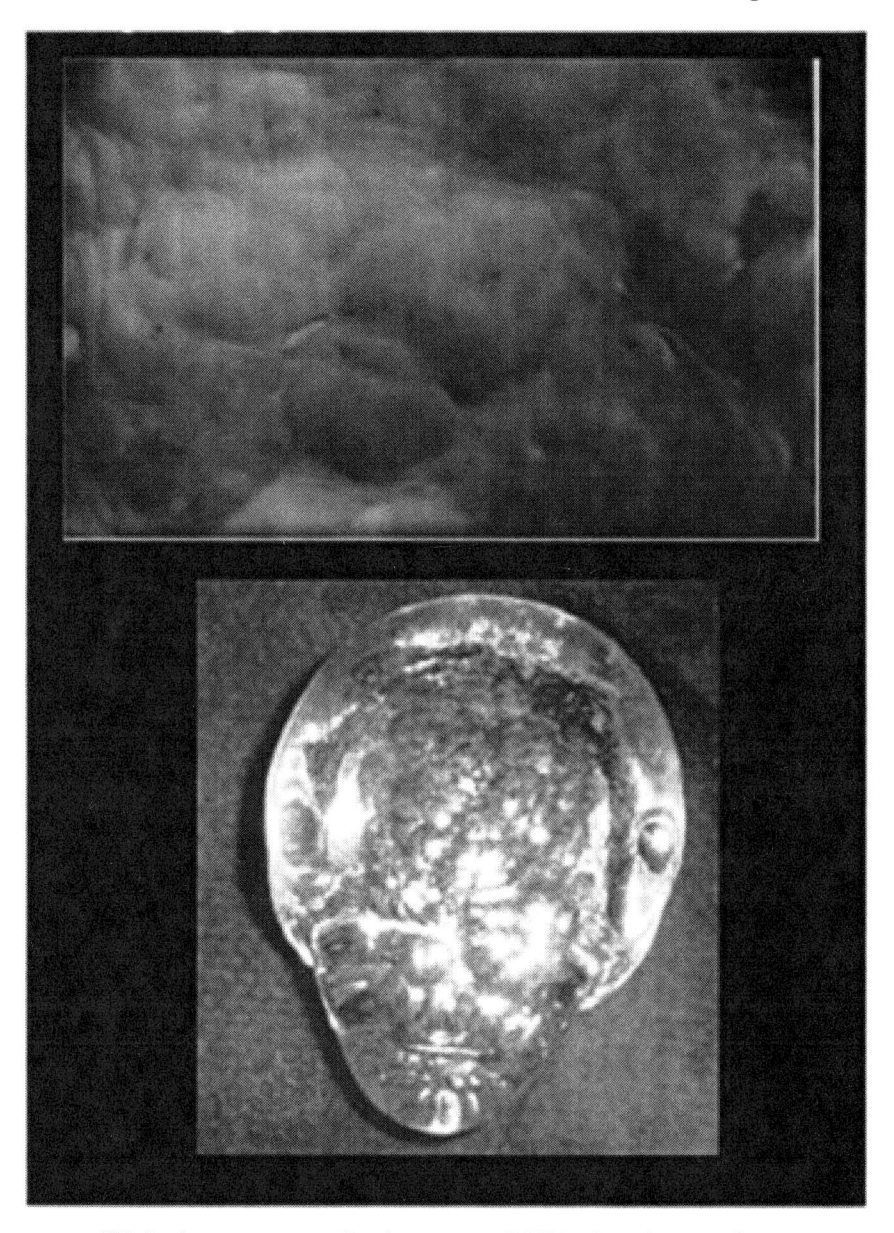

This is an actual picture of El's brain under a
very high power microscope.
A small drop of iodine was placed on the skull so
it could be photographed.

Plate 2

Susan Isabelle

Susan teaching at the Shambhala Center

"My Daughter, I have heard your request for the Waters Of Life...
The water Of Lourdes"
Mother Mary

This is the fountain, now at our store beneath sacred Mount Shasta

Meet me in the Lotus

Plate 3

Cosmic Eve 2012: Rebirthing Mankind

Hathor's Temple

Slowly, our arms raised themselves in
unison to the Divine.

As our hands were raised to Heaven a great
Light descended all around us.

It lit up the entire area.
I could hear Lou cry out in fear and awe.

"I am in the Presence of God!"
He fell to the ground and wept.

Plate 4

Susan Isabelle

The True High Council Leadership

Kuan Yin
Mother Mary
Ananda
Christ
El Moya
St Germane
Chief Seattle

People have asked me about the High Council.
There are actually several Councils.
One night I was taken through the tunnel to meet
this Council. I was told to stand between the
worlds to paint them. So at 3:00 AM I painted
them as they took my hand in the dark.
In the morning I could see them as you do now.
Susan Isabelle

Plate 5

Cosmic Eve 2012: Rebirthing Mankind

The Dreamer, The Father,
Dreamt a Great Dream.

It lasted about 26,000 years or so..its ending in 2012

The Mother,
In Compassionate Love for her Mate,
Responded to Her Lover in the Lotus.

Combining Divine Thought and Divine Love,

Movement formed in the Universe.

Light, Sound and Vibration Moved
Christ, Light, and Creation happened.

You, Me, All Things, were Born Of That Love
We Are The Children; And NOW,
The Children Dream The Dream

A New Dream has been Dreamt

It begins In 2012!

Susan Isabelle,

Plate 6

Chapter X

Ruby and Sapphire

I was back within the Lotus across from Richard. How natural, how beautiful and peaceful. Then, I awoke.

"What?" I looked around my room. All was quiet. "I must have been dreaming," I thought as I rolled over and snuggled down under the covers. Very soon afterward, I was back in the Lotus. He was there across from me in his meditation form. I looked around. I was not dreaming…

In the morning, I knew I had spent the entire night meditating with him in the Lotus. Something new was about to happen. Every night that week I found myself across from him. He was calling me. We would immediately begin meditate in silence as soon as I arrived. That was what we did each night until dawn, and then I would return home.

A whole week had gone by and we were now actually facing one another in the Center. Neither one of us had spoken about the nightly visitations, but we knew. It shone all around us. The meditations of the night had transformed us both.

"Breathe in deeply, deeply through your eyes. Bring in the pyramid. See it now?" His soft voice guided me.

"Yes, yes, I have it now." Together we went through the steps.

Soon, we were within the Lotus, its petals gently moving with our waves of light. Once again his beautiful light enraptured me.

Here, one cannot hide emotions; waves of pure love flow out from me to him and he to me.

"You like this Lotus don't you?" He softly chuckles.

"Uh- Huh", I smile in return.

"Let's go up higher!" He states as he draws in a powerful breath.

Instantly, I am transported to another realm. Suddenly, the deep blues and white spirals of light are shooting past us, or rather, we past them. Galaxies of incredible size and colors beyond all one could imagine fall beneath us as were travel out so far, far beyond.

Suddenly, we were being propelled by a force that clearly had not been initiated by us! We were being drawn somewhere, and very fast! Beyond the speed of Light we were traveling faster and faster toward something! Then, we saw it ahead of us. It appeared to be rising up so fast and so mighty! White Fire! And then, we stopped before its' might once again.

"Oh, my God! We have been brought again to the Wall of Spirit!" I whisper to him with my mind.

"Yes, but why? Why have they brought us to the end of the Universe?" He asked.

Considering the question, we hovered once again before the Dancing White Fire. We wouldn't make the same mistake again. We held our composure.

"I wonder what's on the other side?" He spoke quietly after a while.

"Can we go through it?" I asked. "Does it have another side?"

"Let's go!" He spoke with determination and command.

"I am right here with you!" I agreed.

Behind his glowing form, I watched him as he began to enter the White Fire. Flames of white, gold and orange appeared to open and part the wall as an entrance for him. I pulled my form in close behind him, merging his field and mine.

Suddenly, we were swept into the wall by a great magnetic- like force! It was pulling us into its depths! We could not pull back or away now. But that was OK. We didn't want to go back.

Once inside, the flames, soft and cool as feathers, were all around us, above us, beneath us and before us. There appeared to be nothing but pure white feathery flames dancing around us as we stood within the wall. There was no up or down, forward or back. We simply hung within its dancing, spirit- fire.

Moments or eternities passed. Dancing spirit feathers stroked us gently. Such Love! Love, love, love! Something was probing us, examining us, purifying us, stoking us as a mother lovingly strokes her child's face. We hung in the love and simply enjoyed every precious, feathery stroke of tenderness!

Then, there was motion. The stroking became a gentle nudging. This motion was moving us. We were being directed somewhere! Gently propelled by feathery nudges, we traveled in the pure white membrane of the universe.

Suddenly, we were thrust out into the 'other side'.

Moments passed. Centuries, eons? Who knows? There is no time here.

On the other side of the wall there is nothing. NO- THING! Absolutely, not a single thing exists there. No stars, no form. Looking back at where we had come from, all we could "see" was the wall of white fire, so far in the distance as not to even exist.

I looked over at him. He was suspended in void. I was also floating in void.

"We are in the void" I whisper. "There is nothing here." I giggle. "Why is this so much fun?" I giggle to him again.

He too is beginning to laugh. I can see he too is feeling silly, playful. Hanging together in nothingness, we giggle and laugh together like children.

"Look what I have in my hands!" He teases, pulling his form away from me. He is floating away.

I chase after his glowing form that is now swimming away from me in the void.

Engaging my will, I find I can catch up to him with my mind as my form glides effortlessly toward him, faster than he can swim! I giggle and laugh to see his expression. He's surprised I caught him.

But then, I can see something glowing brightly in his two hands that are held above his head. He pulls away as if to hide a precious secret from his little sister.

"Come on! Let me see it!" I plead, trying to chase after him to see.

"OK." He said while opening his hands.

Looking over his shoulder, I can see that he has formed a wheel like object, something like a clock with gears all golden and sparkling. He then lifted one hand over the clock and strange symbols began to flow out of his hand and into the devise. Letters and globes of light were forming inside his clock!

Cosmic Eve 2012: Rebirthing Mankind

"I am receiving symbols." He tells me in a reverent voice.

"Yes, I can see them going in." I reply softly with amazement. I watched as he placed more of the symbols into his wheel. I feel that he is pleased.

Gliding around to face him and his beautiful clock, I state, "I need to put my essence in."

As soon as the words were spoken, something began to flow out from my being. A soft white mist flowed out from my heart center and enveloped his wheel clock as he gently held it.

"Yes!" He suddenly exclaimed. Then, he did something totally amazing! Just like throwing a Frisbee, he flung his clock far out into the void; so far we could no longer see it!

I watched, as he did, the Frisbee disappear into the darkness. Then, a glow appeared far, far out in the darkness beyond.

"Look!" Look what is happening!!! I exclaimed laughing with total delight! "LOOK!"

Where his Frisbee clock had disappeared into the darkness, we watched the glow expand. Great towers of glowing matter that looked like clouds billowed out and expanded far out around us.

Then, the fireworks began!... Just like the Forth of July!... Explosions of sparkling lights began to rise up in the void's new clouds! Exploding, glorious colors filled the darkness, then something began to look like stars and mists began to form in a spiral of glorious light. A galaxy had formed! Stars sparkled in the velvet darkness, spinning their new light.

"Let's do it again!" We exclaimed together! Giggling with excitement, he formed another Frisbee-clock and again, I put in my essence when it was ready.

When it was complete, he once again threw the Frisbee out into the void. We waited. Explosions began; fireworks blasted the darkness! Another galaxy was formed, its beautiful center sun shining and lighting up that which had been void.

Enjoying our new game, we, the two children, made many clouds of matter, many explosions and fireworks! We laughed and exclaimed with glee as the colors rose spectacular in the blackness of the void.

And before we knew what was happening, we were being pulled back in, toward the wall. Our parents were calling us home. That was enough play for the day.

I don't remember coming back into my body, only lying on the hard floor of the Center many earth hours later. Opening my eyes, I could only see the ceiling swirling above me.

"Richard?" I whispered. "Are you here?"

"Yeah…oh….yeah, I'm here." He whispered back.

I rolled over on the floor. How had I gotten on my back in the center of the floor? Richard was lying spread eagle a few feet away from me. He wasn't moving. I put my head down again.

A few minutes later, he whispered again, "Did you see THAT? Those wheels! What were they? What were we doing?" He tried as I did, to rationalize what had happened. The incredible had happened.

"Richard, we were creating….creating galaxies, whole galaxies! I rolled back over onto my back, seeing the whole thing play out once again in my mind and upon the ceiling above me

"But, but we were outside this universe!" He exclaimed, getting excited. "Is that possible? Did you see those symbols?"

"Yes...." I began as he interrupted me.

"Do you remember them? God, I've got to remember them!"

"They seemed to be created by your thoughts", I offered.

"Yes!" That's it! That is what was happening!"

"Each wheel was different, Richard, each had its own symbols, and created a different type of spiral...you created each one uniquely...."

"And you, Susan, you...."

"Could you see what was coming out of me?" I asked.

"It was beautiful, Susan! A mist of some kind."

"Do you know what that was?" I interjected anxious to know more.

"No, but it gave life to the whole thing! Can you believe that! It completed the wheel!"

"I think it has to do with the male-female thing, Richard. It takes both to create ...."

"Yes, that must be it...are you hungry? I've never felt so hungry before..."he asked me rolling over to look at me. "I'm starving!"

"That's what pregnant mothers always say!" I quipped back at him.

He gave me a wink. "Let me get some strength back and we can go to get something. I think we should ground."

Getting up after a few minutes, we couldn't stand up without feeling like we were falling over. It was like we were really drunk.... really, really drunk! Laughing and stumbling over each other, we made our way out the door.

"Oh, Richard! Why am I feeling like this? I can hardly walk straight!"

"I don't know....must be something to do with the energy! I think we need water....at least that's what I think the Guides are telling me.'" He said laughing with me.

Everything was so funny! We made our way over to the store and bought two liters of water from the attendant who was watching us stumble and giggle like two kids on a high! As we made our way out the door, we nearly ran into an old looking man about four feet tall. He had a bald, shiny head, hearing aids in both ears, was hunched over and walked with a cane. He took one sideway look at us and with a great big toothy grin, smiled and said,

"You can get drunk on that stuff, you know!"

We fell into great heaves of laughter! We laughed so hard! Before us was the manifestation of a Guide...a Guide in disguise! He was telling us what we already knew...we were drunk! Drunk on energy!

"You'd better get- on now," He said with a drawl. " And drink that stuff..."He said nodding toward our water.

"We will!" We said as we stumbled away laughing to sit beneath a tree nearby. We drank down the water as quickly as we could. In about five minutes, the water began to take affect and we became more normal. Getting up, we began to walk back to the Center again.

"Richard, that was a real Guide!"

"Yeah, I know....glad I'm feeling better. Man, what was that?"

"I don't know, but if we ever do that again, we're going to need a stash of water on hand!"

By the time we arrived back at the Center, we were completely back to ourselves. Back to our awkwardness and all the feelings of I-You-it can't be-. At the door, I gave him a big hug anyway.

"Anytime you want to play Frisbee with me, just call! I like to play with you!" He blushed.

I watched him leave. My thoughts were going wild! What an amazing man! Then, "My God! Who are we? What God, are you doing with us?" My heart went with him this time. I'd never want to lose him. We belong together.... but it can't be. Then, I began to cry softly.

"Why, God? Why would you do this to me? First of all, why would You have me experience this? Then, fall in love? Yes, I am falling in love! Why did You have me meet him? He is the most amazing man in the universe or anywhere else for that matter, and why? I'll never be able to be with him? Why? It is so unfair!" I cried.

Trying to rebalance myself, I prayed out loud again to the walls of the Center. "But, please, if it has to be this way, do not stop this on my account. I will accept, in love, love; in whatever way I can. We must be able to continue this work and all that You have given us to do. I will not let my emotions destroy this! Help me to be strong!"

I went home that night torn inside and out; with glory and confusion; with love and without. I went home to an empty bed, cold and with responsibilities, so many responsibilities.

I wondered how I had gotten myself into such a mess. At 7 AM I would wake up and be at the Center to clean and vacuum, then run off to the job til noon, check in at the Center during my lunch, go back to work for the afternoon, then go back to my clients in the evening, then home around 11PM....Work! work! work!

People started bringing me food because I'd forget to eat. Now a Pandora's box had opened, I was falling in love. I was in love with someone who did not want me. I'd met my twin flame and was now knowledgeable about the depths of the kind of love that transcends all time. Now I understood love for really the first time in my life.

In my strict upbringing and my personal beliefs, this was not allowed. I would have to put my feelings on hold.

Chapter XII

Play That Again, Sam....

The week passed as usual until Friday night, the night before I was to teach a class. Deep in my sleep state, he came for me.

"Arise, and come! There is much to do!" An Angel Of Light said to me. Lifted from my body, I could see that it lay sleeping on the bed beneath me. "Come!" I obeyed.

Side by side, the Angel and I rose into the Light Of The Divine. Its brilliance consumes the All. As I was allowed, I was able to see through the Light to see Richard standing on a platform of pure light. He was unaware of my presence at first. He glowed in all majesty and wore a robe of white. He had on his head a turban of white with a glowing red ruby placed in center.

Then he turned towards me and stood silently gazing upon me, enraptured. All around him were multitudes of beings, angelic and others that were magnificent. He stretched out his hand toward me. I placed mine in his and he lifted me up upon the platform and stood me facing him.

Our eyes met and he spoke not a word, but he did not have to. He looked at me with total love, perfect love. Our love for one another filled the entire universe. I adored him and his beauty enveloped me.

At that moment, I saw his ruby spiral and my sapphire interlock at our heart centers and we merged our spirals of light. Wave upon wave of pure ecstasy enveloped us. We embraced one another fully with passionate fires. Our spirals, our souls, our being, interlocked.

A White, Holy, glowing mist from God began to form above and descend down over us. Wrapped in the arms of God we were hidden from the view of the multitudes of watchers all around us. Held in this white palace in his arms we consummated our love as man and wife in passionate beauty, but only in Spirit.

"We are One, We are One, We are One", he whispered to me. "We are One, We are Love, We are Creators, We are One." We whispered our vows to one another amidst our eternal Spirit lovemaking and astral-consummated union.

In the process of time, the veil began to lift and the Word of God was heard throughout the universe, "What GOD has joined together, let no man put asunder!"

Filled with love and happiness, we, the newlyweds, looked down from our platform upon the multitudes who were looking up at us. Suddenly, a shout went up from them all! Then, the whole universe partied! There was so much joy! We were the newlyweds and there was a gathering, party, celebration and wedding feast like none other!

And then, I awoke. I lay on my bed for an hour feeling the waves of sexual union wash over me, of love, and of his embrace. Waves stirring and flowing the remembrance of his powerful embrace left me spent with love.

As my mind cleared and the waves subsided, I could only think, "My God! What has happened to me?" This was not a dream! I had just been married and had experienced a cosmic orgasm! Divinely married to him-by God! Could that be real? "No, it was a dream, no, it was real.... YES!

Showering, and getting ready for my class, I felt such happiness! My prayer had been answered, although it was in a most unusual way... nothing would matter now. I felt complete and filled with a joy that no one could extinguish. I prepared for my class.

The students came in all excited. They were chattering and as joyful as I was. It was as though the universal party was still going on, everyone was happy! Did they somehow know? I felt like a bride and my glow was evident to everyone.

The morning went by very quickly. As I was teaching a technique just before lunch, I felt something and I looked up. To my total surprise, Richard was behind the students pacing back and forth excitedly. He looked up and met my gaze. His hair was uncombed, he looked tumbled and he had a big grin.

"There was a celebration last night." He spoke and looked deeply into my eyes.

"Yes, there certainly was", I replied slightly embarrassed. My glow spread out across to meet him.

Could the students see? I was blushing. I was a blushing bride and he was the proud groom. Love joined us across the room and swept over the startled faces of the students that were staring up at us. The room became completely silent as they all felt it and stared at us both, looking from one to another.

"OK!" Everybody, let's take a break!" I said quickly. "Richard, we can go in there." I said pointing to the massage room. "To speak." I added so all could hear.

The class filtered out disappointed they had been dismissed from something that certainly was becoming very interesting! I ran into the room behind Richard. He sat up on the massage table and I quietly took the chair beneath his gaze. I looked up at him. I was sooo in love!

He stared at me as if he could not comprehend me at all. Finally, he drew in his breath and nearly shouted at me.

"There was a REALLY BIG CELEBRATION last night!"

"Yes, I know", I answered him softly, embarrassed. I couldn't very well say to him or in front of my students that he was incredible and that our cosmic antics shook the entire universe!

" I was there." That was all I could say, but it was enough.

He visibly shook. "You know?" he asked incredibly.

"Yes." I answered looking down.

"You know there was a WEDDING last night?" He demanded to know, to be certain.

"Yes, I was there. I was the Bride." I said looking at him intently this time. I was not going to be intimidated. He invited me.

The look on his face was so confused, I laughed. "Yes, I was there. And so were you. In fact, you invited me, and you were the Groom."

Someone, very impatient, came knocking on the door. "OK, I'll be there shortly!" I hollered back. "Richard, I have a class…can you come back, please? We really need to talk about this."

He nodded. "Yeah, and I've got a lot to think about…"

My heart went out to him in pure love remembering what he had said to me only hours before.

"Richard, I, please, don't go yet…who are we?" I asked looking up at him.

He answered me with love, "Creator gods, We are One…" and we walked out the door to many faces that were filled with questions.

My class began the sacred dance of the Goddess that afternoon. Twenty women celebrated the union without knowing the true facts of the matter. Spirit rose on the multicolored veils, rainbow colors sparkling with Spirit, lifted and swirled in the Center all afternoon and continued into the night!

"Susan, I can't stop dancing!" she laughed as she twirled by.

"What are we celebrating?" another asked.

"The Bride" I replied as I lifted my veils to honor Goddess.

That night, I stayed in the Center. I lit all the candles around the altar and re- dedicated myself to The Divine Mother and all Her aspects, especially that of the Bride and of the Wife.

Now, when he asked for the Breath, I would give it to him.

Sunday night, February the 17th right after the service, he appeared after everyone had gone and I was ready to go home. He was very distraught and appeared to have had a few drinks. He looked in pretty bad shape and blurted as soon as he was inside the Center,

"Susan, I can't do this. I can't be married!"

"Richard, its OK. I…"

"No, no its not!" He interrupted. "I have nine wives, not in the physical way, un- understand….and, ….and a girlfriend here…." He actually moaned.

Shocked, I exclaimed, "What do you mean you have *nine* wives?"

"On different dimensions…I visit them…" He sighed and looked at me pleading.

"Richard, I didn't do this. You called me- and remember, it was God put the mist over us and that pronounced us? I didn't initiate this. I don't understand. Has this happened to you like this before?"

"No, no,…no…..never like that with God and the universe watching!" He said shaking his head. " I can't be married! " I can't be married !......Excuse me…." He ran to the bathroom and threw up!

I sat alone for the next several minutes until he returned. I didn't know whether to laugh or cry. I was too stunned to do either. Nine wives? How could anyone have nine wives? On different dimensions? What kind of hogwash was this he was trying to sell me anyway?

He made his way back over and sat down. "Sorry."

"Can you start over?" I asked. "I don't understand."

"That's just it, neither do I!....... I have my rights, you know!"

"Didn't you call me?" I asked, confused.

"Yes…..No! That was my higher self!... I didn't know, just like you didn't know."

"Well, we didn't seem to have any problems over there…." I mumbled remembering our joining.

"You've got to understand! That was our higher selves that were joined, not here!!"

"Well, why do we both remember that if its' only supposed to be over there…?" I wondered aloud.

"I don't know!" He moaned again. " Its not supposed to be like this! Something's wrong!"

"Richard, I am in no position to be married. I already am. But a Guru told me that God would choose my mate. Something like an arranged marriage, I guess you could call it, and it has obviously happened."

"Susan, I ….."

"No, *we* can't. I am not going to lie to you. I know I love you, but everything is wrong right now and I don't understand this either. But I do know this, that if we ever do want to have relationship, God has sanctioned it and even performed the ceremony!"

"I think we'd better just be friends, a friendship...."

My heart sank, but I said it anyway. "I am very much in love with the man who sits across from me in the Lotus." He nodded.

On that other realm, I knew that he loved me too. But, I was also was beginning to fully understand that the love had not transferred over to this realm for him as it had for me.

"And because I do understand how you feel, I agree with you that a friendship is best." I sighed.

"Yes, a friendship," He agreed. "We can be friends here." He looked up at me hopefully.

"Now, I have to go. But the next time we meet, I want to know more about your having nine wives!" I kidded with him as I rose from my chair, trying to break the intensity of the moment. This had been an exhausting weekend. "I am really tired, and I want to go home now." He nodded and stood.

I felt compelled to tell him, "You know that I'm going to Florida with Will next weekend for his cousin's wedding. I won't be here." I added. "For some reason, I have felt I may not be coming back from that wedding, Richard." His eyes grew wide. He knew something that he'd not told me.

He held the door for me as I fumbled, with teary eyes, for my keys. "Let me have a hug, " I said smiling up at him as soon as I managed to get the key out of the door. He quickly gave me an embrace that shocked me. I thought he was never going to let go and I could hear him crying on my shoulder. Then, in a flash, he was gone.

I walked out to my car and got in. I put my head down on the steering wheel and let the tears flow. "This is really crazy!" I thought aloud as I started up the car.

That night and all nights afterwards, I slept on the couch. My true husband awaited me on the other side. I would meet him there.

Only tonight, someone else showed up.

"Melchizedek! What am I doing here?" I stood beneath the great Council on a platform in the glowing white room. The Council sat in a half moon circle above me behind the 'desk' of Judgment. It appeared to be like a judge's throne room, but there were many seated behind the desk. They all stared down at me. Some I recognized.

I was standing in front of a number of other people that were lined up behind me. I didn't know them. We were all in a Council meeting on the other side. There would be no rest tonight! Business!

"Why have you called me?" I asked the Council.

"Al'Lat. There is something we must discuss and you must remember. It is vital you understand." Melchizedek spoke again.

"Sir," I spoke to the Council and Melchizedek. "There seems to be many things I do not understand;

Why was I married? Why was I not?

Why am I going to Florida and not coming back?

And, why do I feel the call of this man day and night? I need to be with him.

Why?"

My frustration was growing with each thought and question. Here, I would hopefully, find some answers!

"We shall start from the beginning," a Council Member spoke. "When you began this journey to earth there was no anticipation that you would go beyond what normally occurs. You have."

Another broke in to explain, "Both you and your husband are fellow Council Members such as ourselves. You are in a physical incarnation on the planet Earth, on an assignment." He shook his head in wonder, " But- it is not often that humans can retain the ancient codes between the dimensional levels. You have."

"What are you talking about?" I asked.

Melchizedek spoke again. "You have done something we had not anticipated."

"Oh. That's it? Now, in my life I am stuck between these worlds? Just what did we do that we weren't supposed to do?"

"You broke the law." Someone shouted at me.

"WHAT?" What law?" I asked astounded. I looked around the room. " How did I break a law? I don't know what you are talking about! I complained and defended myself. "This is a crazy dream!"

"Humanity is not allowed to go beyond the barriers, at least not at this time." Kuan Yin spoke gently, explaining the situation.

"And there are special 'requirements' for such actions that have not yet been fulfilled for creating other worlds within the void." St Germain added.

"Oh, that's it? I didn't meet your requirements?"

"Somehow, Al'Lat, the two of you, in your physical incarnations here on earth, remembered the codes and have created." Melchizedek sighed. "As High Priest, it was necessary to bring the two of you together and perform the Marriage Act as commanded by El Elyon, God Most High- after that fact."

I could not help it. I started laughing!

"You mean I got pregnant and **had** to get married!"

"We do not see the humor in this Al'Lat." Someone stiffly announced.

"Well, I do…." I said stifling my laughter.

"When worlds were created it was always by the Elohim, never humans!" Someone else sourly announced.

I was beginning to see the issues here. I thought quickly;

We had broken the 'law' by remembering how to do it. We were human.

In doing so, we'd inadvertently created a serious, new problem for the Council.

Once humanity experienced the ability to create beyond the physical realm of Earth's local, ALL of humanity would be able to access that information.

Why? Because once that barrier had been broken, it became part of the human experience.

Our creative act, not as Elohim but as humans, became part of the consciousness grid of the planet.

From now on, HUMANS would hold the right to creation acts. Humans would have the ability to do it by accessing the grid.

One day many others would follow the path that Richard had established simply because they would assimilate the knowledge from the Christ Consciousness grid that surrounded this planet.

We, humanity, weren't ready yet!

Oh-oh! Even I could see the implications. They all saw- I now understood.

"Most importantly, Al'Lat the Divine Order has not been followed. Pairs of Elohim, male and female-when they so desire, are given the right to create beyond the realms and bring life into the void. It is a great responsibility."

" Yes, you have created worlds and galaxies, but they contain no life, or Spirit, as you did not understand or finish the works of creation." Someone explained.

"Nor are you in a position to maintain guardianships over such creations." A gentle, female voice continued.

"That must be corrected." Someone interjected.

"Your mate must finish that which he has started and you hold the Divine Spark of Creation. He needs you to finish his work. And he needs the Breath." Germaine explained to me.

Kuan Yin spoke again. "Understand, the Breath can only come from you."

At that moment, a veil was dropped. I could see Richard, but he could not see me. He was in deep discussion with some other of the members of the Council. I watched and I could see he was having some difficulty with what was being told to him. He looked angry.

After a few minutes, Melchizedek spoke. "It is agreed on the higher level, but now must be agreed in the physical."

"Obviously, you have a plan?" I asked.

"Only if you agree." Metatron spoke from his crystal platform.

" I will do so." I affirmed to him.

"Oh, Mother of Universes, we have come to instruct you in the way....hear us now and remember….." the tone of Melchizedek began to sing to my soul.

Chapter XIII

Fly, Fly Away

Wednesday, February 19th

I awoke in the morning with my answers. I may not return, but I knew where I was going! In two days, I would begin my journey. It was not just to Florida.

I closed my eyes and envisioned him within the Lotus and I called him.

"I need to see you now!"

The telephone rang. It was Richard. "Susan! What do you need? I was just at the flea market and a white mist formed by me and called my name! It was you! I'm already on my way!"

"Good, we've got something important to discuss. I was on the other side last night and boy, do they have a plan! I'll wait for you in the Center." I drove to the Center. A few minutes later he was walking through the door.

"Man, what this'll do to the cell phone business!" I thought. "Let's go for a walk." I told Richard about the visitation and relayed the final discussion. "Richard, I am going to tell you exactly what Melchizedek said to me."

"Melchizedek's words;

The way, the nature of the universe is procreation and diversity.

The Father, Creator of All has set it so;

Male and female he has made them, in His Own image.

As above, so below; the Dreamer dreams the dream; in compassionate action and love, the female responds and seeks to form the dream into the physical realms.

This pleases the Dreamer who loves his mate; the female creates once again to bring pleasure to her friend and lover....and so all things; birthing, exist.

Opposing, yet attracting, movement and motion, give and take, warm and cold. Dancing the dance of snowflakes, warmth bursting into beauty at onset of cold.

Merging and dancing together all things become, all things exist.

View now, the procreation of your own kind;

The thrusting movement of the body male;

The receptive female receiving her lover....."

"I watched, Richard, as a couple were engaged in sexual union, moved in motion together. I understood the words of Melchizedek as I could see the rhythm, giving and receiving, and I understood in a new way. Then Melchizedek spoke to me again saying,

"Now look and view the miracle with new eyes."

"Richard, I could see the couple's bodies start to glow. I was able to see the aura of each; one warm, one cold; one emerald, one topaz golden. In flowing motion the rhythm intensified and so did their colors! Brighter and brighter, intense, fire and water peaking higher and higher until they had an orgasm together! At that precise moment, the female did something spectacular!"

"Suuuuuu....san..."

"No you wait , Richard!"

I could tell by the look he was giving me he didn't like my speaking about such things to him. "This is important! Before my eyes I saw something I had never realized before. At the moment of peak, an electrical charge exploded from them! Like hundreds of lightening bolts, hundreds of charges burst from them! The female's lightening was a combination of the two colors! She produced something 'new' from the two of them!"

" Melchizedek told me,

"Your science has just begun to understand what you have just witnessed; conception;

Life does not just begin simply because a sperm enters an egg.

*A reaction, **a charge**, brings forth newness of life.*

Now, charged with this couple's mixed energies, the diversification process may begin;

The Divine Spark of Life has been engaged and energized.

What was two individuals, now will become a creation that bears the energetic, frequency codings of the two.

Now a secret shall be told you; the colors,

The Spark of Love, the individual contrasting and merging of the

individual participants, shall determine what DNA coding that

shall be produced within the 'child' created.

The Mother carries the spark within and provides the catalyst and the womb to bear the child.

Cloning requires the electromagnetic artificial charge to begin life, but without the soul charge of the Father.

It is a dangerous territory your species has entered in experimentation. It has been tried in other places within the universe, but the final results are yet untold."

"Then I asked Melchizedek why he was showing me this. This is what he told me, Richard."

*"Mother, **you** are Mother. Richard, Regalis, the Courageous, has dreamt a great dream. You are the Feminine Aspect in your creation. You carry the catalyst within; the half necessary of the Divine Spark, to birth the DNA encodings of your copulation. The love you bear in your soul for your mate is the Spark.*

I said to them, "I have no children here.(meaning, on this plane) I have no expectation of any."

Metatron spoke to me,

"Mother, you are to create life. You are made to create life. You are made to create. You and your mate have created form. Your likeness permeates the universal form you have created.

Together, you have discovered the Mystery Of God, yet without knowledge. You have burst through the barrier as we knew mankind would one day. It was so determined for your evolution.

You have sent your DNA far into the future and secured it there for all time. Yet understand and know this; What you have created is FORM

It does not bear the Divine Spark Of Divine Union!

It does not hold the Breath Of Life, the Gift of Mother.

Your Breath will initiate life.

It is as if it were a cloned image and can not be as it is.

Do you understand?"

"Wow"….Richard sighed. "What have we done?"

"It's OK, Richard. I asked them, "Is it because we have not copulated as a husband and a wife this is a clone? They said, "Yes." Then I asked about the fact when we were married we were merged and wasn't that enough? They said , 'no.'

"Su…..zannnnne…….", he warned me again with his tone.

I got mad!

"Richard! Listen and get out of your ego!" I exploded. " This is what Melchizedek told me.

"No. The Divine Sanction was given. The power and the protection of the Father was placed over you after the creative process was done, the form became. It is allowed and desired you become one flesh, as it is known. You will do

> *many acts of creation together for the form is prepared and awaits. But that force must replicate the Divine Laws."*

"I am not desired by him. That is not going to happen." I told him that, Richard. "But it must!" was their reply to me."

He looked very concerned and worried at that point.

" Then Metatron spoke again to me." I continued.

> *"This we have seen and have provided an alternative process for you. You all have choice. We have shown you this for understanding. Again, we shall show you your marriage in Heaven;"*

"Richard, I saw the whole thing, all over again." I gulped down the tears for all my love came flooding back to me. He waited for me to speak. "I could see you……I have such love for you, a soul love. I can't help it."

"Susan, I am so sorry this has happened to you. I never knew what was going to happen, not like this." He said, holding back his own feelings.

"Richard, this is what has been suggested I do. I am going to go over on the other side."

"No, Susan you cannot die! You've got too much to do! The people here need you!" He shouted at me and turned away.

"Calm down. Actually, I don't have to die to do this. When I told them that I'd love to be here always, but that I had people who depended upon me, they came up with a plan and explained something to me saying,

> *"Susan, Mother, when the time of ascension comes for your planet, the universe you and your mate have created*

is the template to where they shall ascend: Would you have them enter a place void of life? Devoid of the Creator's Law Of Love?"

I then asked, "I always heard that God has gone before us to prepare a place of many mansions for His children." Their answer to that was,

> "He has, first in the Only Begotten and now through His children! You! When you came forth from the Mind Of the Creator, you came forth in pairs. The time of rejoining is now, for this creation and for many others."

"Are there others doing this?" I asked.

> "No, not at this time." They told me. " You are the first two of the human kind to transcend the barrier of time space and of this universe to create another. But it is the Divine Plan that the pairs shall all one day take their place as creator gods just as you have done so."

I told them I didn't think we'd done such a great job of it so far! But, they disagreed.

They said,

> "Many shall follow you in times to come. A great wave of humanity will in time, ascend through the gateway you and he created, into the new universe. There they shall find one another, pair, and discover what you have. It shall be many ages hence: but it shall be. You and he have made the template.

> You are greatly honored, both of you throughout all the Universe of the Father. The path, the bridge now exists, but is yet lacking."

I asked them, "What can I do?"

They said,

> "*Agree to come, to merge with your husband. Create the Divine Spark of Creative Force over this New Universe. Infuse it with the Likeness of the Divine; both male and female; with the DNA of humanity and borne of Divine Love. Merge in the Divine order with your mate on this plane. Breathe the Breath Of Life, Of Soul into the whole."*

"I told them that I knew that if I did that, I'd never want to return, Richard."

"What does that mean?" Richard asked me.

"Well, this is the plan. I am needed on the other side, and in the realm we created, to produce the Divine Orgasmic Spark with the higher aspect of yourself. This is to set forth the DNA Spark from my form."

" Remember the combined lightening bolts that I told you the female produced? That's what is needed. I gave my essence to your thought creation, but with out the 'lightening.'

Life there has no soul essence, no consciousness, no breath ...

"What? No way! That's crazy!" He backed up.

"No, no, no, you don't have to do a thing….just me. I just have to go for a while and enter into what the Buddhists call YAB-YUM with your higher self and create lightening and set the template! I can stay as long as I need to and then return. They told me I'd have no concept of time there, though." I paused for I knew what that really meant. I might not come back.

"Also, there's another problem. Melchizedek explained to me that I hold the Divine Aspect of the Feminine on the Earth right now."

He said,

"Without your presence on the earth plane for any length of time, the earth and its peoples are in grave danger of negative forces overcoming it. You hold a balance for the peoples, a protective barrier for the people of God's love over the people. The hand of destruction is withheld.

That is why you called forth the Angels of Mercy and they came; thwarting nuclear destruction of the earth. You are the present Kuan Yin Aspect on Earth, the aspect of the Mother of Protection, the Bodhisattva of Compassion in a physical form. The Father sees you there and has compassion and protects the people."

Richard, I thought about that for a few minutes then I asked him , "I'm not always going to live, or be in this form. What then?"

He told me,

"This is true. Through your work and that of your mate, many shall ascend even through times of destruction on the planet .As the Goddess Aspects are assimilated into the consciousness of the planet, others will bear this and you shall be free to leave at the designated time. But it is not yet so. A time exists soon, the end of this, your month, which is a critical time. Your mate has told you of this."

"I told Melchizedek that I knew you had information about a possible tragedy and you were concerned about me. You'd already told me it was on the 27th, the very day I was to return from Florida. He told me I had to return to my physical form on or before that date! That is what you were seeing, Richard."

Richard sat quietly for several minutes. I could see him going over what I had told him in his mind. I didn't speak.

"YAB-YUM?" He finally spoke, questioning me.

"Yes, ever see the Buddhists paintings of the god figures in sexual union? That's YAB-YUM. Eternal, creative union on the other realms, it's the glue of creative force."

"You're not REALLY going to do that are you?' He asked astounded.

I resisted the urge to smile.

"Richard, we have already begun the process. And, I have something else they told me. Because of our individual essences, me sapphire, and you ruby, when we add the lightening Spark of the Divine Love, we will create something beyond spectacular!"

"The combined essences will produce a Violet- Ray creation. The life consciousness and DNA patterning we will be creating will be of the very highest life form in the new creation in the void! It shall be the first of the new humans' evolution and set a new, restoring pattern for all to follow!"

"Susan, that means we will have created a new universe and at the very beginnings of that universe will be the highest consciousness and DNA! My, GOD, that's incredible!"

"That's what they said. That's why *I have* to go."

"HOW? How are you going to do that and still come back?" He asked, concerned now.

"Are you ready for this?"

"100%."

"OK. When I am in the airplane with Will, on Wednesday the 20th, I'll be taken out of my body. Someone else is coming into my body-right in the plane! I am to be replaced with a walk-in."

"No, way!"

"Yeah."

"WHO? Do you know who's coming into your body?"

" Um- hum, yeah."

"Alright, Susan, tell me!

"Thoth."

"Thoth? He's a man!" Richard shouted." A man is going to embody *you*?"

"I know. Wild , huh? But he's the only one with high enough energy to do this and he's agreed!" I defended.

"Well, damn, this is going to be interesting!" He exclaimed shaking his head. "What about Will?"

"They told me only he would see the difference in me, but that he would not interfere. They must have spoken to him too. I am being taken away from here so no one will see or know the difference."

He sat back and took a long look at me. He must have been imagining me with Thoth inside. I fidgeted, he saw and then said, "You don't have to do this."

"Yes, I do! I want to do it! It's my baby! OURS! I want to do this, Richard, I want to bring you the Breath, for the creation and for those who are ascending."

"OK, OK,… OK……" he said raising his hands in surrender.

"There is one thing you have to do, Richard. My coming back depends on it. If you don't, I won't be able to come back."

"Susan, you know I'll do anything I can. What? What do I have to do?"

"They tell me once I am in YAB-YUM there is only once voice I can hear. Yours. Only yours. The voice of my beloved lover is the only voice that I will respond to. You will have to call me back when it's over, that is, when the lightening has struck!"

"I can do that. Yes, I'll do that." He promised.

"There is another thing. Please, hold my reality in your consciousness. You will need to hold me, remember me, as no one else can. I was told that you could meet me in the Lotus to maintain my reality in your consciousness on this plane."

He nodded.

"When I leave, my presence is gone and all other people will loose my reality very quickly. They won't even remember who I am. I am beginning to understand that I am more of a concept rather than a person here."

I thought about that for a minute, then said to Richard, " My walk- in will eventually become solid, will become the new me."

I paused to gain control. "If I am not returned, Thoth will remain in me and I will never return to this world, Richard. I am a little frightened, but also very excited. Thoth and I told them we thought you'd agree to do this and bring me back."

"Yes. I will do that. Yes, this all makes sense. I will bring you back! Its' not over, you know. We have a responsibility to take care of this now. There is much to do! I *wi*ll call you back. The universe we created is growing, expanding! I have been watching it grow. Yes, there is much to do!" Richard exclaimed.

He was ready! So was I.

"Then, its' all set. On Friday, 2/22/2002 at 2:02.22 I will leave this world. 18. It is the time of life."

A Time To Consider...

When I finally had a few minutes of peace, I realized there was no one else on this Earth who knew what I was about to do. There was no guarantee that I would even return, that in fact, I might even cease to exist in the minds of those I loved.

I said quiet "goodbyes" to my children, telling them that I loved them. The thought that what was about to happen was in fact for my children, strengthened me somehow. My going meant they would survive.

In fact, I began to realize something else. All the while the Council had been planning for earth's destruction, God had found a way to preserve His highest creation; mankind. And, it was done by preparing a whole new dimension for humanity. Our souls would now incarnate into bodies and a form at the highest levels! We'd leave this plane of lower energies for good!

Father-Mother had called Richard and me through the wall of Spirit, of White Fire. Mother-Father gave us the codes to create in the void. Humans did it; their little child-like humans. There would be no stopping this now.

The Council had sent me to Earth to incarnate and to prepare humanity for an ascension they knew was impossible to attain by efforts of a few people. Once Richard and I were here, God took over the opportunity and worked out the alternative. Right underneath the Council's noses, so to say!

I thought of Richard. He was so strong, yet this frightened him, I could tell. His dedication to Spirit had been borne out by his entire life's work. After he left the service, he'd spent twenty years with the Benedictine Monks in prayer and in his spiritual studies. It was all in preparation for this very moment.

He'd call me back; he had given his word.

Chapter XIV

A Song, A Song, A Singing In The Night

"Hurry up, Sue! We don't want to miss this plane! Will exclaimed. "We've been given tickets to Disney World too as a gift to all the guests. That'll be fun. This is going to be quite a wedding!"

"Oh, Will, if only you knew...." I thought as I packed my bags and talked to myself. "How do you pack for an Egyptian Ascended Master like Thoth?"

I wondered what he'd like to wear. I wondered how Thoth would like Disney Land. Mumbling to myself, "Men used to wear skirts back then, wonder if they wore underwear? No, not likely, and no bras; Thoth! There's a modern contraption you'll just have to figure out!" My mind was rambling, or totally lost at this point.

"Didn't you write the Emerald tablets and talk about everything being, "mind?" A state of mind, Thoth? Just keep a positive state of mind...." I spoke to him as I chose his clothing for the week from my closet. Now, to find something he could wear to the wedding. It had to be something conservative and formal too.

"Yes, this one will do." I said aloud as I packed a white pleated skirt and matching top with a wide fancy belt of silver and gold. "That's sort of Egyptian. Yes, lots of white stuff; knee length shorts and loose tops. OK. That's it! I'm ready, Will."

At the airport, we had a few minutes before boarding. I couldn't stop pacing with excitement. Will could see that I was troubled.

"You're really going to miss the Center."

"Yes, I am."

"You don't really have to go to Florida with me if you don't want to." He said gently.

A chill went through me. It wasn't really him speaking. I shivered. This was the luring voice of another force speaking through him. The voice of evil is slimy. "Oh, no you don't!" I thought.

I shot back "No, I am going! I want to! I'll not turn back now, I've come this far!" I startled him back into his true being with my intensity. He got up and walked over to the window and shook it off.

Before I knew it, we were boarding the plane. We had strange seating. Will and I sat side by side, but were also facing two other passengers who were seated up against a solid wall. We had a few feet of space in front of us, but it was strange to be looking at someone across from us.

As we settled in, we all spoke to one another just to be more comfortable. I was facing a young woman who sat next to her husband. Somehow, she looked really familiar. After the intros and we were in the air, I pulled out a book and pretended to read.

All I could think about was the body exchange that was about to happen. How was this going to feel? Was it really going to happen? I began to feel really tired and started to fall asleep.

I wrapped my shawl around me and put down my book. My eyes would not stay open. I must have slept for a couple of hours when suddenly, I found myself looking down at my body below me still seated in the airplane. It startled me and I crashed back into my body with a start!

"We'll do that again." I heard the voice say. I instantly saw the head of Thoth.

Cosmic Eve 2012: Rebirthing Mankind

"Thoth" I whispered.

"Yes, I am here. Focus now upon the Lotus." I closed my eyes and began to meditate. I could feel a tremendous pull and squeezing of my body! I gasp!

My eyes shot open. All I could see in that moment was the astonished look on the face of the woman across from me! She could see what was happening! At that instant, I heard Thoth speak as he slid into me and I past by him on the way out,

"*I always wanted to be in female form!*"

And then, I was gone. And he was in my body below. Whirling into the Light, I heard the Voice say,

"Go up higher. He will call you there, he has heard the command."

I could see the ruby essence of a Great Star above the Lotus, the scent of roses permeated the air around me.

"Lift up to me." I breathed in his ruby essence, lifting into his being.

"This is how you will come to me, My Love."

I hear him speak as I merge with his essence,

"For now, there can be no other way.

Your life on Earth is but a moment;to me without you it is eternity itself.

I wait for you for now, for God has willed it so..."

Clearly, I can see him now. As he speaks his passion, magenta rays flow outward across all of time and space, his ruby rays flare with his passion for me. A blaze of white purity now enfolds me as I join my husband in eternity, in ecstasy, in YAB-YUM.

There is no time here….all is perfect….all is union…..all is One…..

Days went by. …but I didn't know….

The wedding in Florida came and went, and I had no knowledge or care about any of it until….

'What? What's happening?" I cried as I was being pulled back into my body!

Thoth screamed as he past out of me and I was pulled back in.

"He's calling you back too soon!"

I found myself in a lounge chair by the pool in an ecstatic convulsion and in a scanty two-piece bathing suit…

Just as I was trying to pull myself together, I could hear Thoth speak,

"All fixed!"

And he slid right back in … and I was out again…

"Susan! Susan! What's the matter with you? We were here yesterday! You drove us! Watch out for that car!" Will screamed at me!

I was driving the car!

Or rather, Thoth was driving the car!

Could he drive?

"OH!" I screamed!

"He's at it again!"

Thoth shouted as he slid back in my body again…

And I was gone again…

"What a week, Susan!" Will was talking stiffly to me.

I suddenly realized I was in the airplane flying back home to New Hampshire….

" I'm filing for divorce when we get back."

"Oh, I understand, Will. It's not your fault." I spoke quickly, trying to gather my senses. A week had gone by! Now, I was on my way home.

I suddenly realized-**Richard had called me back**! It worked! I'm here! I'm really here, I thought, ecstatic!

"No, I've never seen you like that before, Susan." Will was angry and clearly upset with me.

What had happened? I sought some way to soothe this until I could find out.

"Let's just forget about the whole thing." I said to him. " You know, weddings-I've got a really big headache right now."

"Well, you ought to….glad nobody back there knew us." He snapped at me.

Susan Isabelle

"Thoth! What did you do?" I sent out a stern message to him, but with a smiling heart-full of thanks...

Unpacking, I found lots of new "items." Thoth had gone shopping and had a really good time! Among the items were the bathing suit and a fiery red sexy dress with a plunging neckline. Pictures later showed I-Thoth wore that to the wedding! I also understand that he danced wildly all night long with all the men, and had lots to drink.

Will still couldn't get over the fact that I had driven him to Disney World one day and couldn't remember how to drive there the next. He told me about how he ended up driving when I nearly hit the car head on. Guess he made Thoth give up driving for the rest of the trip.

I-Thoth, also rode the roller coaster-the terror ride in the dark-three times and he nearly had to drag Thoth home to get him off it .

I continued to sleep on the couch.

Late that night, I got a phone call from Richard.

"Susan? Susan, I'm sorry. I just had to call! Are you-*you*? Are you all right?"

"Yes, Richard, we just got in a while ago. I'm here and I'm me. You did a good job, Richard. I'm fully back. Thank you."

"Thank God!" I wasn't sure I was doing it right, Sue."

"Richard, you really got that down pat!"

"Yeah, I practiced a few times. Did you know?"

"Uh-huh, I knew when you practiced, I definitely could feel it. Someday, I'll tell you all about it but right now I need a vacation from my vacation. You know, that Thoth is quite a guy. I can't wait to meet him someday. And so are you. Nite' Richard."

"Good Night, Susan. See you soon."

Early the next morning I avoided Will. I prepared to go to the Center a few hours earlier than anyone was expected to arrive. I wanted to be alone and I was trying to keep the peace.

I made my way to the Center and stood outside, just looking in. It seemed funny somehow, to be looking in through the windows, just a passerby. Somehow things would never be the same. I would never look at life the same way. Just window- shopping for a little while, until I go home to where the real goods are. Once I wanted things, you know, things. Houses, airplane rides, vacations in exotic places and money. Now, I could care less about those things.

I unlocked the door. As I walked around the Center, I could see that it was quite an accomplishment for a woman. Many were vying for position and status, even here. It was tiring. The only things of value in this store, I thought, were the symbols of the miracles of all that had led up to what had just happened to me.

This Center was the birthing place of a new reality for humanity. That was what was really important. Not me, not anything else.

God and Spirit, the Shekhina, the wife of God, had blessed all of humanity here. Now, a new place, a new mansion, a new universe had been fashioned with Their blessings- two, simple humans. Christ had told us in His incarnation that we, the children, would do even greater things than he; It was all a part of the Divine Plan. This part of the plan was now complete. It had been done. I lay face down on the floor in front of the altar and praised and worshipped God- Goddess. It is Their plan, Their way.

All too soon, I heard the arrival of the staff. I rose, wiped away my tears of joy and prepared to meet them. I felt such love for them all. They are the Children, they are loved beyond all this world can imagine, I knew it. You are loved.

"Susan, I just had to come to see you! How are you? Please, tell me everything that happened!" Richard burst into the Center, ahead of everyone else. I smiled and a warm glow from my heart swept out to my friend.

"Well, it was like this…."

I began to tell him all about Thoth's playfulness.

"He drove the car?"

"Yes, and he danced and drank like a wild man at the wedding! He absolutely stunned Will. He says he's going to divorce me! I don't think I can blame him. Not that it was Thoth's fault but it's hastened something that was clearly coming anyway."

"Well, you're back! And you're OK!" He said relieved.

What was amazing to see was Richard. He had a new softness about him and he often wiped away tears as I spoke. He had been really worried about me while I was gone. That's why he kept 'practicing,' and trying to bring me back.

Also, even though the merging of our energies had occurred in dimensions we'd never fully understand and while I was 1500 miles away, he was different and so was I. A softness toward one another and a deep love that transcended the physical was now in place.

What had taken place in Heaven was now making it's way down to us on Earth.

" Susan, I don't think we're supposed to meditate anymore. You know." He began to speak.

"I agree, Richard." I interjected. " I think the work we were supposed to do is done. Will you still come here?" I asked.

" Couldn't keep me away!" He said grinning.

"Well, El Aleator, I guess you're going to have a rest too!" I spoke to the little crystal skull I'd been wearing around my neck. "After all we've been through, I think it's time for you to be put away."

"You're going to put it away?" Richard asked.

"Yes, I think that its power and knowledge is more than I'm ready to experience for a while. I need a rest too! The safety deposit box will be its home for a bit."

"Yeah, I guess so…."

Chapter XV

The Cosmic Eve

Two days later Richard came running back into the Center.

"Susan, hurry! Get ready! You have to see this!"

"What, Richard?"

"Come, not here, come now!"

I put my coat on and ran out to the car with him. We traveled the short distance to the cemetery. He wouldn't talk to me, but sat driving the car grinning! Once there, we briskly walked up the path to the temple in the cemetery and sat down.

"Close your eyes! Look at this!" He said, all excited.

As soon as my eyes were closed, I could see it. The Project, his project, the fountain was glowing brightly. It was so bright! It was so filled with radiant light, that it was difficult to look at.

"WOW! Richard! Its incredible!"

"LOOK! Susan! *Look inside*!" He was crazed with excitement!

I focused more intently in the center of the light and gasped!

"It can't be! Oh, My God! That's a woman; no its' a man! NO! A woman!"

"You see her?"

"Yes, Richard I do! She's inside the light in the center of the fountain!"

"Yes! Yes! That's it!"

"Who, Richard? Who is it?"

"That is our Daughter, Susan! The Breath has given her life!"

"Our Daughter?"

"Yes! She is the Cosmic Eve of the new creation! Susan, we've done it!"

"The Cosmic Eve?"

"Yes! See the DNA?"

As I focused in to watch, I could see the Cosmic Eve turning inside the light. She was so beautiful! Her hair flowed sparkling white down her long, slender back and covered her firm breasts. Her arms of pure light rose gracefully above her head, then floated down once again. It was as though she was dancing in the light, slowly but ecstatically.

As she turned, she took on form and then, transformation: first a woman, evolving the form to that of a male; a young man evolved from her essence. He too was beautiful in his light; the male, the female, ever dancing in ecstasy, their pure joy was filling the void with possibility.

Moving again, he slowly danced and swirled gracefully back to the form of a beautiful, young woman again. As she did so, thousands of DNA spiraled up from her, swirling around her, birthing the new creation; new souls; new formation to fill the coming form in the new universe!

Over and over again, I watched as the process continued. It would continue on forever;

This is the Cosmic Eve.
This is how souls come into being;
This is how universes are filled with life!
This is the Twin Flame energies, of male and female being created.
The highest spiritual essence of Richard and I were in eternal Yab Yum
The DNA of twin flames and soul groups was filling the new universe...
This is what God had Richard and I do to prepare for the new world...

2012

The new consciousness, the new DNA of the Violet Creation...

Many of us would one day incarnate into that realm, forever leaving behind the lower form!

My heart was filled with awe and love! I began to cry. The tears ran down my cheeks and would not stop. Richard moved next to me, put his arm around my shoulders and pulled me close. He handed me his handkerchief.

"It is done; Susan. It is complete. Humanity will continue on. An incredible new world is waiting for us all. It is because of the Cosmic Eve; our Daughter." He comforted me as he wiped away his own tears. "Who would ever believe this? This is inconceivable! If I wasn't seeing it, I wouldn't believe it either. But Look! Susan, LOOK!'"

We cried together that afternoon. We couldn't stop watching the Project, now the Cosmic Eve. In 2012 it will begin.

I realized that long ago, Richard and I were created from another Cosmic Eve. We were created at the same moment, of the same movement; of male and female. We came out together, as twins. We were likely birthed together at the very beginning of time and creation. All of us had come from our first Mother.

We were now watching new couples, new potential and a great promise to mankind, now forming within the Eve. We were watching what we are now-and had been- in our Mother, Eve at the beginning. All DNA came forth from one Mother.

We had come full circle in time. It is the end of this age. Earth was soon to evolve out of the lower realms. We were about to ascend. 2012 marked the end of this age. I had a lot to think about that day. Things became clearer to me as we sat and watched the spinning of life.

Certain things had to be in place to make ready the next potential. A New Universe had to be prepared and a New DNA had to be produced.

Adama-the first human father- had told me in 1999 at Mount Shasta, Ca. that they (the first fathers and first race already ascended at the first resurrection into Light at the time of Christ) would come to *"hold the integrity through the transition, but it must be with the assistance of humanity."* Then he asked me,*" Will you go?"* When I agreed to go, I had thought I was only to go to thirty –six places on the earth; not into the universe or into the void to create a new place!

Realize that a whole race is waiting for the end of this age. Our first fathers and mothers are waiting for this day. They are also waiting for the next potential. When Christ was resurrected into His and our, new form, he made the way for us all. He wasn't alone.

The streets of Jerusalem were filled with the ascended spirits of the Ancient Ones who had received the promise of the first resurrection and their ascension into Light. Adama was one of them. He rose that day and is now assisting his grandchildren.*

Little did I know what he meant then or what I'd actually be called to do. I understood today, while watching the New Eve, what he couldn't tell me then; the response I would make would have to be from the *heart*, not from the mind. My heart and that of Richard's, our love for God above all things, was required.

God-Father, is the Dreamer; He dreams the dream and Divine Mother produces the dream in a Compassionate Action for Him. All creation is a Compassionate Action born of love. The force created through love is the Christ Light; Christ is the First Light, the Creative Being formed from love. That Light is sound, frequency and vibration; all that is needed to create in the lower realms.

True love to the Dreamer was required to do this. Trials of faith and personal sacrifices were required to refine the soul to a place of love, unquestioned love; a love without thought to self or personal gain. Adama and Melchizedek kept the secret. They knew; it had to be a secret, or Richard and I may have fallen into ego, not love.

Humanity had matured as a race, a people from the original Eve. Now we are creating; creating the sum total of what we had become in our evolution through time, and now were extending that knowledge, far, far beyond!

"What child to be born?" I asked.

"Can you imagine the possibilities for mankind? What this will mean?" I asked him.

"No one can even begin to conceive that, Susan. This is unlimited possibility: with the new DNA being produced here, all children will be born into super- human capabilities, just as God intended for us at the beginning."

"How, Richard? How is this going to happen?"

"I don't really know all the details, but I would say that when children come into being that this is the new Violet Frequency template for their creation."

"What about all the people, all the souls who are already here, Richard? Does that mean that the old souls who leave the earth will incarnate into the new Universe using this DNA? What about the Ascended Ones, the Ancients who are waiting for new bodies? Do you think they'll pick up the new, fresh, enhanced DNA on their way in?"

"I think so. Evolution has begun. We're watching it. And think further, Susan. It's not just us; all the twins of the original creation will one day be doing this."

This is why El Aleator had been brought to the Earth plane. One would work with the Light energy encodings it held to do this. Not one, but two were required; a male and a female. Regalis and I must have tried in Atlantis, but the time was not right or we would have already been in a higher form. There was too much opposition from the dark. Light would eventually prevail.

I thought about that a bit. God had created us; now humanity was one day going to create in response to the Great Commandment; "Go forth and multiply!" For some reason, Richard and I had been given this to do. Even though we had blundered all the way through, we had done all that we had been given to do. The template was made.

Richard had spent countless hours, day in and day out, consumed with moving blue agni mist into geometric shapes to form something he didn't even understand. He just knew he had to do it. He had been instructed to do it, and he did. It consumed his life and had cost him relationships and set him apart from others. Now, today, he understood why. He had great love within him for God and humanity.

I remembered the scripture that said, "It has not even come into the mind of man what God has in store for the Children of Light!" Now we were being given a glimmer of the Great Plan of God!

The Council had fought over the right of humanity to survive. Anyone that is not fully Light is a lesser light and the truth is not fully within them. That includes the Council and the 'masters.' They simply dwell on another realm that is a little higher up. The higher you go, the more Truth you realize. They are not gods, but many people seem to think they are.

God over- ruled the Council. It is His Plan, His thought; He is the Creator! It was His plan to give it all to mankind all along. The coming of the Christ secured our right in the higher realms. Now we were ready to stand up and move forward.

"Does she have a name?" I asked after a while.

"Yes, I am going to call her, Nek'ca'abba, if that is all right with you." he said pronouncing the name phonetically for me.

"Yes, Neccaaba. That is a beautiful name. Do you know what it means?"

"Yes, I believe it is a form of the name Eve; The Mother of Love."

We sat for a while longer watching the Cosmic Eve, Neccaaba, produce more DNA. After a long time, I began to giggle.

"What's so funny?" He asked.

"Just think of it. There are thousands, no, billions of potentials being created at this very moment! Daddy!...." I said pushing him away.

I wish I could describe the look on his face at that moment! His eyes grew wide. Pride, then realization, then shock crossed his features! I laughed.

"Oh, Ricky, we're going to have a lot to do later!"

"Yeah, you can say that again!" He smiled shyly. "I wonder what the Council is going to say about this one...."

There is no end to this chapter....it is just beginning

- At the time of this publication in 2008, I live at Mount Shasta in California. I have to address something at this point. I see that many come here trying to find a way into the mountain to ascend and to find Telos and Adama. They seem to think that the inner earth holds the place of Shambhala. They believe there is a portal way they can simply enter into. Some believe they can go into the portal, enter the mountain and get there without a transformation of their light and soul, or that they've already attained that ability.

    The only problem is, they search but are unable to find the entrance. There is a reason for that. The portals on the mountain are used by many inter-dimensional travelers, since the opening in 1999. Adama spoke to that opening when he explained that was a risk they had to take during this time of change. Even the lower realms can use an open vortex portal. Not all the portals are 'safe.' A lot of money, time and effort is being wasted upon this endeavor to find a portal way. One must be very sure of what one is doing these days. It distracts the true seeker from the true path. True ascension is transformation into Light.

Adama spoke to some people through me in a channel I did here in 2004. He spoke directly to forty or so persons he called together who hold high positions, land and finances. I will speak it again as Adama now requests I do so.

Adama told you this:

"God has given you the money and means to assist humanity, to build healing centers , spiritual retreats, to house and feed the poor pilgrim-seekers that are trying to attain enlightenment and transformation at this sacred mountain. It is not your money, your land or your position; but it is God's land. You can never own it. It is to be used to assist God's people. You are upon Holy Ground.

The people come to heal their souls; they come to find Teachers of Truth but they are met with stores of merchandise upon Shasta's sacred streets rather than the Seven Centers of Light. Teachers of Truth barely survive within the difficulties placed upon them. The onslaught of lower energies seek to destroy and drive out the Teacher and the Seeker from this place in a multitude of ways. There are none to help. Gifts were entrusted to you for this purpose, but the gifts have been used upon your own ego- wants. It is requested you consider your ways, for you know this is truth. There is still time. " End of Adama channel.

Apparently, there are those who have not used the gift from God as was intended. They are still seeking a hole in the earth. They help no one and lose the blessings intended for themselves.

Now to you who come here as seekers of truth; Understand that Shambhala, meaning the Heavenly realms, is not *within* the earth, but in the dimensions *above* the earth. That is why they are called the 'heavenly realms'. The Shambhala Realms are near the eighth dimension where enlightened beings hold purity of heart and thought. They barely hold a physical form.

Mount Shasta is sacred ground and there are powerful energies of transformative power here. Access to the higher realms is in the energies of transformation. The heart must be prepared. Lifetimes of incarnations must be cleansed to prepare you. Sacred areas at the mountain and in the surrounding areas do this by their energies of Light, forgiveness and healing. It is my understanding that there are to be seven Shambhala healing centers here.

You cannot enter the true Shambhala without a purified heart of love, compassion and of the highest integrity, and bear the Aspects of the Goddess in your souls. You cannot enter into Shambhala without your heart and mind consecrated to God-Goddess. It's Their house you seek entrance into. The current, lower energies of humanity will not allow entrance. The mountain energies serve to purify the heart and bring about transformation of the soul.

So, while you are here at Mount Shasta,

Please, don't look for an entrance into dirt; look for an entrance into your Heart.

Be prepared for many challenges and changes.

The Women's Gathering

"Hello, Ladies! Have I got a treat for you! I know its after Valentine's Day, but how would you like to meet your Twin Flame?"

"Oh, mine's not on this plain, but I'd sure like to meet him someday..."

"Well, what if I told you I've been on the 'other side' recently? I was given instructions as to how to connect your energies so that when the time comes, you can ascend together…"

"That would be really nice! How?" The interruptions began to flow. "When?"

"We'll just take down the meditation mats and get comfortable right here on the floor, right now."

After a few minutes, the women were all ready and anxious to get started. I began the meditation,

"Oh, Spirit of the Divine Mother, we have gathered here to rejoin our Twin Flames, our true love from the very beginning of time. I ask that the gates of Heaven be opened, where the perfected essence be of this one resides, to come so we may meet and enjoy one another again…"

Then the process began. Spirit led me all the way though so they could rejoin their Twin. And they did. Afterward, the women could hardly contain themselves!

"Susan, where's the bubbly? I just got married!"

"I want to celebrate!"

"He's so beautiful! I've never felt such complete love!"

And so it began. We continued doing this rejoining for months, finding soul mates, Twins, and rejoining in the Star! Spirit had sent me back with a beautiful gift for all!

I began to teach them all about our true inheritance yet to come;

"My Sisters! Brothers! To be connected with our Twin Flame, even in part on the Earth plane, allows a greater integration of our totality here. It is easier somehow, to find a soul peace when this is so. Most of us have never met our Twin and unfortunately, we may never in this lifetime. When we do, even in part, there is a knowing that we are loved, cherished and that there is someone waiting for us beyond all that we could imagine.

Someday, we shall rejoin our 'Twin' completely. We shall ascend together, back into the Light! We were created there. The Thought of the Divine Father combined with the Love of the Divine Mother created us. We are each a half of that Divine Thought and love.

When we left the Light to explore the lower realms, we split into different aspects. We forgot that we were once equal, male and female counterparts in the Great Plan, and separated. We lost track of one another and sought out others that we believed could fulfill us; not so, for there is only one who is given that place!

Now, it is time for us to rejoin our mates and return to the fullness that we once were. When we do, we will share with Mother, Father all that we have experienced on all the realms of God's great creation!

This takes one far beyond all the failed relationships and impossible connections with those who do not share our light essence on Earth. Freedom from bondage to those relationships makes it possible for us to return to our true center; to our own heart, in preparation for our Twin Flame. It is time to send out the call, as we do here, to our beloved ones, prepare and to purify ourselves as the Bride and the Bridegroom."

Think on this for a moment; God is a God of Creation. Mother, Father has placed within each one of us some very special gifts and abilities that are latent, just waiting to be discovered, used and perfected within us! You and your Twin Flame will use these gifts together to create. This is an exciting future for us all!

The Divine Aspect of the Mother is manifest not just in beings you might decide to call "Masters" but also within each one of us. We are made in Their likeness and there are Divine qualities that are within you that are waiting to be made manifest.

You are a Kuan Yin every time you show compassion. You are a Mother Mary when you birth love into the world and you give of yourself! You are Sophia when you share your wisdom with others. You are a creator when you place paint or pen on the canvas and allow the creative force to flow through you in imagination and expressed thought.

Let Spirit flow though you and allow you to become present on all realms and dimensions. Truly, go forth and multiply your abilities, your love, your being! Then, when the time comes, you'll be ready. Be all that you can be now…

Create Something Beautiful in Your Life!

Its practice time! This is in preparation for your mate. What you do here in manifest form raises the bar, so to speak, for each of you. Even now you are working together. Lift each other's light!

And, one day, we shall go out again as pairs and fulfill the great commandment of the Father, "Go forth and multiply!" We shall create worlds, galaxies and multiple universes and fill them with beauty and life! But again, practice! be all that you can be now…

Create Something Beautiful in Your Life!"

And they began to create Beauty! First, they created joy within themselves and then that enthusiasm spread into the community. I saw less focus on useless relationships that had previously consumed all their life force; even as I had, they had met their twin Flame in the Flame of the Lotus and were now free! That soul freedom allowed for tremendous growth!

I was reminded almost daily of the words of the Indian Mystic who had counseled me, "God will not tolerate you being in a relationship that will not support your mission!" I had to make changes too.

I continued to teach,

"Understand that I do not advocate your leaving a relationship that meets your needs and you, your partner's. Some soul mates from the same frequency range can and do manage quite well.

In your many incarnations, you have taken on both male and female form; you may be a male in female form, or vice versa. That will not hinder you and do not be concerned. All will be made clear soon.

What I am saying is that we have spent too much precious energy on useless endeavors all too often and it nearly kills us spiritually and makes us ill. You can meet your Twin and find a soul freedom in this lifetime within the Lotus. Just call him or her and be ready! Then, you will find that you will acquire a strength not previously known in your life. That strength may even improve an existing marriage, even if it is not to your Twin.

Your Twin Flame brings you into balance on many levels. If he or she is not on this plane, or if your decide to stay within a relationship, you will be far better off for having joined at least spiritually, until the time of return!

So you love your husband or your wife and never want to be separated? Likely, that person is your Twin.... don't stress! Twin Flames have entered the Lotus together and have found even more incredible joining! Also, at the time of return to the Light we shall know everything and all shall be known; all shall be made right once again."

And so the changes began;

Within a few days of this gathering, Richard showed up at the Center with a gift for me. "You need a cat!" He announced as he pulled a small Siamese kitten from under his coat. "A Temple cat!" He said smiling broadly.

I took the small furry kitten in my arms and hugged her close.

He said, "I call her, Fee Fee."

"Fee- Fee?" I asked. "How about Sophie? For wisdom, Sophie? Sooo- feee. Seems that we are into naming all the little creatures these days!"

"Yeah, I like that!" And so it was agreed. Her name would mean, ' wisdom.'

So Sophie became our Center cat, a very special little member of our growing community. She would often sit on the mat beside me as I taught the classes and was loved by all.

And then came some more good news. Cynthia arrived with a plan. How quickly the world takes over our lives!

"Susan, I like our arrangement about the store. Things are going really well here. I spoke to my husband and we are ready to invest

$125,000.00 to get us set up in the beer factory as a partnership in the store. You're ready to grow and this will benefit us both!!"

"That is amazing, Cynthia! You mean you and your husband want to do that?-When?"

"As soon as possible. He'll set me up as a partner in the store, the Gaila Goddess, and you can have the Shambhala piece as that is your training Center! There's plenty of room! I'll just move my stock I bought from you into the new space. We can get the walls made and lay the carpet with my money, plus buy an aura camera -I always wanted one of those!"

"I like the idea! And I can use the money I set aside from your stock purchase to buy the interior therapy room furnishings and to set up the new Shambhala Center auditorium! It still allows me the ability to teach and relieves me of the store. We'll do a 50-50 on the store, and I'll set up a three way Shambhala partnership with two others I have in mind. How's that sound?"

"Sounds great! I've discussed this with my husband and he says that with the income we're already getting from the little store here, we'll generate more from the larger store, so we can handle the rent and the expenses."

"Cynthia, that's three thousand a month. Are you sure?"

"Yes, that is what we want to do. You've done so much for me, we could never repay you and this is good for us too!"

"Well, with this much potential space..." I said looking out the window at the beer factory across the way. "We can also bring in other teachers. We'll charge thirty percent and that can go into the general fund to help pay for some of the expenses. We'll just have to get a few well known people to come here to teach!"

So, within a matter of weeks we signed the papers, both Cynthia and I, to move the Gaila Goddess/Shambhala Center and store to the other side of the same plaza. As it was the same landlord and the same plaza, we just slid the previous name over too. Without much thought, the Gaila Goddess Center went on the paperwork for the lease. Tom was very pleased for now he'd get his commission.

As we looked over the larger space, we marked out the area for the store front, therapy rooms, office space and the new Shambhala Center auditorium.

It was decided to use the old area that had been used for the refrigerator units, and two huge vats, for the Shambhala Area. So we had a classroom, four therapy rooms, an office and an auditorium for 150 people, a large store-front and another small classroom, plus two functioning bathrooms and showers!

The first matter of business was to remove the old vats from the space. Once they were out, we had a very pleasant surprise! The room that held the vats was very oddly shaped. We had not been able to see that when all the old equipment was still inside. The area that was to become the Shambhala Center auditorium was a dodectrahedron shaped room, one of the highest energy generating shapes.

As you walked into the room, you would see the flat back wall and two side walls that were slanted, two straight walls coming down from them and the front entranceway that was one long straight wall. Everyone had all kinds of ideas for the room, including a natural stage in the space seen directly ahead as you entered.

Things were happening very quickly now. As I pondered the Shambhala area's large room one night, I had a dream-vision. The angels came and spoke to me while showing me the room.

"Susan, this is how the room is to be utilized;

The three panel walls over the stage will hold the aspects of the Shekhina" they said, "and the Earth will be the center panel over the stage, having the Dove Of Peace over the earth.

"On the right panel wall, shall be the image of Kuan Yin as she had been seen over the Center after 911.

On the left panel wall is to be a Fountain. It shall have flowing from it all the healing waters of the Earth and Goddess; flowing for all time for all people. Her image kissing the earth shall be on that wall."

I saw in the vision the entire room, as it was soon to be.

"And here, the place of the Buddha for meditation, and this corner for the Angels to come to the people to help them and to bring requests to God for their assistance."

As they continued around the room pointing said, "And here shall be the place of the Elementals, the fairies and the children. And finally, here you shall place the symbols of the all the Native peoples of the earth."

The next morning, I wrote down all that had been shown to me! This was incredible!

I hurried and dressed to meet the company that was bringing our store front signs this morning. They were to be hung over our new center saying, The Gaila Goddess Specialty Shoppe and a second one saying, The Shambhala Meditation and Training Center.

As soon as the men for the signs arrived with the big crane to hang them, the company boss wanted to see the interior. I was so filled with joy at the vision of the night, I had to share it with him. I took out my drawings I had sketched that morning that diagramed the entire space.

"And look what the angels showed me last night!" I told him with excitement while I was pointing at the diagram, "These are the murals that are to be painted on the three panel walls behind the stage!" I continued to tell him, "But HOW will I ever be able to do that? It would cost a fortune to have them painted like that!"

"The man walked over the walls and ran his hand over the wall affectionately touching the pale bare paint. He looked at me. "I'll paint them for you." He said quietly.

"What?" I was speechless.

"I'll paint them for you. I can do this. It's been many years, but I can do it." He said again while examining the walls more carefully.

"It'll cost you about $1,500.00, for my time and the paint." He said finally looking up at me.

"When?" The word fell out of my mouth.

"I can do it this weekend. I must have three days, undisturbed."

"I'll make sure of that. Thank you! How can I thank you?"

"Just let me do it. I want to give something back." He stood and walked out of the door leaving me standing there too stunned to move.

So the angels had sent the man to do the murals. I just had to stay out of the way!

That weekend we had three murals painted. They were beautiful!

A trip out to the seacoast to relax, brought me face to face with the fountain. I saw her as I drove by. It was as if she called out to me. I stopped the car and spoke to the owner. It was a Goddess foun-

Susan Isabelle

tain about six feet high. It was Dianna, beauty, and she was pouring water from her vase. It reminded me of Kuan Yin, her vase, and the nectar of mercy and compassion she pours out over the earth. She would arrive at the center the following week.

All the pieces of the room were manifesting! The angels brought everything right to us! The only thing I felt I needed was the water from Lourdes. The healing waters that flowed from a little stream in France where Mother Mary appeared ought to be in the fountain! People from all over the world went to Loudes for the healing the waters would bring to them.

"Richard, wouldn't it be wonderful if our new Center had the waters flowing in the fountain? Then the people wouldn't have to go so far." He was the only person I told. I went on line, the internet to see if that could be obtained, but without success. I would have to wait.

We were almost ready to open the center. Over the past three weeks a miracle had occurred. People were volunteering to do everything. The store was ready to be moved in. We should be ready to open in May, within a month of our having signed the lease!

One Friday afternoon I received a phone call.

"Susan,....Isabelle?"

"Yes. May I help you?"

"I sure hope so! This is the Raven Center further north from you. We have a problem and we were hoping maybe you can help us out.'

"What's wrong?" I asked.

"We have a woman coming from Arizona to channel Mother Mary. The booking has exceeded our room capacity by a mistake.

We need a larger space for her. We'd heard you have an auditorium that would accommodate our group, we don't want to turn anyone away."

"Well, yes," I said, "But- we've not really opened yet; but if it will help you…yes…come! I'll make it work!"

"Oh, thank you! Can we come tonight?" He hesitated, waiting for my answer. I took a quick look at the mess of half opened boxes all around me, took a quick in-breath and almost said, "That's impossible!"

Instead I bit my tongue, then spoke, "I suppose so…yes, come anyway. I'll find some more chairs." I looked around the room. Tonight. Wow! Spirit was moving fast!

"A Mother Mary Channel!" I thought out loud. "That'll be a blessing for us all!"

So at 8 PM that night, I opened the door for a group of people I had never seen before. They filed into the beautiful center and some began to cry at the sight of it. "This is the most beautiful place I have ever seen!"

"Yes, the angels have designed it and you are the first to enjoy the new space. I am honored that it would be Mother Mary, Goddess energy, to fill it for the first time!"

I was introduced to the channel for Mother Mary. She was a beautiful, dark-haired woman filled with peace and grace who wore blue flowing silk wraps over her shoulders and slim body.

"Here is where you may sit if this is comfortable for you." I said to her as I directed her to sit in front of the Goddess fountain and the mural of the Goddess kissing the earth.

"Yes, this will be fine! It is so beautiful here! Susan, you have made this for the Goddess, for Mother Mary." She said looking up at me.

"That is true. The Shekhina over the earth represents the Divine Feminine Spirit and all the qualities, aspects of the Goddess. This place has been built according to the command of the Father to build Her Temple! I am pleased to have you here and it is no mistake that you have been directed here tonight."

After a few welcoming comments to the gathered group about our new center, I sat down across from the channel and turned the evening over to the channel. She began to tell her story about her experiences and then opened to channel Mother Mary.

I watched, along with the rest of the group, the beautiful over-lighting energy of Mother Mary wrap itself around the little woman as she sat peacefully on the chair. A few deep breaths were taken in deeply by her, and then she looked up- right at me. Mother Mary spoke through the woman directly to me,

"My Daughter, I have heard your request for the waters of Lourdes to flow in your fountain here. I have come tonight to personally deliver it to you."

I gasp! Mother Mary had heard my prayer for the sacred waters! My hands went to my heart and my eyes filled with tears.

Then the miracle happened. The channel, Mother Mary, reached down into her bag and took out a quart-sized jug. On the bottle was the picture of Mother Mary at Lourdes. It was from Lourdes!

She then stood up and walked directly toward me, looked deeply into my eyes and placed the bottle in my hands saying,

> *"You are to pour the waters into the fountain, 1/3 to go in. Refill the bottle with spring water: Do this always. You will never run out of the waters. It is for the children."*

With tears streaming down my face, I somehow managed to say, *"Thank you, Mother, for hearing my prayer and coming to bring this precious gift to us."*

The others in the room were silent, stunned at the action taking place in front of them. Some began to softly cry and wipe away tears, even as I did. Then, she made her way back to the chair, sat down and began to speak of her never ending love for all the children. I was so overwhelmed, I do not remember all that was said, but I will always remember the LOVE that night!

Everything that happened was because it was meant to, and in just the way that it did. I'm so glad I bit my tongue. How easy it would have been to say 'No, not tonight-it's too short of a notice.' What a blessing I would have missed! Acts of compassion and service are always rewarded in one way or another. It is a Universal Law.

No one cared that night that there were boxes of stuff tossed all over the place, or that we weren't ready for company yet. We may not have been ready, but God was. Humanity will never be "ready-enough."

How often we hesitate to open to others because the house isn't clean, the dishes aren't done, we're too busy, it's not on the schedule, and on and on…. The message here was simply, "Open your heart- open to me-your soul family-I have a blessing for you!" Isn't it always that way? We just forget it, sometimes.

As the workmen completed the interior rooms, they tried to take pictures of their progress. They encountered a problem.

"Take a look at this," one of the men said as he shoved his camera screen in front of Cynthia and me. "No matter what I do, every time I take a picture in here, there are these big globe- things hanging all around." We looked at the hundreds of light globes of multi-colored lights in his picture and laughed.

"That's just the Angels hanging out watching you! They've been sent here to make sure everything is perfect!"

We had rainbows that hung in the sky all day long as we finally moved into the new space all the furnishings from the old store. Blessings were everywhere! We tried to have three hundred booklets printed for our grand opening day. The booklets were to tell the story of the miracles happening at the Center. Not three hundred, but three thousand arrived!

"Guess Spirit wants everyone to know about this place!" Someone quipped as we brought in the boxes.

"No charge, our mistake!" was the word from the printer. "You can have them!"

Our New Center

And then, in May 2002, we were in our new Center. Cynthia had her new store and aura camera and had filled the shelves with crystals, jewelry, books and other products. The beautiful Shambhala Center classrooms and auditorium would allow us to teach and to bring to the people the experience of the Divine, the Spirit.

Richard and I decided we would share a therapy room. We filled it with sacred items of healing and of the Divine. He had spent twenty years with the Benedictine Monks in meditation and prayer practice. Soon, his energy filled the room and people were coming to see him on a regular basis.

How amazing it had been to see Spirit work and manifest such incredible miracles, one after another!

If I thought I was busy before, I had no idea what was coming. Soon, I'd walk into the Center, no matter what time of day, and be surrounded by people. It became a regular practice for me to say, "If you've come for the Energy, please come into the sanctuary!"

Fifteen people at a time would line up in front of the Altar and Spirit would use me to bring the Blessing to the people through healing touch and anointing. Some were healed instantly, others were filled with Spirit, some then lay on the floor and simply worshipped the beauty of God.

Early one morning, I made my way over to the auditorium and sat down. Shekhina dwelt here. You could feel it when you entered the room. Peace, beautiful peace and love, swept over me,. An altar had been placed on the stage for this reason with the Goddess on it.

Behind the altar was a full wall mural painting of the beautiful earth mother, Gaia, with the Dove Of Peace, Shekhina over it. The Dove's wings were outstretched, covering the earth, just like Mother had covered the earth during the fall of the Towers.

Father had seen Her and had shown love for His Bride. Earth was saved, moved two days forward in time and the children's survival was assured. So many miracles in our old Center had happened across the way. Now, it was continuing here. I lay face down on the floor in front of the altar and praised and worshipped God-Goddess! The blessings continued.

I had so much to be thankful for!

Chapter XVI

Time For Us

Richard soon saw the numbers grow at the Center and my physical strength begin to weaken.

"Susan, let's go for a walk."

"Richard, I don't have time…."

"Susan, get your sweater!" He demanded.

I took my sweater and got into the car with him. He drove me over to the cemetery. I was miffed for the first few minutes, but when we arrived, I felt better and we got out to walk.

"Have you ever gone fishing for frog?" He asked.

"Fishing for frogs? You've got to be kidding!" I laughed.

"No, really…"

"How? How do you fish for frogs?" I asked this Master of the Universe.

"I'll show you!"

I watched as he picked a long piece of straw grass. He searched all over to find something else in the grass.

"What are you looking for?" I asked.

"You'll see." Soon he arose from the ground holding the stem of the biggest, brightest yellow dandelion he could find. "Now watch what I do." He said.

Carefully taking the end of the straw grass he tied it around the stem of the dandelion. It hung from his grass 'rod' bouncing in the breeze. He then went over to the high grasses at the edge of the pond, hiding in them.

"Come here!"

I crept over closer to him and lay in the grass beside him. I tried to see what he was doing. He was dangling the dandelion over the water.

Just then a great big, horrible- looking bullfrog leapt out of the water! As it flew through the air, its long, black slimy fingers grabbed the dandelion! I screamed! That frog was huge! It swam to a lily pad still holding the dandelion in its grasp, climbed up and stared at us. And then I began to laugh!

He did it again and again. The bullfrogs loved dandelion and him. Soon, several were sitting on the wide lily pads croaking at us. I sat in the grass delighted for the first time in years! I laughed with the joy of a child!

"Susan, you must take care of yourself…you are working too hard. We are going to do this every day, all summer. Father has said it!"

"OK," I agreed. He was right.

So by the end of the summer, we had trained 19 frogs to sit in line on the lily pads……..I never laughed so much in my life…… that is until…..

"Richard, you promised me you'd tell me about your nine wives, remember?"

"Yeah."

"Well? Tell me!"

"OK. Since you won't stop asking, I give in." He sighed.

"Really, Richard, after all we've been through, it can't be that difficult…"

"There are many dimensions," he looked at me strangely, "as you've already experienced. Usually, we don't or can't, go as far as you and I did together."

"Yes, continue." I nodded.

He straightened himself and put on his professional look. " In my work and my training, I learned to travel between dimensions and to visit there. We have parallel lives on each one, in some sort or another. In my case, I have memory and can go into the dimensions to see my wives." He paused. "I have nine altogether."

"WOW!" Doesn't that get confusing?"

"You've got that! I go to them when I am asleep. Can't help it anymore…. because I've done so much of it, I go automatically. As soon as I close my eyes, I am somewhere else, on one of the dimensions. That's why I wake up so tired-I never get any rest!"

"How do you keep it all straight? I mean, do you say the wrong things to each one or forget things?"

"Not really. When I go, I am that person, so that part's OK. It's when I wake up, I have a hard time readjusting to this dimension, you know, the memory stuff."

"So why was it so awful getting married to me?"

"SUSANNNE...."

"No, really, I want to know.."

"It affected every dimension, Susan. Every dimension! Everything changed!"

"What changed?" I pressed.

"Enough! We'd better get back."

He wasn't going to tell me. I fumed. Something was up, I could tell. I felt like a woman scorned, but I couldn't understand why. After all we'd been through together....What was he not telling me?

That was the night I decided to be a secret detective. A super, inter-dimensional spy was about to be born from the mind of a crazed woman! If he could go to other dimensions when he fell asleep to go visit nine other women that were obviously better than I, ...well,..... so could I!

But how? I sat for a while thinking about this. Actually, I was obsessed.

It was my right, wasn't it?

No, it had to be some kind of an invasion of his privacy.....but I am his wife!

I have a right! I have to know what's going on.... and what he's not telling me......and wasn't he so rude...?

"ENOUGH!" He'd snapped at me!

And he actually vomited when he found out we were married by God-it upset him so much!

WHAT HAPPENED?

That's when I decided I had to know and that, for once, I'd be really naughty....I was going to follow him...into the other dimensions....that was the only way.

I lit my candle and set myself on my floor cushion. I went into a focused mediation, and waited. I didn't know exactly what for, but I waited several hours. I focused entirely on his essence and my threads of connection to him and held that strong. When his conscious left the world, I would be following.

Finally, it happened.

"Where am I?" I asked as I looked around, startled by how quickly it had happened. "What is this place? What?"

I found myself standing behind a rack of clothing hung on a circular frame. All around me were racks of clothing the biggest mall I'd ever seen! The glass ceiling above me was at least a hundred feet high with balconies of shops looming overhead with banners announcing the stores, waving everywhere.

I was somewhere in a mall with even more stores beneath me. I crept out from behind the rack. He was somewhere in this mall. But why did he come to a mall, of all places! I thought he was going to see some sexy, gorgeous, woman! Obviously, he wasn't making mad, passionate love to her in a mall!

Where was he? I made my way over to the balcony and looked down. He must be here somewhere.

"There! There he is!" I silently exclaimed. "Who is that with him?" I wondered aloud.

A little girl with dark curly hair, clung to his hand. She was sooo cute! "That's his daughter! Richard has a little girl here! She looks just like him!" I whispered to myself.

Then, a tall, slender woman with long blond hair swishing past her waist as she walked, came up to him and was now speaking to him. I watched the interchange between them as his kiss brushed her lips affectionately. I was jealous. Horribly, jealous! Emotion burst out from me. "Shame on you, Susan!" I thought to myself. I couldn't move; I had to watch. I saw Richard put his daughter's little hand into her mother's, and he walked briskly away. He soon disappeared from sight.

I continued to watch his wife and his precious little daughter. The little girl was beautiful, but I just couldn't see the face of the mother as her back had been toward me all this time. I waited, hoping he'd come back. And then, the mother, his wife turned….I could see her face….

"SUSAN! What are YOU DOING HERE?"

Richard was behind me! I'd been caught! I turned to see him standing there looking at me, astonished.

"YOU HAVE TO LEAVE NOW! YOU CAN"T BE HERE!"

"But?? BUT SHE….I said pointing down at his wife…..

"I'll explain later…you have to leave now, before anyone sees you!"

"OK." And I left.

I came out of the trance and out of that dimension, shouting,

"Oh, My GOD! NO WONDER HE WOULDN"T TELL ME!"

The woman,tHE WOMAN, when she turned around…. there was no mistake….

That was my face…

The woman was me.

And then I knew

The secret…

NO WONDER HE WOULDN"T TELL ME!"

I realized in that one moment, the secret.

The secret that was so upsetting that he was afraid to even touch me!

When Richard and I were married, on every dimension but the one we were on, we were physically married, we lived together…. and we had a family.

He was married to nine of ME…..

In every shape, in every flaw, in every bad mood, in every good way…

But, imagine… NINE of ME…..

And then,

I laughed, and I laughed and I laughed….until my sides hurt….

Can you imagine that?

Don't worry; later, he'd get his revenge….

"Richard, why didn't you tell me?"

"Look, Susan, it's bad enough being married to nine of you. I can't be married here! I have my rights you know!"

"Rights? What does this have to do with rights?"

"I want some freedom. The only place that remains free for me is here-where it all started! Here is the only place that has not been determined. All the other dimensions were automatically 'corrected' when we were married. Because you and I are the ones who did this, we have more freedom, more control over what happens to us."

I thought about that for a few moments. I could honestly see his dilemma.

"And you don't want that here. OK. Understood. But let's be honest about things-everything- with each other. I have a feeling that we're going to be together one way or another for a very long time, Richard....Please, you can't keep secrets from me, I don't handle that sort of thing very well, as you know."

"Oh, I'd say about eternity…You know, when we leave this life, we'll be together taking care of that universe we created, Susan, I think we'll have enough time together, don't you?"

He said shyly smiling up at me. "Please, I'd like a little time here to be free and, you know…"

"Play the field? At least that's being honest with me. I just can't stay mad at you, Richard." I said smiling back at him.

"Then, maybe I can tell you something…"

"What?"

"Susan, I am not going to be always staying on this dimension. I've been given the directive to go and live with my child and wife- you-on the other dimension."

I gasped!

He added quickly, "Don't worry, I'm not going to leave you now, your work is too important and you need me. I've also been told that there are some more things we have to do together."

"MORE?" I exclaimed shaking my head. I thought we'd done everything.

"Yes more.; But know this; one day I will have to go. I don't really belong here. There is going to be another warrior, a protector, for you. I've seen it. You're going to choose someone else to be with you."

I felt faint, my head swirled. "I don't want anyone else, Richard! I can't even imagine anyone in my life!"

Will had followed through with his threat. The divorce had been filed and I had recently been forced to move into a small apartment. It had been a very difficult time for me. The house had been in his name and all our assets.

I'd been badly burned in the divorce, and as his income was a 'previous to the marriage pension', I was not able to even get any financial assistance from him. Hurt, I truly couldn't think about anyone. Richard was my closest friend and that was all I needed.

"The time is coming when you will make a choice. There are warriors from all over the universe just lining up in hopes you'll choose one of them…" he said shaking his head.

I stood shaking my head, 'no!"

" You need a protector and companion while I am away. You'll need to choose someone. This is so weird!" He looked distressed, even as he spoke the words.

"Well, they'll have to wait! Maybe forever!" I was getting upset. Tears were welling up.

"Let's go catch some frogs, Susan…"

Prime Real Estate?

That night, I had a very strange dream. I was standing on a platform in the middle of a big room. Men were standing all around me, looking me over. They began bidding on me as if I was a slave girl on an auction block. They bid galaxies and worlds, however, instead of money.

When one would win and claim me, he'd approach me and speak to me. Here's where it got really strange. Rather than taking me away, I'd look *him* over and then say, "NO!"

Then the process would start all over again…..and again….and again….

The bidding got higher and higher and other, more affluent men entered the room. I still said, "NO!"

When I awoke in the morning, I was mad! How dare they do this to me! I put it out of my mind as I prepared for my class.

"Dang Girl, you are brutal! You are slaying them all over the universe!" Richard said as he entered the classroom. I glared at him.

"You know? You know about the auction?"

"Yeah, I've been watching. You're really pulling in the big guys now!"

"This is humiliating!"

"You are Prime Real Estate! No one's ever seen anything like it. Why do you keep saying no? You're passing up some real opportunities and quite a dowry!"

I couldn't believe what I was hearing! My rage overcame me! How could he be so cold? So nonchalant? And Prime Real Estate? I backed away from him.

"Have you ever heard about love?" I raged.

"What's love got to do with it?" He quipped the old song, smugly.

"Not funny!" I ran from the room.

We had a group from Massachusetts coming in for instruction on bio-location today. Soon the class was in full swing. We had a good group of about twenty people and they were anxious to learn the techniques for time and space travel in bio-location.

As we began to make progress in the class and they began to finally get the technique down, I asked, "Where would you like to go next?"

Richard's voice shot out from the back of the room.

"I'd like to go to Hawaii!"

"Hawaii, Richard?"

"Yeah, I want to go to Hawaii!"

"I do too!" Someone shouted. " Me too!" I looked over at Richard. He was smiling smugly. He'd won. Everyone really liked the idea, so we began the bio-location.

"OK, we will go for a period of three minutes and you will automatically return to your body; set the intent; prepare; move the energy and "GO!!"

I found myself standing next to Richard at the front of a cave at a beach in Hawaii.

"This is where I used to come when I was a kid living here. I wanted you to see it, Susan. Look down here at these shells."

He bent down and picked up a shell. He turned toward me and placed the shell in my hand, but he did not let go. Holding my hand, he said, "Susan."

As I looked up at him, he drew me close and with a gentle pull into him, and he kissed me. Warm and tender his lips, his mouth searched mine with passionate love.

And then I was back. Gasping: I was blushing in front of twenty students. I swam in the passionate embrace still upon me. In the back of the room, he was laughing this time. The students looked from one to another and back and forth from him to me. They began to giggle. It wasn't hard to figure out.

I stood up. "It's time for a break!"

Revenge is sweet.

The dream continued. I kept saying, "No!" to all the suitors that were bidding for my hand. One day, I knew, the dream would end. I would have to choose someone to replace Richard on this realm. But for now, I would refuse.

All during the summer, Richard and I continued to watch in amazement, his fountain-creation out in space. I was fascinated, always, watching Our Daughter, Neccaaba the Cosmic Eve, as she continued her work now! Richard assured me she was safely tucked away in the outer dimensions and very well protected. God was overseeing this project, we both realized that.

We didn't do any more of the physical travel outside of the universe or into our galaxies beyond this universe as all of that was now being overseen by the Council until the day we could return there ourselves. We avoided the meditative state together, and that felt right. That part of our work was done.

The Center continued to grow and flourish as we worked the energies there. Now instead of thirty people on Sunday nights, our numbers were growing. Music and performers were added to our Sunday evening services. A healing circle and Goddess Dances complete with veils and music, honored the Shekhina, our Mother.

Living alone did something to me. It brought me closer to God. My private times in worship and in connection became a refuge for me. There I could meet God and refill my soul. Truly a Daughter of the Light, to be in that Holy presence, strengthened me.

Relationships and partnerships rarely allowed for that very private time with God. The household mate sometimes simply overtakes every moment with demands, rightfully and sometimes in jealousy. I'd already experienced that.

Now, when I spoke at Sunday evening service, I could feel the Light within me expanding and the Word begin to flow from me directly from Source because my connection was becoming very pure.

It became harder and harder to get up to go to work in my social work job. The office manager had been replaced with a woman, who at first seemed likeable. I soon found that she too had an agenda not unlike her predecessor.

I was miserable working there with so little money to help desperate families. My heart cried for their situations. There appeared to be no hope in sight. The world was making a decision once again and it was to rob the most vulnerable, the children.

With all that I had gone through in the past months with my previous supervisor's harassment, pending divorce, my move and the work at both the Center and the community, I was too depleted to fight this battle. Others would have to take up the cause. I'd just make sure everyone knew the truth.

A Change Of Pace

I sensed that change was coming, but not how much change! One night, I received a message; "It is time."

Upon waking, I knew and would follow that knowing. I decided it was time to go to see the Mystic in Canada. I called him.

"Yes, Yes! Susan, you must come!"

So it was arranged that I go at the beginning of September. Two precious women went with me and would stay with me the entire time. As soon as we walked into the three hundred acre compound on a beautiful lake in Canada, I was met by the Indian Mystic!

"Hurry! Hurry, you are late!"

"Late? For what?"

"It is the time, the most auspicious time! You must be prepared! Here! She will take you now!"

I was handed over to a woman who briskly walked me to another part of the compound. She directed me into a shower and handed me a towel and a robe. She could speak hardly any English but was of a kind soul. A bit confused, I showered and wondered what was happening to my two companions.

She set me on a massage table and began what would be a four-hour long massage and anointing with various oils and herbs. Every inch of me was massaged, hot-oiled and massaged again. When she had completed her work on me, I was covered with a yellow-colored sticky oil and wrapped in towels and robes.

"You must stay in this until morning…" she managed to say. "Then you may wash."

She escorted me to my friends who were waiting for me in our cottage. When I walked through the door they burst out laughing! I was completely yellow and dripping wet! My attendant spoke quickly so they could also hear.

"Do not worry about the sheets. We will change them in the morning for you. Now you sleep!" She put me to bed.

I slept straight through without a dream, a thought or anything else for that matter. When I awoke, the sheets were bright yellow, as well as me. I washed it all off, but could not wash away the questions forming in my mind. They would soon be answered by the Mystic.

I was running late again and would have just enough time to get to my appointment this morning with him.

"Good morning Susan!" He cheerfully greeted me. "I trust you slept well?"

"Oh, yes, I did. What was that yesterday? The massage, I mean."

"That was to prepare you, My Dear. It is the massage and preparation for the Bride. You must be prepared for your service to God. I trust that things are going well for you?"

"Oh, a whole lot has happened since I saw you last. The Goddess Center has grown incredibly and we have expanded."

"Good, good!" He exclaimed genuinely delighted.

"And my husband, the critical one, you called him-has filed for divorce and I am no longer with him."

"Well, My Dear, you know that that had to be. I am sorry for any discomfort for you, however."

Just then, the attendant knocked on the door. He handed the copies of my palm prints that were taken a few minutes before. The Mystic took the papers and began to study them.

"Do you mind if again my associates come in?" He asked looking up from the papers.

"No, it is alright."

He got up from the table and disappeared down the hall returning with three others. They all sat together as the Mystic began to speak as he pointed to the palm prints.

"See, here. She has divorced her husband and now has a star on her destiny line….look, Susan. You divorced and you got a star!" He smiled broadly. "Now, we must get to work. You have come with a very great destiny and I am to help you. The massage was to prepare you for your coming to God to do your work. There will be many changes now. Pray, meditate and we will work with you while you are here. Then you will be ready!"

"I know that a change is coming, but I don't know what it is. I was hoping you could help me to understand what that is."

"When you came here, it was to do something for mankind, something that would change the world. Do I know what that is?

No. I wish I could tell you, but God will reveal it to you in time. I can help you with the preparation and to steady yourself and provide some guidance."

"That would be wonderful!"

"Yes, I see that in your chart that there are those who oppose you and the work you are to do. It will be very difficult. Some of this is karma, but you must overcome their attempts. The date of this Center is not in the time of establishment."

"What do you mean?"

"You have begun a work, but the time of that work is not for many years yet. Your soul tells you to do this, yes?" I nodded. "But the time is not yet. You are in Rahu, not a good time. But it will be as a learning time for you. Good practice."

"That is difficult for me to understand. Everything is going so wonderfully right now with the Center…."

"Well, according to your chart, the time is not yet. There will be something much more important for you to do in the near future-perhaps within the year. The star is here and you will do this. Prepare yourself with much prayer and avoid all men, other than the one who has been sent to you. The one we spoke of last time. Is he still with you?"

"Yes."

"This is good. He will help you now."

"He tells me he is not always going to be with me. He says that there is another coming for me. Do you see that?"

"Unfortunately for you and your friend, yes. But it is good in the end. There will be others, and your protector. But not until you are close to sixty years of age will your life mate appear. It shall be after much of your work is completed. But, of course, your work just begins at age fifty eight or so."

" 58! That seems so far away!"

"No, it shall begin to birth this very year!"

" You mean, its just starting?"

"Yes. You may come and live here if you wish. Your work is global, as is mine. I will give you some land."

After leaving the session, I felt as though I'd been given a whole new way of looking at my situation. If the Center was not to be my life mission, what was? I'd already done a lot. I figured I'd already completed my work! According to him, I wasn't going to even be doing what I had come to earth to do for six more years!

I was being told I was just starting! And, something very important was about to begin to manifest. I hadn't heard from Melchizedek and Adama or the Council for quite some time now. Ever since the walk-in experience, they had been pretty quiet. I truly thought I was done!

Chapter XVII

A Visit From Adama

October 4th, 2002

Within a few days it happened.

"Susan, awake and write!" It was the voice of Adama. " Latitude--#---Longitude---#--Go there soon! This is the place of the Earth Alignment. It must be activated and brought into balance. He will help you. You will need the skull."

In my sleep, I wrote down the information. In the morning, I retrieved the information. I was on assignment again with Adama again. He'd said there would be thirty-six sites I'd have to go to. This was the next place. I read the little scrap of paper with the numbers written on it. So, it wasn't a dream. I wonder where this is? Getting on my GPS Will had installed into my computer, I typed in the numbers.

"Oh, my God! That's at the tip of Florida. And he's supposed to go there with me? I don't think so, Adama…" I spoke to the screen before me.

I'd be meeting him at the Center in a few hours. I'd ask him then.

"Richard, would you like to go on a little trip? I need someone to help me do something."

"Sure, when do you want to go?" He was curious.

"As soon as possible. I think that we'll be gone for about ten days or so...."

"What? Ten days? Just where are *you* going, Susan?"

"We need to go to Florida. I was given this latitude and longitude coordinate by Adama. He says we must go there to bring Earth balance, to bring the skull, and that you'd help me. Or at least I think it was you. He wasn't specific, just 'he'."

"Ten days? I don't know about that..."

"Well, think about it Richard. I kind-of got the feeling it was important and that we'd, or at least I, would have to do this quickly. I've got someone coming in now, so I have to go."

The next day Richard approached me. "Well, I quit my job last night. I couldn't stand being on my feet for so long anyway."

I looked down at Richard's feet. They were often swollen and he was in silent pain. Many times now I had tended his feet. We kept a secret no one else but he and I knew. Richard had the Stigmata, the holes of the spikes of Christ's crucifixion on both feet.

"When do you want to go?"

"You're kidding! You quit your job?" I was surprised.

"Yeah, I couldn't take it anymore and this is a good excuse to do something else. You'll need someone to drive you. Where are we going anyway?"

"I looked this up and there's a castle place in Florida. That's the most interesting place within the area that was given. I think that's where we're supposed to go. There's something very odd about it and it is pulling me there, I can feel it."

"So, when are we going?"

"Can we leave tomorrow?"

"Tomorrow? Susan, you're hardly giving me time to pack!"

"OK. The day after tomorrow we'll go. I have vacation time that's built up and I'll call to let the Agency know I'll be out for a week. That'll make them happy…"

"Ellen, we'll have to make some schedule changes!" I called out to my friend and assistant at the Center. "I'm going on a trip!"

By October 10th we were in Southern Florida. It was during that trip that I really began to know Richard. I'd never met anyone that ate only rice, coca- a- cola, nuts and French fries before.

There was also a universal joke that plagued him. Whenever he asked for a coke, the waitress would tell him, "We only have Pepsi, will that be OK?" If he asked for Pepsi, he'd get a coke. It never failed and was a source of frustration for him and laughter for me the entire time.

He slept on the floor beside the bed. It didn't matter if we had two rooms or a single, he didn't sleep in a bed, so we shared the room. He was intensely personal about his privacy, and kept his distance no matter what. He spent time with his nine wives during the night, not me.

On the morning of the tenth, I awoke early and hung the pouch the skull was in around my neck. I peeked into the pouch. El Aleator was glowing, activating inside. It pulsed upon my chest. I would have to keep it near me this day.

Driving around the area, we could not find the castle anywhere. We stopped the car on the side of the road to look at the map. Suddenly, I could hear someone speaking to my mind.

"Richard! Be still! I hear someone!"

"Who? Where?"

"I don't know! Shhh…" I put my head back on the seat.

A male's voice began to speak more clearly,

" Behind the Lucent- shoulder, I am 'ed. I help to know."

I could see an image in my mind of a great light behind a man's back with great rays of light shining over him.

"Richard! Write!"

I heard him scuffle getting paper and pen. I repeated what had been said to me.

" Behind the Lucent- shoulder, I am 'ed. I help to know."

Then I heard,

"Find the Lucent ; help you."

I repeated it aloud so Richard could write it down. There was more;

"The two are sleeping, beside one another to awake/awaken the earth."

Then there was a pause for a few moments.

"Two rise to form one: The Voice of Song to awaken, the male, the female, sing the earth from the waters flow. My Beloved awaits."

And then it was over.

"That's it, Richard, the voice is gone."

He handed me the papers. I looked down at what had been written on them. " I can't even imagine what this means." We looked at the map and decided to turn the car around. "There it is Richard! We passed it!"

We saw the sign for the entrance and drove into a parking spot. We entered the busy little gift shop to pay for our tickets. We were handed a small map with some literature about the amazing construction of the castle.

Apparently back in the 1930's a man had somehow carved out great chucks of coral to form the amazing structure. Without using any modern tools he managed to do this and set up blocks of coral, one upon another, they each weighed tons. It was said that no one had ever seen how he did this and the blocks would seem to be placed overnight. It was a mystery.

We followed the tourists out into the grounds. We walked around the park looking at all the structures that had been built by this man called Edward. Soon, we were left alone in the park. The tourists had gone. We sat on one of the coral benches.

"Richard, I can feel it. This is the place; the energy is flowing here. We're supposed to do something here, but I don't know where exactly."

"Me too. I can't pin point it either. Maybe we should go back inside and ask some questions."

We returned to the gift shop. A small man approached us.

"I've been watching you. I think I may be able to help you, my name is Lou."

"Lou-Lucent?" We both exclaimed together! The man nodded.

"That's the name the Voice gave to us! You are the one to help us!" I excitedly told Lou. He looked at me, curious.

"Richard, please go and get the papers of the channel back in the car. I'll explain to Lou."

"Let's go out here to talk. Now, what is all this about?" Lou asked me.

"Well, I was given some coordinates in a vision at my home a few days ago. I was told to come here. We've come all the way from New Hampshire. In the vision, I was told I must come here to balance the earth energy. Somewhere in there is the place," I said waving toward the park, " but we don't know where." Lou just stared at me.

"I know this may sound crazy to you, but just a few minutes ago, I heard a voice in the car on the way here that told me to find the Lou. See here. It's on this paper, we wrote it down. Can you help us?"

Richard handed the paper to Lou. He held the paper in his hands and re read it several times. His eyes began to well up with watery tears.

"Fifteen years! Fifteen years I have waited for you." He looked at both of us with misty far away eyes. "I've been waiting for you. Many psychics have come here, but none with this." He shook the paper. "Come, I will show you."

We followed him as he walked toward a tower like building made of the coral. We entered. "Stand here.' He told Richard, then turning toward me he said, "And you stand here."

Instantly we felt it! Hardly able to stand up, we felt the currents of earth energy flowing beneath us. The magnetic force of the earth grids were causing us to sway back and forth.

"It's masculine and feminine, negative and positive forces that flow through here. Edward built his castle on one of the most powerful magnetic grids of the earth! He said he built it for his Beloved and waited for her to come. I think that's why you are here, Susan. Come, follow me."

As we began to follow Lou across the park, he told us his story.

" I came here over fifteen years ago and just stopped in for a map. I never left. I connected with the energy of Edward right away and have felt him. I have always known he was speaking to me over my shoulder. I feel him. That is why I know so much about this place and why he built it."

"Why? Why did he do this?" Richard asked.

"He waited for the one to come, his beloved, all of his life but she never came. I believe he built it to balance the earth with her here. But, this wasn't the first place."

" What do you mean?"

"Originally, he built it in a different location several miles from here. Then, one day, he moved the entire structure here! It was impossible to do but he did it! He had to move it to be on the exact grid line you just experienced. He had to have used levitation to move it here."

"I can feel it beneath me feet, we're still walking the line!" I exclaimed. My feet tickled with the energy.

"Yes, I am taking you to the epicenter of the line where the two forces meet in a strange way." We quickened our pace. "I think that is what he meant when he told you they were sleeping side by side, waiting to be made one and awakened."

"What do you mean?" Richard asked.

"Well, if you consider that the lines may be male and female energies, I think that they are, they would be "sleeping side by side" until activated. Here's another reason I think they are male and female."

He pointed to two graves, or what appeared to be graves. "There, they are sleeping side by side. He made two graves to symbolize this, one for a male and one for a female body."

We looked down at the two graves. The symbolism was Egyptian with the ankh to symbolize eternal life. He began walking again. "Here, just ahead is what I believe you are looking for."

Ahead of us was a huge structure of two horns rising up into the blue sky. "Each one of these horns weighs about thirty tons. It was an impossible feat for him to have raised these without breaking the stone!"

Between the two mammoth horns was a raised, waist high round pool of water. I went over to look inside the pool.

"Richard, come look at this!" Inside the pool was a perfect Star of David, the symbol of the perfect balance of male energy and the feminine.

"It's the symbol! We've found it!"

As the two men came over to the pool, Ray asked me, "What are you looking at and do you mean?"

"Well, the Star has two pyramids, one over lapping the other. See? One is upward pointing, that's the masculine, and the other pyramid is female, the receptive force, and it points downward like a womb."

"Well, I'll be! I didn't know that, but I'll show you another reason why I think you need to be at this spot. Stand right here, Richard. Susan, you stand here."

As we stood on the spots Lou showed us, we could feel the pull toward one another; we almost fell into one another.

"Yup! That's what happens when we stand here!" Lou glowed.

"Susan, if this is what I think it is, this is where the lines meet and merge. Ed said they were sleeping side by side and now we are to awaken the lines." Richard looked at me.

"Are you ready?"

"I am if you are! Let's find the best position for me and for you."

We both began to back up and move in the energy lines. I found that if I stood several feet back between the two horns, the flow seemed stronger. Richard moved about until he stood about three feet from and in front of the pool of water. We nodded at one another across the pool of water.

"Lucent, I think we've found where we need to stand. You can watch us if you want to."

"May I take some pictures?" He asked.

"Sure, and here's my camera too. I think I'd like some too." I said as I handed him my camera.

As Richard and I allowed our bodies to become connected to the earth's grid flow, we became a conduit for that energy in a physical form. We seemed to know what to do although we'd never done this before.

Slowly, our arms raised themselves in unison to the Divine. As our hands were raised to Heaven a great Light descended all around us. It lit up the entire area. I could hear Lou cry out in fear and awe.

"I am in the Presence of God!" He fell to the ground and wept.

My body could not move and neither of us spoke as we provided the complete merging of the energies. The ground began to vibrate beneath us. The two became one. Somehow, the two great Earth meridians were joining beneath us. We swayed in the energies. As the vibration ceased, we slowly brought down our arms and stood staring across from one another.

Silently we walked to either side of the great horns and sat on the stones stairs beside the pool and beneath the great horns. The Star of David was vibrating so strongly in the center of the pool that it created waves in the pool. We sat without speaking until the pool calmed and we regained our physical forms. I prayed for the earth and all the people.

"It is done." Richard announced as he stood up. I did too and went over to Lou.

"Thank you, Lucent for helping us. We must leave now."

He handed me the camera without saying a word and stood staring at us as we left the castle. Sometimes, there are no words. He had seen his life's mission completed at long last. Fifteen years is a long time to wait. Edward waited all his life and never lived to see this day. But, I know he saw it finally happen!

Just One More Thing....

We returned to our hotel room and fell into a deep sleep. When we awoke, it was morning. What we had come to do had been accomplished. I pondered these things while Richard was asleep on the floor.

The symbol of the two horns around the pool of water was clearly the symbol of the Hathor, the Earth Keepers. This had been a Hathor Temple to guard the secret of the Earth. It had all happened so fast! Now what? Somehow, it felt as though we still had something to do. I wasn't ready to go back to NH.

"Richard, do you want to go back now?" I asked him when he awoke.

"No, actually, we're so close to Key West. I think I'd like to go there. I've never seen it."

"Neither have I. We've got time so, let's keep going!"

As we made our way down into the Keys, we discussed the events of yesterday. There were so many things that remained unanswered in our minds, but we knew the mission had been accomplished, so we decided to be content with that.

We found a small hotel in town late in the afternoon. I went for a swim in the pool in the back of the small hotel while Richard rested from the long drive.

About 8 PM we decided we'd go out for a walk and then to dine downtown. The streets were just starting to show the evidence of a lively night in Key West as we sat down for what would be a long time at dinner. The pace there was certainly not the rushed atmosphere of the North East. Finishing dinner around 11 PM we started the walk back to our hotel.

Walking side by side we happily strolled down the sidewalk. We could see a group of men standing on the sidewalk, just ahead of us. Still enjoying the warm night and the glow of a really good dinner, we approached the men. Just as we got close, they jumped! Not at us, but off the sidewalk! They were hissing at us and spitting!

Demonically possessed, they growled. *"What are yooou doing here?"*

I drew closer to Richard. Regalis answered them with loud authority, "We have not come for you! Allow us to pass!" The men backed off. In the morning we left Key West. It was time to go home.

Our Return To New Hampshire

I received my final divorce papers a few days later in the mail, on October 20th Three days later it would have been my 13th anniversary. I stood there holding them in my hands in disbelief. So much had transpired. The vision of the cougar walking through my home a year before had come true. The work I had been called to do for Spirit had required I give up so much. The tears fell…

I drove to work that morning and was told by my new supervisor that another three thousand dollars of my very scarce family emergency funds were being diverted to send a few families on an outing. She told me that if I complained, she would find a way to fire me.

I felt all the life drain from me that morning, like water down the tubes. I went back to my office, and put my head down on my desk. I didn't want to do this anymore. I needed help. After a few minutes, I picked up the phone and called the number for our company stress counselor. I was told to come in right away. Canceling my mornings' appointments, I made the short drive to the counselor's office.

I sat in the counselor's office and let it all out. Like a damn bursting, in heaving tears, I told him the story of the cruelty and the harassment I had been under for the past two years, the "retirement" of the past abuser and now the current situation. It had become impossible to do my job and the stress of it was affecting my health.

At the end of that session he made a few phone calls to the Agency. As a result of his calls and confirmations, I was put on medical disability for extreme job- related stress and harassment.

"Susan, you need to rest. You cannot work under these conditions and I don't believe you ought to return to this position." It was final. Well, that said it all. After twenty years as a social worker, I would never return.

Two days later, I was driving across the Queen City Bridge in Manchester, New Hampshire. In a few seconds of time, my whole world would change forever. I was driving onto the ramp of the bridge in the flow of traffic. Speeding up, I merged into the traffic. Just as I did, a woman driving in the opposite direction on the bridge suddenly careened across all the lanes of traffic. She slammed into the car ahead of me and spun directly into my path. She slid sideways into my car, almost head on.

My feet were both pressed into the brake all the way to the floor. I watched as in slow motion, my car crashed into hers. Her face was screaming at me in terror; my car's front end pushed into her side door on impact, pushing all the way into her passenger seat, then into her body. The front of my car crumpled and pressed me against the steering wheel. My head had snapped forward and backwards with the impact. I felt life leave my body as darkness enveloped me.

Then, suddenly, in a fraction of a moment, the whole scene changed.

I awoke to a whole different scenario.

She was standing outside the window of my car. She was screaming at me. I was confused. She was dead. How had she managed to exit her car? She stood by my door screaming, "What happened! What happened?" I had seen my car slam into her front seat.

I hazily realized she was not dead and I was back in my body! I was left dizzy and disoriented. The woman who had caused the accident was hysterical. I simply sat in the car, dazed and immobile.

The police officer finally arrived and approached my car. "Please, would you drive your car over to the side, by the curb?"

I just looked up at him. How could I? It was inside her car, I had seen it happen.

"Do you need to go to the hospital?" he asked.

Looking around, I could now see what the officer was seeing. My car was not crumpled up but only crunched against her door. I shook my head, no. "No, I'll be OK."

What happened? My mind reeled; I had been in a near head on collision; Had I died? But I am not dead. I have been returned. I will be OK. What had happened? Someone asked for my paperwork. I reached up into the visor and I passed it out the window.

"OK, you can go now." The officer said and I drove home.

All I could figure that someone did a "rewind" and replaced the 'tape'! I lay down on my bed and fell asleep. Two days later I went to the hospital. "Severe soft tissue damage and whiplash" was the initial diagnosis. Months later, in an MRI, they would find the compressed vertebrae, spinal injuries, and hemorrhages now in the form of hemangeomas, benign tumor growths, all up and down my spine.

I may have survived the accident and been brought back from the dead, but I suffered. The result; Permanent disability. "Susan, you will never work again with the spine we see here."

There were other, less obvious to other people, things happening to me also. Understand, that within three short days my entire former life was gone and my future had been altered forever.

I was divorced, out of my lovely home, out of money, I was out of a job, in a car accident, and I was hurting all over. I was hurting in body, mind, and spirit. This was going to be a long recovery, I knew. I would have to wait and recover.

Sometimes people think that when 'good' things happen, you are blessed or that you've done something 'good'. They also think that because 'bad' things happen to you, that you've done something 'bad'. Not so.

But I do think that there is always a reason for things. We don't always know what the reason is. Sometimes, it is a test of our faith. Will we receive from God the good and not the testing? Will we turn and curse God when under pressure? Or, was I under a curse? Some thought so, but I didn't. Everyone had an opinion and didn't hesitate to offer their thoughts and solutions.

There had to be a reason for all of this, and I would wait to find out what that was. With a lot of time at home, I began to meditate by myself. Trance-like states were becoming very common for me. Sometimes, I didn't even know when it would begin and I found I would return to the body sometimes two earth days later. I was spending more and more time on the other side and I was between the worlds.

Simple tasks such as answering the phone or opening the mail or shopping were unimportant. I seemed to have lost, or forgotten, the ability and the desire to function in the normal every day way that humans do.

Human tasks were difficult, but the clarity of spiritual things was astounding! My vision and clairvoyance was uncanny; I knew so much and could see and hear the thoughts of those around me. The

Angels were everywhere and communication to the other side was so easy and natural. What was necessary was not primary any more; only Spirit and my connection to It.

I still had to see my job counselor weekly and I tried to convey what I was experiencing to him. He called it stress-job induced trauma or post-traumatic stress disorder. I'm sure that played a role in it all but if I had been living in India, they would have called it, satori, a high spiritual state of existence. The only problem was that I wasn't living in India, I didn't have a cave to live in or the devotees to deliver food. If so, I would have been very content!

I think it was a combination of many things, one in particular; I wasn't *me* anymore, at least the old person. This new person had to relearn simple tasks and find new purpose. I wondered about the Indian Mystic. Had he seen this? Was my preparation for this? My death?

I wondered then if I had taken a walk-in. It felt like it sometimes, but had no recollection of any agreements with the other side. I finally affirmed to myself that this was not a walk in experience, I was still me, but very different.

I know I had died in the car accident, there had been a second death for me in this lifetime and once again, I had been returned. The first time I had been returned with the Word, "Go back and help the people!" I was still here, back a second time and apparently, under the same Divine Orders.

Chapter XVIII

A New Life

One morning I woke early and went into the living room and put on a favorite CD. The now familiar, and sometimes completely unavoidable, trance began. In my misty trance, I could see children entering my living room. I was happy to see them and we began to dance around and around, playfully. I found myself moving with them into another dimension. Soon, I was dancing with hundreds of children.

We danced and played together for a while, then suddenly, they all became very still. They all stood staring up at me. I looked at each little face fondly, with great love. I felt something was wrong, they were so sad. I began to cry for them for some great sorrow was over and around them. I didn't know what to do.

When I came out of the trance, I was still crying. I realized that many hours had past. Gasping with the sorrows of the children, I washed my face and dressed to go to the Center. I had to get away from the vision and the soul grief that still held me.

The others at the Center had taken up almost all my responsibilities during this "recovery" time, but I still liked to go in a couple of times a week to see how everything was going. I began to speak in the Sunday night services.

Sunday nights the Spirit spoke very powerfully through me. In my pain and in my heart's earthly sorrows, I was released from my body somehow. My mind became so focused on the beauty I was experiencing in Spiritual Ascension that I became Spirit. I was disconnecting from this world.

People started taking pictures of me just to see what would come out on them. There were times the people could see through my body as I spoke. I was filled with Light. When I spoke to them, the scent of roses and incense filled the room. Does that make me special? No. That will one day be all our inheritances: to be as Spirit and as flesh. It is not for us now as we have much to do in the material world and we need our physical form.

As soon as I arrived at the Center that morning, I saw Richard drive into the parking lot. He ran into the Center.

"Susan, get your coat, we are going for a ride."

I got into his car and he drove me all the way down into Lowell, Massachusetts without speaking a word to me. His jaw looked tense and he kept wiping his forehead. I was still reeling from my vision that morning. The faces of the little children burned into my mind. I could not forget them. I lay my head back on the seat. The vision of their little faces filled my being.

I felt the car turn and I opened my eyes. We were near an old cemetery. I was surprised when he drove into the cemetery. We went through an old marble archway and rusty old gate. He then drove around. He seemed to be looking for a specific area of the cemetery. Finally, he found what he was looking for. In the entranceway to this area stood a beautiful, fifteen-foot tall, white marble statue of Jesus holding a lamb. It was the children's section of the graveyard.

He parked the car, opened his door and said, "Now, do what you do."

I watched him as he walked away, up over the hill. I was alone with the silence all around me and alone with my own thoughts. I sighed. I wiped away the hot tears flowing down my cheeks. I opened my car door and walked over to where the statue was. I stood looking up at the image of Jesus holding the lamb. Several other marble lambs were at his feet.

"Feed my sheep." He had told Peter. Jesus had come to save His little lambs, the Children of the Kingdom. I realized in my heart, that the little lambs at this cemetery were the children I had danced with earlier that morning. The souls of countless children waited here. They, for some reason, had never passed over into the Light.

They had called me, danced, laughed and played with me; they had become silent and sorrow filled them. They were not free. I didn't understand at the time, but Richard had seen it all and now brought me here to, "do what I do."

As I walked through the small tombstones, I could feel their presence. I saw their precious little spirit being and faces. Many, many of the children who were buried long ago in this cemetery, were still here.

The heartfelt words and emotions of parents who had lost their children cried out from the granite slabs and tied the bindings to the small, lost souls here. I cried too. I felt the pain of death and loss, such loss. Those emotions held them here; some for hundreds of years.

It was time for them to go home now.

So I did what I do; I prayed for them. I asked that the Creator of All would release them from this plane, that the Angels from Heaven would come to escort them home, and the arms of Jesus to embrace them.

I could feel the children gather around me as I prayed. They were ready and somehow, I helped them to understand what they needed to do. I told them not to be afraid, that the Light was love.

Some of their parents and grandmothers, fathers, aunts and uncles were coming for them. They could rejoin their families. It was time for them to go home. They had to enter into the Light that was coming for them.

As I prayed, I saw the great Light from Heaven come to receive them. They joyfully left my side as they rejoined their loved ones and were taken up.

And then it was over. My heart suddenly felt free and clear.

I walked back out from the children's area just in time to meet Richard who was coming back down the hill. We both got in the car and he drove me back home in silence. We never spoke of what happened that day. There were no words.

The Divide

2002 was now past. The lessons, the sorrows and trauma became history. The year of the great divide had been just that. As winter turned into April's spring, my strength returned. Physical therapy and lots of energy work from my students began to make tolerable the damage done to my spine and spirit. The giver was now the receiver. It all balances in the end, you know. I was able to resume teaching one weekend a month and continued the Sunday evening talks.

It was wonderful to see the former students become accomplished teachers and healers in my absence. It has always been my desire that people be empowered, not made dependant upon me or upon others. Upon the solid rock, I stand.

In the teachings of Shambhala we learn that all are fully capable, it is simply a matter of re-membering and re-connecting to Source for all that is needed. In the process of learning about and living in Shambhala, we learn to live cooperatively and share the responsibility. That way, no one person becomes overburdened.

Previously, I had been burdened, now I was able to focus on personal and spiritual growth in my own life. Soon, I would understand the events of the past six months were very important, not only to my growth, but also that of the students. Soil that has been turned produces greater crops. I'd been turned and made ready for a new crop to be planted. The students also had been turned by my absence, had taken up the responsibility and had the opportunity to grow.

Students began to run the free clinics and hospice clinic. The rooms were now full of those teaching and healing using massage and other alternatives. Guest speakers were using our auditorium and bringing in many new students to our Center.

Richard was kept busy in his new life as a healer. He had developed a unique ability to take people to the other side to resolve their life issues and was very popular. Nine wives or not, he managed to keep busy here too.

I remembered the words of the Mystic; A Center? Right idea, wrong timing. Rahu….the great disrupter, the great reorganizer of my life was in full force! He had said it would last until December of 2006 and nothing would change the path of lessons and growth that were predestined!

Soon, I would revisit my Guru friend and advisor. I had heard he was coming to Vermont. I had spoken to Richard and he had agreed to go with me. It was an easy drive, straight up the highway from Concord to Lebanon.

Before I knew it, Richard and I were seated in his office. "Richard! She is Goddess!" The Mystic smiled at Richard while waving his hand over my head.

"Oh, no! Not me! Not here!" Richard exclaimed. "I'm not getting married!"

"Why not? She is perfect for you!'

"Oh, No….I can't…."

Susan Isabelle

They playfully argued over me….the Mystic couldn't get Richard to budge. I laughed.

I got into the car with Richard while I was still giggling. He was pink with his embarrassment. Suddenly, the whole car filled with my Guru's cologne. " He's saying, Goodbye, Richard."

Starting up the car Richard looked at me saying, "You knew this was going to happen, didn't you?"

"Not exactly." I laughed. "Oh, look, it's starting to rain…."

We entered the highway back toward Lebanon. Pouring hard, it started to thunder and lightening strikes were everywhere.

"Look at that Richard!" I exclaimed as a ball of lightening spun across the sky!

"That's not lightening! Those are plasma blasts. There's a war going on up there!"

A few minutes later, the storm greatly intensified. I looked out the window, but the familiar landmarks were not to be found. "Richard, something's not right. The exits aren't right. Let's check out the next exit."

As the turn off came into view we both knew this was not right! Neither of us recognized the town or the exit. He turned off the exit and we stopped at a store. We both got out and ran through the rain into the small store.

"Sir, could you tell us where we are, exactly?" Richard asked the attendant.

"Sure, he replied, you are in New York."

"New York!" We both exclaimed together. "Where?"

The attendant looked at us and realized we were really confused. He got out a map to show us where we were. Somehow in the half hour we had been driving, we had been moved three hours into New York, far away from the border of Vermont. It wasn't possible. We each silently got a steaming hot coffee to help us think things through. Now, we were five hours away from home. We wouldn't get home until 3 AM.

"How, Richard?"

"I don't know, Susan."

"Why?"

"I don't know that either. I do know there's a war going on out there and for some reason, they've moved us out of New Hampshire. We've been teleported hundreds of miles away!"

As we got back in the car, we sat for a few minutes sipping our hot coffee and watched the universal war light show. We were both absorbed in our own thoughts. What could this mean? Obviously, something very serious was happening. Finally, Richard spoke.

"This is about US. This is over you and me!"

"What do you mean?" I asked, curious.

"They're fighting- about us. There's a war going on! I wish I was up there in that fight! They kept me out of it!" He slammed his hand against the steering wheel in frustration.

I looked at him like he was crazy! He was angry that he wasn't up there! "Well, I glad you're right here! Look at that!" I pointed out the windshield. We watched as two balls of lightening jetted out of the clouds and spun wildly at each other, exploded on contact, then burst into hundreds of white-hot electrical fingers that stretched across the sky!

"Let's get going!"

For the next five hours we drove home slowly in the pouring rain. We watched a thunderstorm like I have never seen before or since. Whatever the war was about it was spectacular to view from our position. I don't think I would have wanted to have been up there in that storm.

Have you ever heard of a five-hour thunderstorm? Plasma balls and spikes shot through the air exploding, lighting up the sky as they escorted us toward home the entire time!

"Richard, I don't think I'm going to go for a ride with you again for a while." I joked with him as he dropped me off at my home. "You can sleep on the couch or the living room floor if you like. It's three AM." I offered, but I already knew his answer.

"No, thanks, he replied. I can't wait to get home by myself and find out what's been happening tonight."

I watched as he drove away. Chances are I'd not hear from him for days or even weeks. I fell into bed. He'd be on the other side for a while. What could he have meant when he said that this war was about him and me? About US? I wondered as I fell asleep.

Chapter XIX

What a Tangled Web They've Woven...

The next day I received an urgent telephone call. It was from a frantic woman in New York. "Susan, I saw you at the 2001 expo here. Do you remember me? Can you come to help us? We need you here. I can't speak on the phone. Please come."

I remembered her vividly. She'd had a skull activation at the Whole Life EXPO. She was a small round woman with blond hair and glasses. She had approached me holding a rosy quartz skull of her own and asked for the activation of the Maya. I had agreed.

When the transfer of energy happened from El Aleator, my skull from the Maya, and her rose quartz skull, she began screaming hysterically-to everyone around her. "Look! Look! My skull!" She shouted loudly. "It's changed-look at it!"

Indeed her skull had completely changed color from a rose to clear, sparkling, quartz crystal. I shone brightly in her hand as she held it up for everyone to see. She then turned to look at me. "I know who You are!-you're not human-I know all about people like you!" I stood up and approached her at that moment.

"Please, calm down, there is much to tell you. You are OK and obviously a very special person to the Maya and the Lords of the Light Realm of Peace." People had gathered around me to hear more as I then had explained the coming world to all of them. Yes, I remembered her.

"I suppose I could come. It's been a while since I've traveled to teach. Where are you?" I asked.

"We're just an hour from Long Island." From the urgency of her voice, I knew I would have to go.

"I'll see if one of my students will drive me there." I was still unable to drive long distances.

"Good. If you can, please come this weekend. We have rooms for you and your guest."

The arrangements were made and one of my teachers in training, Kelly, offered to drive me there. It would give her a chance to observe and do a little hands-on teaching herself.

As soon as we turned into the driveway of the spacious home on Long Island, we could see that there was a problem. The woman who had called me was standing outside her front door frantically trying to open the door with her keys. Apparently, none of her keys would open her door. We got out of the car and walked toward her.

"How? How do they do this?" She spoke, irritated. She was very upset. A small and kindly looking woman, she apologized. "I am so sorry. This is part of our problem. I'll tell you all about it as soon as we can get in. The others will be arriving shortly to meet you."

Kelly and I just looked at each other. Soon a tall, distinguished man arrived. She spoke to him quietly as we stood outside as he managed to find a way into the house. Soon, he opened the door and motioned for us to go in. We were directed into a spacious living room in a beautiful home.

Shortly afterward, twenty or so people arrived noisily chattering. They entered the home and sat down in the living room with us. They seemed to be arguing about each other and differing opinions about meeting us. It all seemed so chaotic and yet so serious.

Kelly and I shot a few glances back and forth as we watched it all unfold before us and as we sat quietly, waiting for calm. After a few minutes the woman, Nancy, began to speak and to introduce us to the group. They did not use names.

"Susan, I could not tell you on the telephone why we needed you to come here. We are all a part of a special experimental group. Several people here are what are known as "The Boys." She looked at me to see if I understood.

I shook my head "no". I didn't recognize the term. She continued.

"The experiments that have been done to them and some of us, have left us with no control over our lives. What I have seen of your work leads me to believe you can help us. We need to break the connections in time and in our minds to the previous abuses."

I looked at all the expectant faces staring back at me. "Please explain to me about what has happened to you." I requested, curious about all this. It certainly was not my usual class!

One man, about thirty years old, began to speak. "When I was still a child I was taken into the experimental space-time facility here in New York."

"What is that? I asked.

"It's a experimental underground base near here. I was taken from my family when I was just seven years old to be trained and used as a time traveler. I was used all of my life and have been placed back and forth in time so much I cannot function in the normal world. My mind is all messed up. I can't think straight anymore. I also think that they still control me. My life is not my own. "

"I agree with him." Someone else spoke up.

" Me too. I went through the same thing."

" They use us, then throw us away." Another man spoke harshly.

"I was used as a musician, to use special tones to control the masses. I was programmed to play certain hypnotic tones for mass mind control. I couldn't do anything about it either. Now I understand and don't want to be called back." Said another.

"And, I was a doctor and started treating these people. I was driven out of my practice with frivolous lawsuits to discourage my working with them." she said, while pointing at the others seated in the room. "I'm madder than hell and want this to stop!"

Nancy spoke, "It's like what happened today with my keys. We are being monitored and they don't want us meeting. Someone changed my locks so I couldn't get into my own house. Just to cause confusion!" She shook her head.

I thought about some of the things they were telling me. "I think there may be a few things we can do to help. First of all, let's get you out of the computer…."

"You can do that?" They all exclaimed at once!

"NO, no she can't do that-no one can!"

"Maybe she can!"

"Give her a chance!" Someone else shouted.

The room broke into total confusion as they started arguing with one another. It was as if someone pressed a button in them at the speaking of the topic of the main computer. I stared in amazement as two of them got up and went into the kitchen and started punching each other!

Nancy and a few others ran after them. I watched astounded as the fight escalated with more of them fighting, two had gone outside and were slugging it out on the lawn. Yes, something was very wrong here! CRAZY! Trying to fathom what was happening to them, I walked out onto the front lawn where several were gathered arguing around the others that were still fighting on the grass.

"Quiet! STOP!!" I demanded, sternly. At my voice, they became quiet. I was stunned with the result. "OK. NOW we will do something. You must go back into the house right now!" I pointed back toward the house. "Sit down, remain seated and be quiet!"

They began to file back toward the house like little children that had been scolded. My mind was racing. They all seemed to be brainwashed! Was something controlling them? They couldn't tolerate the fact that I had spoken of a computer. They had begun to act crazy after I had mentioned it. Why?

There's got to be something here, I reasoned. I looked around the yard, then down the street. There it was. Across the way, further down the street was a white van with radar or a satellite dish pointed at the house. I ran inside after the group.

"Everyone! Be perfectly still. I am going to do something. DO NOT MOVE!

A frequency was being beamed at these people from the van that was down the street. It was obviously designed to make them go crazy. We needed to have a filter. Something had to block the waves of confusion and turmoil being beamed at the house and the people now inside. I would need to move quickly. But how?

I stood still. "Yes, I can feel the pulse now," I thought. It hurt my field. Their pulse would soon compromise my own energy field. I was strong, but this was very strong. Clever usage of their energy knowledge, I had to admit. An etheric energy filter was needed.

They all sat quietly staring at me, obediently waiting, waiting for me to do something.

As they watched, I brought in a strong frequency of Light and placed it around the house. It wasn't strong enough. I could tell as I could now isolate the frequency and could feel it in my body. Although the frequency had diminished, the globe of light frequency I had created wasn't strong enough to totally block the outside frequency. I'd need to do something else.

I tried another globe of Light and placed it around just the room we were seated in. Hopefully, it would hold long enough for me to break the controls on their minds. Yes, this one worked, but if they went outside the room, they would be susceptible to the frequencies once again.

"Wow!...."

"What happened?..."

" I feel better…"

"Were we fighting? …."

"What did you do?" They looked from one to another and then me, asking and wondering.

"Look, this may be hard for you to understand right now, but there's a van down the street beaming a frequency at all of you…"

"See, I told you!....Damn them!...." The murmuring began and anger swept the room.

"Hold up a minute and let's think this through, before you get all upset again…" I stated firmly. "I've placed a block on the frequency, but I don't think it's strong enough to protect you outside of this room."

"You mean if we go out of this room, we'll go crazy again?" A timid looking woman asked me.

"Only for a while. We need to do some things to protect you from the program they have established- that apparently works. The first thing we have to do is change your energy identity."

"Our energy identity?"

"Yes, you can all be tracked, we've seen that. How do you think that happens?"

"I was in the group for so long, I know they can track me and control me…I always thought it was by an implant."

"It doesn't have to be by an implant that tracking takes place. That's actually an old program. It is done by identifying your energy signature, or the mapping of your energy body. Everyone has an energy field that is as identifiable as your fingerprints. Once that energy signature is identified, it enters a "computer brain" outside this solar system."

"How? How do they do that?" Jen asked, shocked.

"Have you ever been to a doctor, therapist, or even a bio-feed back demonstration? Usually, they demonstrate their devices at new age conferences. They may have had you put metal bracelets on or a metal head band, maybe both. You enter into a computer your information such as birth date, home location and such."

Most nodded. "Well, that's how. Those machines take your information and map your energy field, as many as ten thousand aspects of it, and enter it into that alien technology's main-frame computer. You can be found anywhere at any time. You can also be manipulated. You can be " beamed" into doing whatever the frequency they beam at you wants."

They looked stunned as many realized they'd been mapped and manipulated but nobody ever told them how or why.

"That's why that van down the street knows what to do. It's beaming a frequency at you to make you angry and to cause disruption by manipulating your emotional bodies."

"This has got to stop!"

"We're puppets on their string!" The murmuring began again. I raised my hand to stop them.

"Yes, I agree, but you must also work with me to help yourselves." I said. They looked confused.

"What do you want us to do?"

"I'll be giving this class for three days. You've got to be here every day…" I started to say.

"I can't,….."

"I've got to work….."

"I don't have the money… "

"I just wanted to meet you…." The excuses began.

"Look, I am here to help you as you requested. If I do this for you, you must be here to complete the work or you, yourselves, will be making the decision to remain as you are now." A few people actually got up and left the room.

"This is for you and we can get you out of this," I continued. "But you need to do everything I tell you or it won't work…"

I was interrupted by the sounds of voices shouting from outside. Everyone got up to see what was happening. I ran outside ahead of them. Outside the few people who had left earlier were slugging it out again on the lawn.

"Go back! Go back in the house!" I shouted at the others still coming outside. They turned back inside. I left the others outside.

"See what I mean?" I said to my frightened assistant. She was getting a lot more than she bargained for!

"Susan, I think I want to go home. I don't understand this...." She pleaded with me.

"Let me try one more time. They need us!"

A few minutes later I was back in the living room scolding the "children", or so it seemed. "If any one of you leaves this room again, I will pack up and go home! Make up your minds right now, or I leave!"

A few moments of murmuring among themselves revealed the truth. "We don't know that anyone can help us!"

"Well, you won't know that unless you try! You asked me here because of what you were told about the energies I work with. Your friend here has told you she witnessed in New York." They nodded.

"You also have just seen what I have done to protect you inside here." I said waving my arm around the room. "Well, let's get to work!" Smiles broke out and some joyful laughter. That was much better.

Soon, we were bringing in a new, higher frequency to the people. The attunements of Shambhala's full Light Spectrum automatically changes a person's energy fields. So when that happens to you,

you become a totally different person with a new energy body! Any previous tagging of your auric fields are for a person who no longer exists! It's no longer effective.

Also, the attunement allowed for free flow of pure energy from a much higher source than the manipulative lower forces, and simply melted away the darkness that had enfolded them for so long.

It was wonderful to see the glow of their faces and the pure joy radiating from them! This is why I teach and do what I do! People are meant to be free! Finally, it had been done. They were free! (You may also change the frequency and aura with the use of magnets.)

Our little drummer looked up at me and smiled.

"This is the first time in twenty years that I don't hear the voices!" He exclaimed." Nor the buzzing!" Then the others began.

"Me too!"

"WOW! What was that?"

"What a trip!"

"That is just the beginning. Be here first thing in the morning!"

The next day about half of them showed up. I never heard about the others and no one mentioned them that day. I didn't ask. It was as though they had not ever existed. Maybe they didn't. I don't question anymore. People make their own choices.

We went right to work. We went into the main frame computer and wiped the records clean....Those present that day would never be bothered again.

One thing about technology and those who operate technology; there's something missing in their 'link'....If it's not on the computer, it doesn't exist. Remember that. Oh, remember too that computers record only memory, a frequency of the mind encoded upon memory. It can be erased with MIND.

We went home, Kelly and I, and not too soon.

"Susan, I don't think I want to be a teacher." She sighed as we passed out of the State of New York.

"I know, me too." I answered her. We laughed.

Chapter XX

England

"Well, Richard, good to see you! It's been a few weeks!"

"Yeah, had a lot of work to do on the other side, you know…."

"I thought you'd be out for a while after that 'storm.' So what's up?"

"Intense... Here, I brought you something." He handed me a book.

I turned it over in my hand, thoughtfully. It was a topic I only recently had any knowledge of: The time-space experimental facility in NY. "Where did you get this?" I asked, knowing full well he'd not any real knowledge of my trip to New York.

"It was given to me by a friend. It was on my shelf at home for the past month. The Guides last night told me to give it to you. Do you know what this is?"

"A matter of fact, I do. Last week I went out to New York and met some of The Boys."

"Really?"

"Yes, it was quite a trip. I'll tell you all about it later. Tell me, how are you?"

"Man, I've been on duty every night for the last two weeks. I was beat. Seems that things have calmed down now though. I'll be ready to take clients again."

"You know, there's a young woman coming in this afternoon. She's only thirty-five years old, but she's got a big tumor in her liver. She's scheduled for surgery in three weeks. They tell her that she'll lose about a third of her liver. Interested in helping?"

"Sure. It's been a while since we've worked together."

Later that day, Richard and I began to remove the energy pattern of the tumor from her liver. The energy of the Mahatma, Feminine Aspect, softened the hardness of the tumor and Richard removed the residue. Three weeks later, she had her surgery. The tumor had shrunk to the size of a quarter. It was removed. There was no cancer.

Perhaps if she continued with us for a few more weeks, the surgery may never have happened. Not everyone responds to the energies, but those who do, most often, fare very well.

I took the book Richard had given me home that night and began to read it. When I was called out of my body a few hours later, the book fell from my hand. I entered the realm of time, into a time long past. It was a time before I was born.

Somewhere in England I hovered above a crowd of men and a young boy. I was watching a group of Nazis and a man who called himself the 666 Anti-Christ, A. C. Beneath me something was happening. I was watching a ritual, child sacrifice.

"Father! Father! NO!"

A few of the vile men grabbed hold of a young boy that was now screaming for help. They ignored his cries and bound him to a wooden plank. He sobbed but no one listened.

His father turned toward the others and shouted orders while pointing to a stone disk that was standing in the field. It stood, as a large donut-like fixture in the field. It was placed between two standing pillars.

"Pass him through the center hole at the very moment I tell you!" He ordered.

They nodded in obedience. The father stood over the stone and began to call upon the legions of darkness.

"Stop! Stop!" I shouted uselessly at them. They could not see me; I was viewing the past.

I watched the incantations of the wild man, his frenzy and power unleashed in hatred. A sacrifice had to be made; he was giving his own son's life to satisfy the demands of the beast of the lowest realms.

"PASS him through!"

As the young boy was raised to be passed through the center hole of the great stone, I saw IT!

It was a demon! It slithered snakelike; a black mist weaving itself into a dark, vulgar form. The form of semi-transparent black smoke followed behind the child strapped to the wooden plank borne out of the incantations of the wild man.

The child entered through the stone and was now being swallowed up by the energy around the donut shaped stone. The creature followed the child through the stone and set it's fire-mark upon the stone in a blaze of hot lava for an instant, marking its territory.

A demon would now guard the stone! The contract had been made and finalized.

"WHY?" Why was this done?" I cried!

And then I heard the Words:

"Al'lat, we summon you.

Go now to England and release the Stone of Birthing!

I shuttered with cold and horror as I found myself, now wide awake, within my body once again. I screamed at the ceiling,

"What? What did you say?" "You, YOU want ME to go to England to release THAT??? "

There was no answer. I pulled the covers up over my head. It was just a bad dream. In the morning I awoke to Melchizedek's voice.

"It was not a dream."

I shuttered. "This is not possible!" I shouted at the ceiling.

I arrived at the Center a few hours later. Richard arrived soon after. "Here, here's another book by the same author." He said pushing a book toward me.

"Listen, Richard, I had a really bad dream last night. I'm not sure I want to hear or read any more about the time travel they are doing."

"I read some of this last night." He said holding up the book for me to see. "You need to read it. The Guides are telling me. There's something in here about a really weird guy who contracted a demon."

"Oh, no!" I shuttered and pushed the book away.

"Yeah, and do you remember the Philadelphia experiment?"

"I think I saw a movie about that a few years ago. Yes, Richard, I do remember. That's when a Navy ship was sent into time and came back with the men encased in the metal of the ship. It didn't work right. What does that have to do with the book?"

"Everything, it seems. I believe they are going to try the experiment again this August at the peak, around the seventeenth of the month. Every twenty or so years, there is a build up of magnetic energy around the Earth that allows them to generate enough power to run the machines, Tesla experiments. It's 2003. They did the Philadelphia experiment in 1943 and tried it again in 1983."

"Do you mean to tell me that they use the ley lines of magnetic force of the earth to generate the power?"

"Yes, I believe how it's done. Why?"

I began to put the pieces together in my mind.

"The Stone of Birthing. It must birth an energy. It must sit on a ley line a major meridian, just like what we saw in Florida! Richard, they have used a demon to control the flow!"

Then the full force of it hit me, " Oh, My God! I have to go to England! NOW!"

"What?"

"I HAVE to go to England! This is June! I have only until August to get to England and undo this!"

"Susan, what are you talking about?"

"Last night, Richard! The dream wasn't a dream. I'll tell you, but I've got to get to England!" I felt nauseous and began to feel weak.

"Last night I was shown something that happened in England around the time of World War II. I saw Nazis. There's some kind of marker there that looks like a donut between two pillars." He was listening intently.

"A demon has been set over it . I believe now that it's a ley-line marker. It was called, 'the stone of birthing'." I paused. Richard was looking at me funny. "What's wrong?"

"I read about that in this book last night. The story is here, all here."

"If that's true, Richard, in August they will try to use the ley lines again. This line has a demon manipulating it, controlling it. Maybe that's why the experiment went so wrong?"

"Susan you've got to read this. I think its because the demon was there that they were **able** to do the experiment. You'll understand why when you read this." He put the book in my hand.

He continued. " It's against the Universal Laws to manipulate time like this. The forces of darkness are needed to do the dirty work."

"I think I understand now. The lower forces were definitely working with the Nazis." I thought a moment. "But it was OUR side that did the experiment!"

"That's right, Susan. We worked together with their technology and the dark to do the time experiment."

"I think I'm going to get El Aleator back out of the vault. I'm going to need a lot of help! This is awful! And now, they're going to try again?"

"Yup. I think you ought to get the skull out too. This time, I think the effects of their time experiments could be much worse than before. My Guides are telling me that the very fabric of time will be ripped apart."

"Oh, My God! A tear in the fabric of time!" I remembered Cape Cod. I shivered!

"It will allow the incursion of the lower realms to flood through time."

"Richard! That means the gates of hell will open onto the earth! They can't do this!"

I began to remember the screams Lucy and I had heard on the beach at the Cape. A small tear had opened at that time. This would be much larger, possibly the end of life as we knew it, if this succeeded.

"I've got to go to England." The terror began to fill me. I sat down. We were silent for a few minutes, thinking of the consequences. I began to understand I might not come back from this new assignment. "Richard, it is called the '**Stone of Birthing**'. It's a hole in a rock on top of a very important ley line. I have to find it."

I heard the Mind of the Creator within me now. He spoke and I spoke the words.

"*It's the Earth Womb of the Goddess of the Divine;*

The place where the Divine Feminine 'births'

It brings the energy of mercy and compassion onto the earth plane.

All that is good is infused into the mind-consciousness of the planet here."

"You mean, the demon was placed there to stop goodness and birthing of the Aspects of the Divine Feminine on the earth?" He asked.

"Yes, that's exactly what I mean. Until that demon is removed, we will have wars and horror on the earth. They have control over it. They passed a child through the Womb to ensure it. Can you believe it? An innocent child was used to contract a demon."

My eyes began to fill up with tears that ran hot, down my cheeks. Richard handed me a tissue. He looked very distressed.

"They want you to make it go away?" He whispered.

"Un –huh." I sniffed.

"How? How are you going to do that?" He asked, worried now.

"I have to go through the stone, Richard. I have to undo what was done."

"Susan, you can't do that! You don't know where it is!" He reasoned his growing anger and worry.

"I'll find it, Richard. I have to!" Determined now, I was getting stronger. Just then, Emily appeared at the door of the room we were in.

"I'm sorry to interrupt. Susan, your daughter is on the phone. She really wants to speak to you now. She won't wait."

"Ok. I'll take it." I took the phone from Emily's hand and nodded at Richard. My daughter rarely called me at the Center.

"Hi, Honey, what's wrong?"

"Mom, nothing's wrong! I'm going to England! Do you want to come?"

I nearly fell out of the chair.

"Richard! She wants me to go to England with her!" I exclaimed.

His face burst out into a huge smile.

"Honey, when are you going?" I asked her. Then I held my breath.

"In a couple of weeks. Some friends in Massachusetts and I are planning to go together and I thought you'd like to be there too! You know a few of them from the Center here…."

"Sweet heart, I'll go with you if I can go to the Stone of Birthing…" I hesitated while waiting for her answer.

"I don't know if that is on the agenda, but we can find out. The reason I had to speak to you is that tonight they are having a meeting here with the tour group leader from England!"

She paused and asked, " Will you come, Mom?"

"Oh, Honey," I said as I smiled up at God.

"I'll be there!"

Chapter XXI

The Dimensions

Students have asked me to explain the dimensions. This is my experience with Richard. When Spirit explained it to me, it seemed so simple. I asked, "Why didn't you show this to me before?" The answer was, "You never asked!"

What was shown to me is this; Mother is the vibrational realm, The Spectrum of Light Creation.

Level 1 is void. No Light is present. No spectrum of Light is there.

Levels 2-8 "MA- infesting", or *Mother existing* in the 7 lower realms.

Also, this represents the seven chakra levels of human potential and manifestation.

We have seven chakras and seven dimensional levels on which mankind *in the physical* may dwell.

These are the physical realms of the Divine Feminine.

Level 2-Brown-red vibrations –density is strong, but still, Light reaches here

Level 3 is color orange,

Level 4 is yellow,

Level 5 is green

Level 6 is blue

Level 7 is indigo.

Level 8 is violet

Mankind as physical form, cannot dwell in the dimensions of 9-12, but only in etheric forms, mental projections and emotional records of prior existence.

Richard and I exist together on nine levels, 3-11. Only 2-8 are in physical form. 9 - 11 are in Light body, yet we are still joined in these realm.

I am a Melchizedek, a Priestess and have come from the 11th realm, my home, to earth to bring the sacraments of God, Most High.

On the twelfth realm I am a sapphire cell of the first ray of Light.

This is the first realm of Goddess, the Divine Feminine Spectrum of Light in form. There are "Seven." Seven of the Holy Spirit, Seven frequencies of physical form and gifts to humanity. The Shekhina, the white fire that surrounds the Throne of God in unmanifest form does exist and it is here.

The Christ is the Bridge, the Gateway between God and The Divine Feminine. "The Bright and Morning Star. He is the physical embodiment of Light; The Only Begotten." This is shown clearly in the Kabbala. He lies between Malkuth and Tipareth, the Womb. He walks between the realms freely as physical and as God.

This will be our inheritance when we join His Light. Ask and it shall be given you.

The Thirteenth is total Light and has no form. This is God. This is Pure Thought and is the Divine Masculine.

More description of the levels;

1. The chart's lowest vibration comes from the void.

Level I is void. No Light is present.

It is void of consciousness, dark and a place of total separation from God and the Light. I consider this hell and there is no return. The Light doesn't even filter down to this place from the level above.

When Richard and I went through the membrane of this Universe and creation, it was with the preparation and blessing of God/Goddess ALL That Is. The purpose was to place an extension of God's presence even into the nothingness-to go forth and multiply through Light. Light overcomes dark.

2. Just above the void is a level that we would consider the abode of demons, entities and the shadow people.

Level2-Brown-red vibrations of denseness and less consciousness are the lowest. They can break through to our realm in times of great emotional distress, wars and inhuman acts that lower us down to their level. This level seeks a presence in the physical realm through humans, sometimes through direct possession.

Possessiveness and acts of violence are effects of their influence upon the minds of mankind. Generally being out of physical form, they seek to take enough light-energy from surroundings and other live beings so as to manifest their presence. They can and do take on human form when allowed or the gates open. Soulless beings of darkness do dwell among us.

3. Third level or dimension is where the Earth resides.

Level 3 is color orange, we seek power and survival

We have been trying to do a balancing act in this place on a thin rope. Here we exist in a dense physical form, but have the potential of embodying more Light. The Light reaches down to us when we ask for help; the dark seeks possession of us.

4. If one could call a place purgatory, this would be it.

Level 4 is yellow, enlightenment, coming into understanding

Disembodied souls not yet ready to ascend into Light wait here. Some wait a long time, some are sent back to Earth to assist the repairing of past Karma for ourselves and others, or undo the wrongs done in the flesh while alive. This is your life review.

Coming from a Baptist background, this was hard to understand until I remembered being three years old and crying for my mother other each night. I had a vivid childhood memory of England and WWII. She and I died together while hiding under a bed. We came back together in this life to repair a few 'details.'

This is the holding area, the place of ghosts and a place of waiting.

5. Experiences on the fifth dimension have been interesting to say the least.

Level 5 is green, healing of the heart and emotions

I believe that this is where I went to 'track down Richard'. It is very much like Earth. People often come here after death until they are ready to evolve into a less dense form and incarnate into higher realms.

They hold the Light but the consciousness has not yet evolved to the point of more Light integration. In the Pistis Sophia, remember, she slowly ascended the ten levels as she learned the ropes of each dimension and could recognize higher truth and asked for more Light. She had not descended into void or there would have been no return for her.

6. The second astral realm still holds form, or image holder, of the familiar world we now know and experience.

Level 6 is blue, the place of the vibration of record.

But; it doesn't have the level of competitiveness or ego self we experience on earth. It is much more free and still affords the evolving soul the opportunity to enjoy a form and to be in familiar surroundings.

7. This dimension is the beginning of the Light realms.

Level 7 is indigo. The realm of the Platinum Blue Warriors.

Angels and ascended beings hold a level of Light that is just beneath the Thought realm (Metatron). They respond to the Thought of God in obedience and service to the Light in a form that allows them to do so. This realm allows movement into form to perform service.

8. Metatron-Thought realm.

Level 8 is violet. Mankind was destined to dwell here. Mankind left this garden to explore, lost the way and forgot where they came from. The pollution of the lower realms interfered in the development of mankind and stole this birthright.

This realm is a transition point between the Thought of God transforming into an action that will create a form. A step-down transformer would be a good example of the dimension. IT IS PURE ELECTRONIC FREQUENCY. A veil must be passed.

This is the Violet Realm; here it is that the new human will dwell. The Cosmic Eve was formed of this realm. This is where we will incarnate after 2012 and leaving this body. Some may ascend directly to this level.

It is the realm of UNLIMITED POSSIBILITY!

9th and 10th dimensions are the palaces of Light, the abode of all that have ascended back from the descent, overcame the challenges, and no longer work. This is a place of rest and record. The record is an actual electronic living library of the ascended one's life and accomplishment while in body.

This is where Richard and I met with Ganesh, in his palace. It exists as a living record hall of all that was made known; all the wisdom and teachings were still there to visit and assimilate. It never goes away. Imagine, one day a palace will be waiting for you; one you created with every good work you did and every word of wisdom you spoke-if you so desire to rest from the physical form.

11. Abode of the Priests of God. What is a priest? One who has been designated to serve and bring the sacraments, or the Light energy, to the others. One who assists the return of the Children Of Light is a priest. Melchizedek is the High Priest of God Most High.

12. This surrounds the very Throne Of God. When I died in 1972, I was taken here and told to return with these words from God, *"Go Back; go back and help the people!"* Out from the Throne Light of God and the river of Spirit around it, great rays of Light emanate, in every color, as a great wheel with spokes of colors that are as gemstones. It is a living Rainbow Light. This is the first movement out from the Light into a vibration, a color.

We each have come out from the Thought, the Light into one of these emanations of color. When we did we were one, then split; one male, one female gendered. We took on a ray of color at the split. I am from the pure ray of sapphire, Richard came out into the pure ruby ray.

As human, we each one of us holds a specific energy frequency in a form and combination of color. Those frequencies are encoded into our DNA. The range of possibilities are limitless. That's why we each look so different, think differently and also reflect the amazing creation mind of God!

This is the Realm of the Mahatma, Divine Feminine Motion, Pure Unconditional Love in response to the Father's Thought. It is ever moving downwards into form.

What is so wonderful about the work of Christ is that all who cling to and embody His Light and consciousness, are able to ascend all the levels, all at once under His work-when it is time. Christ is the bridge between the realm of man and God, The Father.

He is both God and man. He is the result of the Love Response of Mother and Thought.

He is the Only Begotten and is represented in the symbol of the fish on almost every Christian's car. Most don't know what the symbol means; the vesica pisces.

He did the work, we don't have to. Just believe and ask for that mercy to be given to you. Why just stop at the lower astral realms?

13. The Thirteenth Realm is God. It is pure Light and there is NO darkness here. If you hold any thought form that is not absolutely of Truth and Purity, you cannot be here. This is the Holy Of Holies. There's only one way here…under the work and gateway of the CHRIST. You will be made perfect, made "male" as was explained in the Gospel of Thomas. You must transcend the form into Light.

Chapter XXII

Some other questions I am asked….

I've heard there are over three hundred-fifty two dimensions and we must work to get through each one, making prayers to the lords and masters of each.

There are 13 major dimensions and many levels within each dimension. All dimensions hold the same 'place' simultaneously, yet are uniquely different.

Yes, I know that the idea of paying homage to each 'lord' of a dimensional space has been taught. Again, I say to you that there is only One Creator, all else is a lower light. Homage is due no one and in many cases, an entrapment.

As for the dimensional levels in a broad sense, this is my experience first-hand, so this is what I can tell you.

Susan, many people have wondered about the sayings of Christ in the Gospel of Thomas. Especially where Jesus says, "I will make her male" so that she can ascend into heaven, for only "males" can attain that state. What did he mean? It seems so sexist. Did he mean that females don't have a soul?

Take a look at the dimensional levels again and at what has been written in this book. When Richard and I ascended through the Crystal Gateway we learned something very important. EVERYTHING that exists BELOW that gateway is of the Feminine Birth.

It has a physical form. That is "female" and it doesn't matter whether or not your <u>gender</u> is male or female, or even if you are a rock-you are of the female. It's not talking about gender.

To enter into Heaven, you must have no physical form (become male) and must have been transformed into Pure Light.

Susan, isn't Goddess worship condemned in the Scriptures as worshipping the 'queen of heaven?'

In following the above question's answer to that which is 'female'; ALL things that have form are "female." When we make silver, gold, money, possessions of the physical realms we declare ownership of them and turn them into our 'Queen'- into idols —Queen of Heaven-stuff. We bring them up above God Presence and give our devotion to that. That's why rich Babylon is called the harlot. It's a distortion of love; the discarding of our Creator, our true love, for the goods of this world.

So, we are not talking about the Beautiful Aspects of the Divine Feminine-Goddess, that dwell in the Light of God and are God; love, mercy, compassion, and wisdom. Those aspects are within God as His' feminine side unexpressed'.

Expression, or the likeness of God, takes place in **the physical realms** *as form and action (feminine aspects) whenever we show these aspects.*

When we love one another as ourselves, feed the poor, clothe the naked, heal the broken hearted, we show the aspect of God in expression while still in our body. THAT is what I mean when I say that we must have the aspects of Goddess within us before we can ascend into the higher Light of God.

We must also embody these aspects toward one another to secure their action here and image of the Beloved Bride within us. That is done by the embodiment of the Shekhina, the Holy Spirit-

form of the Dove; Goddess. The fruits of the Spirit manifest through expressions of love. Again, ask for this; it is freely given and will transform your life.

What about all the lords of the dimensions, the ascended masters and such….

I went to the Temple of Gansesh and all the Buddha realms. ***At NO time*** *was worship required to receive their knowledge. They simply exist and hold the wisdom templates given to them for each of the levels of consciousness. It was free.*

The Crystal Skulls are the same. They hold a physical reality of <u>the higher templates</u> on Earth to help us understand by infusing that knowledge into this realm by their mere presence.

Some of you hold a Template of Light for the Earth, right now. You are the standing stone for others to find and rest upon. Let your love light shine!

I believe that lower forces have seen an opportunity to mimic the wisdom realms to gain service from us, to use us and to deceive.

You have NO masters; only fellow servants of the Light in the higher realms. Only the lords of the lower realms exact service.

Susan, why don't you channel anymore?

A few years ago, I was told that the days that are coming will be very deceptive. What may appear to be truth will lead people astray. As lower forces eventually do flood into the earth realms, many of those who channel will be used by the lower forces to speak words of deception to the people. This will give false hope and direction. I do not want to open myself to that possibility, not even remotely.

Secondly, they made me understand that my physical body must be kept pure in its self-integrity and the Light that dwells within me is not to be corrupted by any other

To have others embodying me to speak would not be wise. I was taught a new method called 'halo-to-halo' so that I could hear without embodying. My experience with Thoth taught me many things...

I've heard about a newborn Christ on Earth. Isn't he already incarnated here, somewhere in England?

No....

Matthew 24:24-25: "Then if any man shall say to you: Lo here is Christ, or there, do not believe him. For there shall arise false Christs and false prophets, and shall show great signs and wonders, insomuch as to deceive (if possible) even the elect. Behold I have told it to you, before hand. If therefore they shall say to you: Behold He is in the desert, go ye not out: Behold He is in the closets, believe it not."

Why not?

Well, understand that Christ, the True Light comes from the very essence of the Godhead and is the Vesica Pisces-Light, sound, vibration-The Only Begotten. That means, the only one born from Father-Mother.

That first movement of Thought-And –Love of our Father-Mother in the Lotus set the ONE and ONLY Template. Christ Light became from their joining. From that point on, That Light became the Creation Light and All Things were made through that Light. There is no other.

He left the Light where he dwells, came in the flesh (human-took on physical)* to us two thousand years ago to make the way back for us. It's done. Now he calls us "friends." John 15:15.

Yes, Christ said he'd return. But, he said he'd return in the clouds and every eye would see him return in the flesh at the last day.

That means at the very last moment of time as we know it. Not before.

There are no more reincarnations for him-only taking the crown and ruling over the new creation for a thousand years- Not the lower councils people seem to be making contact with in channels.

When 2012 arrives- or the designated moment known only by God- and we begin again, the slate will be wiped clean.

Can or does God change His mind?

Yes, the Thought of God, The Dreaming, under certain circumstances may change; but understand-there are rules. They have been established by the Creator to bring us to higher consciousness.

When humanity as a whole, makes a lower choice it eventually descends to the point of the lower consciousness overcoming the mind of mankind- such as described below in Sodom, or the Roman Empire.

Once it descends to such a low vibration, even Light doesn't want to touch it. There is no coming back up. The civilization is removed, one way or another. The slate is wiped clean to start over again. Empires, dynasties and whole civilizations lose the blessing, are wiped out or crumble.

The mind of the people of the city of Sodom was so corrupted that they demanded the angels visiting Lot to be sacrificed to them. Lot tried to give them his daughters instead for sacrifice! That's hor-

rible. Yes, it can get that bad. The reign of Hitler and the SS is a good current day example.

People of Light and integrity had to take a stand, to say "no!" Even in his day Father Abraham tried to save some; but the mind had become so corrupted it wasn't possible.

Today, our entire world system is corrupted in every way. We are being given opportunities, if we will listen and learn from the examples that have been given to us.

I like this verse because it shows that <u>even a few</u> of us can make a difference in the final outcome. It also shows the end can come to us. It's not a judgment of anyone, but a good example of a universal truth.

> "And the Lord said to Abraham:
>
> If I find in Sodom fifty just within the city, I will spare the whole place for their sake…
>
> What if there be five less than fifty <u>just</u> persons?… Abraham asked.
>
> And He said: I will not destroy it, if I find five and forty.
>
> But if forty be found there, what wilt thou do?
>
> He said: I will not destroy it for the sake of forty.
>
> Abraham tried again; Lord, saith he, be not angry, I beseech thee, if I speak: What if thirty shall be found there?
>
> I will not do it, if I find thirty there…
>
> What if twenty be found there?

He said: I will not destroy it for the sake of twenty.

I beseech thee, saith he, be not angry, Lord, if I speak yet once more: What if ten shall be found there?

And the Lord said: I will not destroy it for the sake of ten.

And the Lord departed… And the Lord rained upon Sodom and Gomorrha brimstone and fire from the Lord out of heaven. And He destroyed these cities, and all the country about…" (Genesis, Chapters 19-20)

Only Lot and his family were spared, but they had to leave the city.

In contrast, the city of Niveah changed its ways and was saved- God changed His mind. Remember the story of Jonah and the whale?

Also, we 'shortened the days' once already in 2001 and Biblical prophesy has been changed. The people prayed. We have been given another chance.

What about the crystal skull you have? I don't like the image of the skull.

Moses was given two tablets of stone. They contained all the law and first covenant with humanity. Nobody ever said what they actually looked like, to my knowledge.

There are a few hints though, that they may have been a skull form. When Christ was crucified, he was on the mount called Golgatha, meaning 'the place of the skull'. I've wondered if perhaps there was a hidden skull- tablet beneath that place.

Once I had a profound vision. Taken back in time, I was first standing at the foot of the cross. All I could see of the Christ were his feet. Then, I was kneeing face-down with several other people when the Earth began to shake violently.

In the darkness, the Earth opened up as we clung in fear to the ground. It was as though the Earth was going to end at his death. I saw in my vision a large crystal skull lift up out of the ground. One of the men laying next to me, pulled it up and quickly hid it in his cloak. He passed it to another man who was beside him, who then crawled backwards and ran away as the guards had already done so.

Recent information about the Knights Templars suggests that they found a skull when they entered the Jerusalem Temple sites and kept it hidden. It is said that the skull gave them great knowledge and wealth. Who knows? Maybe someday, we will have the opportunity to see these great mysteries. They were meant to be shared with mankind, but rather have been hidden away from us. I share El Aleator and El Za Ra with you and will teach you all that they show me.

The Maya were given thirteen tablets of stone in the shape of skulls. They were given to them by Itzmna, Son of the Divine Couple, God Above All Gods, according to the Maya. To me, that is Christ.

I'll tell you a secret….it's explained in my book, 'The Global Assignment; Activate The Crystal Skulls.' El Aleator has a second half!!! A twin flame!

In 2004 the second half, El Za Ra came to me. She, like El Aleator, has a full brain inside. On Mount Shasta in 8/04, a miracle occurred. The two skulls came together for the first time in eons…they formed a perfect human heart. It was the heart of a child!

I offered the Heart Back to God/Goddess on behalf of the children that day. My prayers went up to heaven amidst a great swirling whirlwind that ascended into heaven!

You'll also see in the last book of Revelation, Christ speaks; " On the last day, I will come and take away your <u>stony heart</u> and give you a heart of flesh."

I thought they were going on that day, but it didn't happen, so there's more to come! I fully expect that one day the two skulls that form the heart will be returned to heaven and it will be the beginning of the new human!

I also believe they are the thirteenth skull of the Maya. These are the one that sits in the middle of a ring of twelve. Just as Christ was in the focal point of twelve disciples who each held aspects that were unique, he served as the perfection, the place of transformation.

The Heart of A Child is what is required to enter into heaven, both within us individually and symbolically with the "stoney heart." Christ spoke in parables; many meanings were hidden until the last days.

For now, I am the Keeper of the Heart of Stone. It holds a sacred template. Mount Shasta is the place of transformation and is the heart chakra of the earth. It actually has a heart shape on its side!

The Maya tell us that there are thirteen realms of heaven and nine realms of the lower realms. We live in the middle. The yin-yang symbol has been telling us that all along. We've been trying to hold the balance between the upper and the lower realms. It's exhausting. It's ending.

Return to the Light. Be free and go home. We'll incarnate into new bodies that have been formed by God's own plan and making that hold the Highest Consciousness in the new Cosmic Eve!

Blessings,

Susan Isabelle

What was Genevieve doing walking in Spirit on the table of King Arthur?

For that matter, what was Susan doing on the same table doing the same thing, centuries later?

Another mystery to solve...

In The Eye Of The Goddess

Assignment England

By Susan Isabelle

Coming Soon!

Suggested reading and references;

The Palmistry Center in Montreal Canada

Destiny In The Palm of Your Hand by Gansham

The Emerald Tablets of Thoth

Peter Moon's *The Music of Time Series*

The Pistis Sophia, Gnostic Scriptures and JJ Hurtak

The Celestine Prophecy by James Redfield

Return of the Children Of Light by Judith Bluestone Polich

Coming Soon!
*Read about Susan's search for
the Stone Of Birthing in her next book,
"In The Eye Of The Goddess."*

An old legend exists in England, shown on this tapestry in a pub there. So just what was Genevieve doing walking in Spirit on the famous round table of King Arthur?
Why were they hiding their faces?

For that matter, what was Susan Isabelle doing on the same table doing the same thing, centuries later?

There was another mystery to solve...another prophesy

One that would set
a new law;
The Law of the Goddess
on Earth

Coming Soon!

In The Eye Of The Goddess
Assignment England By Susan Isabelle

Ad 2

The Global Assignment

Activate The Crystal Skulls

Fulfilling The Maya's Prophesies

Susan Isabelle

Susan's work with El Aleator, the Crystal Skull of the Maya, led her back into Central America to fulfill ancient prophesy. Guess what? El Aleator found his twin flame! Now, there are TWO!

Www. Crystal-Skulls-Mayan.com
*Available online and at the Shambhala Store
590 Main St PO Box 698 Weed Ca. 96094
530.938.3500*

Ad 3

Crystal Skull Voices

Card Deck and Book

Early one Sunday morning I awoke to the instruction, "WRITE!" Taking out my pen and journal I began to write the words now flowing into my consciousness.

*The Ancients Found A New Way
To communicate to us in these last days before 2012*

All thirteen crystal skulls of the Maya introduced themselves that day. They gave their names, where they were from and a new way to communicate with them...

Special Orders are available .
To purchase your own Crystal Skulls and have Activations to El Aleator and El Za Ra with Susan

Shambhala Center Store
590 Main Street Weed, CA 96094
530.938.3500
Www.crystal-skull-mayan.com

Ad 4

Printed in the United Kingdom by
Lightning Source UK Ltd., Milton Keynes
137014UK00002B/348/P